Sarah's Last Secret

Jack Trammell

Hard Shell Word Factory

ISBN: 0-7599-0153-8
Published March 2002

© 2001 John Trammell
eBook ISBN: 0-7599-0152-X
Published October 2001

Hard Shell Word Factory
PO Box 161
Amherst Jct. WI 54407
books@hardshell.com
http://www.hardshell.com
Cover art © 2001 Sandy Castiaux
All electronic rights reserved.

Chapter 1
Virginia Tech

I'LL NEVER forget the day I met Sarah. It was one of those rare, soul-defining events that are never fully appreciated at the time, and usually pass into the covered shadows of scrapbooks, or the faded memory of a photograph.

That day was the beginning of many things that would change the world permanently. I realize that I'm trying to pass off a terrible cliche', but that day really was profound. Nothing in my life would be remotely the same if I hadn't met her the way I did, and that may not necessarily be a good thing. I haven't decided that yet.

Of one thing I am certain, though, and it is that I remember that day in every tiny detail and feeling, and I always will until the day I die. That day may be today. I haven't decided that yet for certain, either.

THE FALL OF that year was a busy time for me, as my senior attempt at graduation from Virginia Tech in the pre-law program floundered along, and my parents stressed, overly-concerned about job prospects and my lackadaisical attitude. To get into a graduate law program, I would have to maintain a straight A average for the entire year, and what I perceived as a minor annoyance was an earth-shattering anxiety for them.

I had endured, enjoyed, and survived three years of relative recreation, at the expense of numerous student loans and hard-earned family funds, and was only slightly concerned about the eventual outcome. My family was determined that I become the first lawyer in the clan, while I was more intent on writing (and finishing) my first novel, a monumental flop as I glance through it now. I read Shakespeare and George Eliot on my own, then blew off Harold Nicholson and Carl Marx that were required for a class. I went to see "Gone with the Wind," then blew off "1984" which was required for another class.

My self-justification was that college was what you made of it, and I was making it what I wanted it to be.

My roommate, whom I frequently tagged along with, was no

more concerned about his future than I, although he had already been offered several jobs in his chosen field of mechanical engineering. His grades were worse, if anything, than mine, but his chosen profession by mere chance was much more in demand. His grades wouldn't matter.

Al partied to all hours of the night, then drank himself silly on coffee and studied into the morning hours. I partied with him, then slept through classes the next day, and never studied anything.

It was through Al's influence that I happened to be at one of the female dorms the second night of the fall semester. He was visiting his erstwhile girlfriend, whom he had slept with all year, then ignored completely over the ensuing summer months. The arrangement didn't seem to bother either one of them. They would probably end up married. There was some kind of twisted logic to it that defied common sense.

While they pretended to be amazed at how good they both looked, tanned, a little heavier, and just as horny as ever, I sat down on a couch and absently flipped open the book on International Relations I had drug along for amusement. I really did try to read it for a few minutes. Then the inevitable happened and I slipped out the worn copy of "The Old Man and the Boy," that my grandfather had loaned me, and started reading it instead.

Something made me look up when Sarah came down the stairs. She was deep in conversation with a friend, both taking the steps slowly, as if they didn't want to interrupt their talk with the distraction of stairs. The pages of the textbook on my lap slowly flipped over until the book was shut.

Sarah has always been beautiful, but probably never more so than on that night. She was wearing ordinary blue jeans and a T-shirt from some spring break locale, but she radiated with something extraordinary. My doctor even once suggested that there was something more than ordinary attraction involved; something chemical; something biological, linked with this one specific person. I believe it.

She was about five foot six, with a flawless creme complexion, and nut brown, shoulder-length straight hair, that curled underneath itself at the very bottom. Her nose was small, button-like, and just as perfect, (causing me to laugh since my mother had always told me that beauty started with the nose.)

Her brown eyes—which perfectly matched the color of her hair— met mine at that instant, and for some absurd reason I stood up, silent and transfixed. She smiled at my idiocy, and I immediately blushed at my own foolishness. Her expression was a combination of amusement and satisfaction—as if she expected men to react that way.

"Hello," I called, all the way across the room, tossing my book down with ridiculous bravado. She paused on the third stair from the bottom, smiling, her friend glaring at me as if I had just made a complete breach with accepted etiquette.

"Are you new around here?" I said, walking over as swiftly as I could without tripping.

"No," she said, refusing to give up the high ground on the curved staircase. "Do I know you?"

In a completely unprovoked action, I thrust my hand out to shake hers. "I'm J. K. Baird. My friends just call me Jack." Her hand was soft and warm; not limp, but very relaxed and sophisticated.

Her Barbie-like friend brushed by me, tugging at Sarah's sleeve. "I'm sure we're very honored, Jack, but we were just on our way out."

Sarah smiled again and followed her, glancing over her shoulder with a bounce. "Nice to meet you, Jack."

"Can I see you sometime?" I blurted out, stepping away with them.

"I'm around all the time," she replied, waving, then disappearing around the corner.

Behind me, Al and his girlfriend were making a funny face at me.

"What's got into you Jack? Don't you know who that is?"

I slowly walked over to Al, still staring at the empty space where Sarah Collins had stood. I was in shock, like that King in the Old Testament was when he saw Esther for the first time.

"Come on, J. K., you don't want to get mixed up with her. She's nothing but a big tease. Mickey went out with her a couple of times."

I wasn't sure how that information was supposed to enlighten me. Mickey was no intellectual giant.

"What do you mean, a tease? She seemed pretty nice to me."

Al's girlfriend tried to explain. "Jack, she's not serious about any guy. She just makes a big show of being interested, but never does anything."

I felt myself growing offended, and I was proud of it, because it was a strange feeling. "Are you talking about sex, or something?"

"I'm talking about everything, Jack. You're too nice for her. She's not that pretty, anyway."

As if to confirm that, Al received a warm kiss on the cheek.

By providence, though, or powers on earth greater than me, I knew from that very moment on that Sarah was meant only for me. I had never felt a desire so strong, or a commitment so deep as the one I felt that night. Granted, I had fallen in love with a dozen different girls in high school, and each one had been more intense (and short-lived) than the last. Sarah was different, though, and I heard it right away in the tone of voice of those around me. They knew Sarah was for me, and they didn't like it, or approve.

There had been other girls in college, too. Every relationship had been predicated on some whimsical callousness, or indefinite vision of the murky future. None of them had really touched that spot that Sarah pricked from the first moment on the stairs. None of them had been people who wanted to twist fate—they were more inclined to let fate shape them.

Sarah was suddenly very clear to me. I could see everything about her as I walked back to my dorm room. Sarah was the one for me.

THAT SAME NIGHT, back at my own room, I learned more about my new infatuation.

"Hey Mickey," Al said, playfully hitting me on the arm, "give my stupid roommate some advice about Sarah Collins."

Mickey, who was on the football team, and undisputed brawling champ on the hall, snickered and raised a Sicilian eyebrow.

"Sarah Collins, huh? Is that little thing hot, or what? Whew! Man, I can tell you about Sarah Collins!"

Inside my stomach, muscles began to contract and restrict my breathing. Depending on what was said next, I was ready to die for her at the hands of one of my own friends to defend her. Funny, though, I didn't even know the first thing about her. That's how true love worked in all the classics, though, kind of like Sydney Carton and Lucie Manette in A Tale of Two Cities.

"Tell me."

"Well," he said, rolling his eyes as if scrolling through mental notes, "You can't fault her looks. There's no dispute in that area. But she gets kind of weird when you try to touch her, or even hold hands or anything. I mean, she weirded out on me and left the party."

Mickey laughed and looked at me knowingly. "She's just one of those teases, J. K., and you'll be walking around stiff for weeks for no good reason." Mickey slapped me on the back—a bruising, rattling show of affection. "I'm still walking around stiff," he said over his shoulder.

I was a little stumped. The idea of sexual attraction hadn't really been singled out from all the other attractions.

I joined Al in our room, where he was drinking shots of Jack

Daniels and studying quantum physics. His eyes were bloodshot from one or the other, or both.

"I told you, J. K. Mickey knows her."

"Maybe she's just religious, or something," I said, in a lame attempt to say something positive. I was in the awkward position of falling in love with a girl my fellow brothers said couldn't love in return, or something to that strange effect. Many girls from the part of Kentucky I grew up in were fully injected with a conservative dose of fundamentalist morals, though, and there could be other explanations as well. (Those same girls had a tendency to lose that fundamentalism with a vengeance when they stayed away from home too long.)

"Bickens said he got something from her, but he lies. He says that about everyone."

"I'm not trying to get her in bed!" I said suddenly, with surprising anger. "I just want to go out with her."

Al smiled and downed another shot, then poured me one. "She's out of your league, Jack. I'm not saying that in a bad way. She's just not your type. She probably had one of those parties, or something, where you, ah..."

"Come out? Debut?" I said.

"Yeah, that's it! You're a farm boy, J. K. You're a good person."

"So what?"

"There's no shame in it. You should look for your own type, that's all."

I downed the shot and stared at the picture of a pinup girl above my bed. Suddenly, I felt very childish and angry, and ripped it down.

Al was already back in his physics book. How he studied when under the influence I'll never know.

MY FIRST DATE with Sarah wasn't really a date at all. Because I aspired (somewhat secretly, given my parents' concerns) to be a novelist and a writer, I changed my schedule at the last minute and added an American Literature class. Sarah had the same class, with the same professor, though at a different time.

After a torturous approach in the cafeteria, during which I almost spilled my entire tray of food, I managed to endure the hostile glares of her sorority sisters long enough to ask her if she wanted to study together for an upcoming test. She agreed, neither flattered nor embarrassed by my invitation. I walked away feeling defeat and victory equally. I guess I wanted her to be as excited as I was—maybe she was—I don't know.

I didn't tell anyone at my table what had happened. Only Al noticed my momentary deviation between the dinner line and our seats. His mustache twitched a little bit, and his jet-black eyes blinked.

"What did you do, ask her out or something? Let me guess—she turned you down flat."

"I didn't ask her out," I said, offering nothing more.

Al shrugged, and returned to the pork chops on his loaded plate.

SARAH WAS QUIET when we met at the nearly empty Lee building. The sterile, modern brick building that buzzed with classroom activity during the early part of the day was left open until eleven every night to be used as a quiet study area. She smiled, said a polite hello, and joined me in a classroom near the front doors. She had her notebooks and materials in tow, reminding me of the fact that Mickey had said she was a straight A student.

If anything, she was more beautiful than before. I hesitate to describe her too much, because she is the one person I never could adequately paint a picture of. I can say, however, that I felt a nervous perspiration under my collar that was not at all caused by mere physical attraction, but simply because I so desperately wanted to even hear her voice.

"Are you a lit major, too?" she asked, sitting down in one of the plain, wooden classroom desks that looked positively stale with her curvaceous form curled in it.

"No. Pre-law, political science." I said it almost apologetically, though there was no criticism in her bright eyes.

"Do you mind me asking why you're taking an American Lit class?"

I tried not to grin stupidly, which is what I usually do when I don't know what to say. "I just like literature. International relations and ancient history can get a little stale."

"Maybe you should have been a lit major, too."

"My parents want me to be a lawyer."

She paused from leafing through her notes and squinted at me curiously. "Do I detect the slightest note of dissension there?"

"I...want to be a lawyer, too...I guess."

A curious, far-away gleam suddenly passed through her eyes, and she inexplicably stared out the black windows. She continued staring so long that I became nervous.

"What are you looking at?" I said, trying to see if someone was peeping in the window at us. It was probably Mickey, jealous creep that he was.

"I'm trying to guess what you really want to be." She squinted again, her face so perfect in every expression—even confusion— that I ended up just gazing at her. She finally looked back at me.

"Maybe you want to be a writer."

I stared at her dumbly. She smiled and I just sat there like an idiot. Maybe someone had told her. Al knew about the book I was writing. So did his girlfriend. Somebody must have told her. That had to be it. There's no other way she possibly could have shot a more deadly arrow at me. I was completely smitten.

Later I found out that it was a complete guess, or, perhaps I should call it an insight, for I'm not really sure if Sarah ever guessed at anything at all.

I was already beginning to love her more than I did life itself. And despite my friendly protestations to the contrary, I was also walking around very stiff.

THE FIRST TIME I saw Sarah with another male was two weeks into the semester. The guy in question was a basketball player—the star center, in fact—and he was without a doubt one of the biggest of the big men on campus. They were walking toward the cafeteria, and he was draping his arms all over her as if she belonged to him.

Mickey and Al restrained me, along with three or four other brothers.

"Easy, Jack! It's not like you guys are dating, or something." Something in Al's voice implied that he, too, was ever so slightly jealous.

"I told you this would happen," Mickey said, grinning like a Cheshire cat. "The man who marries her will be looking over his shoulder for the rest of his life."

This particular comment stung with vicious sharpness. In my own mind, I had already imagined being married to her; perhaps living out the rest of my life with her. Since my own parents were divorced, I considered it my sacred duty to find the one and only right mate— Sarah Collins. When I married, it would be forever.

I had only seen her up close half a dozen times. We had never gone out on a real date. The little details were immaterial. Some things you just know instantaneously and instinctively.

The basketball geek tried to slip his arm around her upper torso a little too far, and I strained again against my friends and their presumed better judgement. It was unnecessary, as it turned out, since Sarah casually moved his arm away and smiled as if nothing had happened.

"I'm gonna kill him," I said under my breath.

Mickey laughed. "Listen to Jack, man. I've never heard him talk like that. Say it again, J. K.! I want to hear you say something really mean."

At that moment, Sarah happened to glance in our direction. Though her smile did not alter, her attention clearly focused for several long moments on my awkward wrestling match with my fraternity brothers. She looked away quickly when the geek pulled her again, then they went into the cafeteria.

"Hey," Mickey said, his voice a little hoarse from exertion. "Let's take some bets. How long, if ever, until Jack actually goes out with her?"

"How long until you get beat up?" Al said to me.

With equal parts happy and sad, I must report that both events were very shortly forthcoming.

THE RESULTS OF the fight with the basketball geek were a foregone conclusion. The circumstances leading up to it, however, were of a little more interest. The jock initiated the hostilities because I went out with Sarah, and not vice versa.

We went to the dollar movies downtown in Blacksburg, where smuggling beer into the old theater under your coat was an art developed to unprecedented perfection by college students. Sarah and I, however, brought no unnecessary stimulants with us. I almost forgot to bring enough money to pay for both of us I was so anxious.

It was a chilly day in early November, and she had on an oversized cotton University of Kentucky sweater (by this time I had discovered that we both called the bluegrass state home, an added attraction. How both of us came to be at Virginia Tech is a story in its own right). We walked all the way from upper campus, despite the cold.

On this particular evening, Sarah was in a boisterous mood completely without precedent in our short history. She talked more than I had ever heard her talk before. It spared me a great deal of anxiety, since I was always skipping heartbeats in search of good lines, or funny quips to use to cover up my own innate shyness. None were necessary tonight. A side of Sarah other people said she supposedly didn't have—goofy, talkative, and down to earth—was clearly in evidence.

"You never seem to let anything phase you," she said, pushing me playfully. "When you told me your parents were divorced, I didn't believe you because you said it so matter-of-factly. When people get married, it's a big deal. It was for mine, at least. But tonight, you'd never know my parents aren't still together, would you?"

I shrugged helplessly, clueless about an appropriate response.

"Today was the first time in three years that I've seen my parents together for some common purpose, and I can't believe how nice it was. They actually talked and laughed a little, and were civil the entire time. Better yet, it had something to do with me. I'd say that's worth celebrating, wouldn't you?"

"Sure...I mean, yes!"

She grabbed my hand and I stared at it in shock, as if it were no longer part of my own body. Mickey had said she wouldn't even hold hands with him after four beers.

I was still staring at it when I should have simply been enjoying it.

"This is our first date, Jack. Can I call it a date?" She laughed again, a wonderful sound that revealed in another shade how Sarah Jane Collins was deeper than ten Mickeys. "Can I?"

"Yes," I said slowly, looking up numbly.

"I go out with a lot of guys. Most of them are boring, or want something more than simple fun. It's kind of childish. How about you? I haven't seen you with too many girls. Do you date very much?"

I yanked my hand away, then tried to put it back. It had reacted without my permission, and I attempted to apologize with my face, which didn't work, either. I don't know why I reacted the way I did.

She laughed and covered her mouth with her hand. "That was a stupid thing to say. I didn't mean it as an insult."

"None taken," I said, the words coming out brusquely anyway. "The reason I haven't gone out with that many girls is that most of them..."

"Go on," she said.

"Most of them are boring, or want something more than simple fun."

She swung my hand with an exaggerated stride.

"I don't think that's really what you were going to say, Jack. You're just too nice. Most girls are bimbos. The only reason they came to Tech is to get married or to get laid. I could tell when I meet you, however, that you didn't fall into the usual categories."

"Really? How did you classify me?"

She swung my arm again and looked down the sidewalk, like she had stared out the window in the classroom. "When I saw you at the dorm, you had two books open at the same time. I classified you as a literary type, or an engineer. But your eyes definitely had an artistic shade. I think you're a writer, or will be."

I smiled. It was a shame my parents wanted me to be a lawyer. How did she know these things about me? I thought about Jesse Stuart, or Wendell Berry, or Robert Penn Warren—had they met someone at a critical junction of youth that inspired them to their great careers? They were my idols, and writing was what I wanted to do.

"Well don't mind me if I talk a lot tonight," Sarah continued. "I'm just happy for a little while. It's not often I feel this happy, so I have to celebrate. They're even staying in the same hotel!" She skipped ahead of me, dancing down the sidewalk.

She stopped and turned, hands on hips, smiling, and part of me noted that she already had complete control over me. I was beginning to not only accept it, but covet it.

"I like you, Sarah." I said the words innocently, and with all good intentions, but they still came out rather comically. She laughed hysterically, then grabbed my hand again. This time, I vowed that I would leave it there come hell or high water.

About that time, I glanced behind us and noticed Mr. Basketball striding along with an angry expression. Sarah felt me pulling in that direction and looked herself. When she saw him, she squeezed my hand very tight and laughed again.

"Just ignore him," she said, raising an eyebrow and winking. "He's just mad because I was with my parents all day."

The rest is history. I relate it here only to add to the growing piles of evidence that I was truly in love with Sarah Collins; beyond the reach of any hope; beyond any hope of repair.

I stood my ground and fell, dazed; my jaw nearly broken; but proud for unknown reasons of what I bombastically assumed was my enormous bravery. I never did get to see the movie. I spent the rest of the night in the student infirmary, with Sarah and a few of her less snobby sorority friends "oohing" and "aahing" over me.

BY THE END OF the first semester, Sarah and I were more or less steady. I occasionally received reports of bold competitors elbowing in when I wasn't around her, but I very cockily ignored them. Sarah seemed to respect me more because of this attitude.

Of course it goes without saying that I never looked at another girl for the rest of the school year. Chrisma, in Latin; the end of the line.

It wasn't until the night before Christmas break that a purely accidental conversation with Al interrupted my complete reverie.

"How your grades gonna be?" he asked, busy stuffing a duffel bag with dirty clothes.

I glanced with a guilty look at the piles of schoolwork, mostly unfinished, on my desk. "Okay, I guess." It was, after all, mostly history and politics. My general knowledge in those fields was probably enough to get me part of the way. The rest of the way... ...I didn't want to worry about it, so I didn't, for a while.

Al accepted that, unaware of the sudden door he had thrown open in my own mind. "I've got it all figured, J. K.," he continued, nonplussed. "If I get a 2.5 this semester, I don't have to pass anything my last semester. Pretty cool, huh?"

"Yeah..." I said slowly. "Cool."

From that moment until a conversation with my father three days later, I remember nothing. The talk with my father, I remember all too well.

My father was a retired school teacher, as gruff as the first day he had walked into his classroom, always busy fighting out a few extra dollars here and there on our family farm near Mount Sterling. My mother had left him for many reasons, but partially because of the farm, and she was now living with a wealthy lawyer in Lexington. Both parents were determined that I was going to be a wealthy lawyer, too, though each had different reasons for wanting that. My father wanted me to be his opposite—a Thomas Jefferson type planter and wealthy man of the land; my mother simply didn't want me to be like my father.

I had just given him a copy of my grades, although that was tantamount to masochism. The alternatives were just as bad. As he stared at my grades, he held a copy of the phone bill in his other hand.

Before he even started, I wanted to tell him more about Sarah; wanted to tell him about how close I was to finishing my novel; wanted to tell him how profoundly happy I was. The words never came out.

Instead, I stood like a man and weathered a storm of angry advice about priorities and choices, and this, from a man who was far from what I would call a success in the very such areas of life he presumed to teach me about.

I went to Sarah's house in Louisville the next day, and spent Christmas with part of her family. Sarah helped me begin editing the completed first draft of my novel.

A NUMBER OF people made half-hearted attempts to talk me out of proposing to Sarah during the second semester.

Most of them, like my father, I simply ignored. Al, however, in his brother-like way, and beign with me all the time, was harder to put aside. His opinion was not completely unheard.

"I'm telling you plain and straight, J. K. While you're scrapping pennies to get a nice rock, she's still flirting around like a dizzy freshman."

"It's nothing serious. That's just her personality."

"Exactly! You're not like that, J. K. You're too nice. I set you up with Carla's sister, and you didn't even kiss her goodnight. She wasn't impressed—she was infuriated. For God's sake, think about this. You're about to leap into marriage with someone you don't even know that well."

"That was last year."

"What?"

"The date with Carla's sister."

"You're completely missing the point. Listen, I just want you to be happy, and I'm not saying this to be cruel, but you've just been convenient for Sarah. What's it going to be like to be married to someone who's so restless? For that matter, what makes you think she'll even accept? She's just too restless for you, Jack."

"She's not restless—she's...complicated. And a few months ago you were telling me she wouldn't even go out with me. You were wrong."

Al did something very unusual. He went over to my desk and picked a book up, like the most serious professor on campus. "This is what you need to be worried about. Do you think Sarah is gonna want to be sitting around with some unemployed political science major? She's a lit major, for God's sake. Neither one of you are going to get a job. Look at the clothes she wears, and that car she drives. How you gonna live like that? I don't know her parents, but do they want her to marry a farmer?"

"What's wrong with being a farmer? Besides, I want to write."

I didn't want to be angry with anyone—least of all, Al—but I was close to reaching a crisis with all of the well-intended advice. It wasn't just him either. It was everyone.

Al held his hands up in exasperation. Since he was much bigger than me, and I didn't want to end up in a fight with my best friend, I walked out to find Sarah.

A WEEK LATER, I made the decision to go through with the proposal. Sarah knew what was coming and she still played coy, acting as if she didn't really know what was going on.

We went to a mountain resort for the weekend about thirty minutes west of Blacksburg. I took gleeful pleasure in charging the whole affair on the credit card I was supposed to use only for school expenses. (My father would be furious; my mother would gently lecture me, then pay it off.)

As on other momentous occasions in our young relationship, Sarah showed no unusually profound emotions as we sat down to a fine dinner beside a breath-taking view of a snow-covered mountain ski slope. She was always careful about her appearance, but I imagined that she had taken particular care to put her makeup on just right, and choose a snug, velvet-green corduroy dress that was one of my favorites. Not a single hair on her lovely head was out of place.

"I want to marry you," I said, still holding a menu and catching even myself off guard. I had intended to wait until after dinner. I stared into her eyes and tried to read a reaction. She did smile, but I could tell it was because she knew I was trying too hard to gauge her expression.

Sarah never gave away any secrets before she wanted to. Never.

"Is that a proposal?" she asked, her voice cracking for the first time that I can ever remember.

"Will you marry me, Sarah Jane Collins?"

There was a hesitation that seemed to last for a century. Again, her face betrayed very little, if any, emotion. I had begun to feel a certain anxiety, when she blurted out her answer.

"Yes I will, Jackson King Baird the Second."

I leaned over the table and kissed her on the lips; a long drawn out kiss that tingled all over my face. It wasn't our first kiss, by any means, but it's definitely one that I can remember and taste even to this moment.

"How soon?" I asked, offering her the box with the ring in it.

Without any hesitation she slipped the ring on and studied it carefully.

"How about this weekend?" she said.

I laughed nervously, trying to determine if she was serious. I really couldn't tell.

"We've got to finish school; maybe plan ahead a little."

"I know," she said, smiling gently. "I just wish I could do something now, before all of this ends."

"All of what ends?" I said, alarmed.

"School. It's the first time I've really enjoyed myself. Especially this year, for some reason. It's the first time I've felt like I escaped home, and didn't have to deal with it all the time. It's the first time my family wasn't hanging over me like a shadow."

I reached across and held her hands. "Sarah, I loved you from the very first moment I saw you in the dorm. When we leave school, we can go anywhere, or do anything we want to. That'll be even better than school."

She leaned over and kissed me, a gesture I found profoundly reassuring. I was usually the one who initiated physical contact, although the passion in her embrace was always intense, no matter who started it.

We made love several times that weekend—more than that, actually—throwing mud in the face of all the theories that Sarah Collins was just a tease. It was not a first for either of us in the physical sense of sex, but it was a singular first between the two of us, and emotionally charged with indescribable power.

This began a chain of events that I can't help but remember with jealous desire. After the first barrier was broken down, we were reckless in our lovemaking. I had only to show up beneath her window at any time of the day or night, and then passions took over. I suppose in retrospect we're lucky we weren't kicked out of school, so blatant our obsession became. We managed to find solitude in a dozen different hideouts on campus—some of them dangerously exposed to the outside world. Nothing mattered but us.

Again, it was always me showing up at her room, initiating, but there was no lack what-so-ever of willingness on the part of Sarah. I never once felt a deficit of desire in her actions, or any hesitation to be with me. It was just the way our relationship was evolving. I was the initiator. I always hugged first. I was always the first to move my lips forward for a kiss. I was always the one to start our wild lovemaking. I always wore my heart on my sleeve. I was a the Democrat, and Sarah was the Republican. I drank Coke, she liked Pepsi.

Most of the time.

When the word leaked out that Sarah and I were doing more than studying at night, it resulted in a brief flurry of renewed overtures from would-be lovers who had failed before to solve her mysteries. Sarah enjoyed the attention, it was obvious—maybe even enjoyed it a little too much—but she never gave a single one of them a reason to go any further than politeness dictated. I was flattered and jealous at the same time—a mixture of feelings that I almost grew used to as time went on. I had never experienced dating a "popular" girl, and it made me suddenly feel superior to most of the other guys on campus.

My grades, predictably enough, fell through the bottom. Sarah's stayed at Suma Cumladi, despite everything else going on. When I should have been studying, instead I was with Sarah, or writing feverishly on the novel.

I did graduate, contrary to the warnings of gloom and doom that my father preached by phone every week or two, but I would not be getting into any ordinary law school that I knew of, unless it was for a mail order degree, or some special program where you served as a legal aid for half your life. I might not be Thomas Jefferson, but I still had my sights on maybe being a Poe or a Dickens.

All of our parents, step-parents, boyfriends, and girlfriends met for the first time at the graduation ceremony, and it was a tolerable success. It seemed like life was really coming together.

Sarah and I also were too busy to worry about it. Even as we were walking down the aisle to receive our diplomas, we were tossing potential wedding dates back and forth, talking about who to invite, where to have it, and anything else remotely related. In fact, Sarah showed an unusual interest in the actual mechanics of the wedding, as if it was something drastically important in its own right, regardless of who she was marrying. I fed her excitement about it by listening and agreeing with everything she said.

We caused a commotion on the graduation stage, since Baird and Collins do not even come close alphabetically at a school the size of Tech and yet we had arrived simultaneously. Sarah, in an unusual show of defiance, quietly refused to move back to her assigned spot. They pushed her along with me and she retrieved her diploma later. I suppose in retrospect, that was quite a sign of affection on her part.

Everything from that time on, however, was related solely to the wedding. Frankfort was determined to be a neutral site where both families could come together, and the First Baptist Church near the Kentucky River was chosen as the exact site. It was to be a Capital wedding in many joyous ways—after all, I was marrying the girl of my dreams. It might also be the last time that we would see both sets of our parents together in one place. That, to Sarah and I, was important for reasons that any child of a divorced family can understand. Everything was about the two of us. It was wonderful and exciting.

In time, family would assume even more importance in the circumstances that clouded over us. This was how my relationship with

Sarah Collins came about. It will take a considerably greater amount of time to state how it will end.

Chapter 2
The Wedding

I STAYED WITH my father at the farm near Mount Sterling for most of the days before the July wedding. We argued about what kind of job I should look for, whether I should take more classes and still try to get into law school, and whether mother's boyfriend (the lawyer) could pull any strings to get me placed somewhere as a legal eagle (a paralegal). But even in our bickering there was a small measure of quiet and calm before the upcoming storm of excitement.

My father is a hard man to describe. He was not tall, though he was certainly strong physically. His hair had grayed by this time, although it remained full and wavy. My grandmother compared it to straw back when it was still dark blonde.

He was also a stubborn, proud man, even in matters that I felt he had no right to be. For example, years after his divorce from my mother, he still insisted that most of it was her fault. I know that can't possibly be true.

It still felt good to be home, despite his eccentrics. I baled hay, herded Charolais cattle, cultivated corn, and thought every waking moment of Sarah Collins. Every other day or so, the intensity of my desire would overcome me and I would drive to her mother's house in Louisville—sometimes just for a few hours. Sarah was always smiling and laughing, and occasionally even arranged some kind of small surprise for me to open upon arrival. Once, it was personal word processor so I could work on my writing when I was away from home.

Sarah's parents were both relatively well-off; wealthy when compared to my father. They also gave me things, and bought me a new suit in case I needed to interview somewhere. They were very anxious that I find good work, although Sarah never said a word of worry to me about it herself.

There was, I quickly noticed, a strange kind of tension in the air when her parents were around me, and this I simply chalked up to the nature of divorce. I was very familiar with the discomfort it produced. My parents carried it around with them like a chain. Sarah's parents, regardless, seemed to like me at least tolerably well; particularly her father, who frequently tried to give me things. He also wanted to help set up job interviews.

I remained wholly undecided about what I should do as far as a career. My novel, as reported, was finished before the end of the school year, but I had experienced no success in trying to sell it to an agent or publisher. Sarah encouraged my desire to write, although she never once suggested that it might become a career. I remained in a deadlock; a ship without a course.

But I was ready to marry Sarah. That was the one constant during this time. Sarah made college seem like a distant memory.

The actual wedding day arrived with sweltering heat, and we all agonized in our tuxedos and beautiful dresses waiting for the preacher, who was fashionably late. Behind us, the Kentucky River was near flood stage from recent torrential rains, causing Sarah's mother to panic several times, as she was convinced that the flood waters would rise up and spoil the beautiful wedding she had helped plan (and pay for). Fortunately, the waters stayed below flood level—just barely.

Sarah was radiant. There was no sign of the flirtatious, devil-may-care, flitting and flouncing young college girl I had first met on the stairs at the dormitory. Before me instead was the most beautiful, serene, flawless, sterling example of a young woman that I had ever laid eyes on. When she entered on her father's arm and met my eyes for the first time that day, I could swear I saw a happiness in her face that was never exceeded again. I'm embarrassed to admit it, but as I gloried in her slow procession down the aisle, I began to weep. Al was my best man, and on the video I noticed that he shook his head in disgust. It was the first time I had cried in my adult life over anything, including my parent's split.

Sarah was crying too, but the tears were spilling onto the biggest grin I had ever seen on her face. It was all we could do to stop ourselves from embracing each other fiercely right at that moment. We both laughed, the music suddenly stopped, and the traces of our laughter echoed to the rear of the church. It was a superb moment that the poor audio on the videotape of the wedding does not do justice to.

"Do you, Jackson King Baird, take Sarah Jane Collins to be your lawfully wedded wife; to love and to cherish; to protect and provide for; forever and ever, so help me God?"

"I do."

"Do you, Sarah Jane Collins, take this man to be your lawfully wedded husband; to stand by and to love; to respect and to uplift; forever and ever, so help me God?"

"I do."

The videotape did complete justice to the kiss that followed. Everyone I talked to agreed with me that it was just a little bit too racy for a family-style wedding, but Sarah and I were unrestricted free agents in the kissing arena from the moment he pronounced us man and wife. A few minutes later, we desperately wanted to make love, even in the choral foyer behind the alter as we impatiently waited for the photograph session to begin, but there were simply too many people around, and we soon had to attend the reception. That was a feeling, though, that I never wanted to forget.

It was at the reception that Sarah first began to show some signs of general stress. There were symptoms I had hitherto never witnessed.

"I want to leave," Sarah said shortly after arriving. "Since we're married now, can't we make a command decision and just go?"

"Just give the word, and I'm ready." I hardly even glanced at her as I spoke. I thought she meant in a few minutes. There were so many people around, all of them smiling at us and murmuring things that I couldn't quite hear plainly.

"Well, you go tell my mother that I'm not feeling well, and that I need to get out of this dress."

She meant right this moment. I dutifully slid my chair back and stood up, then was restrained.

"No, Jack, don't do that. I don't want you to lie to her."

"It's not a lie, is it?"

"Jack we can't leave yet."

"But you just said—"

"We haven't even had the toast, or cut the cake, or, or..."

Sarah was not high-strung, by any means, but she was clearly beginning to unravel. It shook me up a little because I was so used to her normally even, sometimes dreadfully steady, keel. She looked as if she were ready to burst into tears again, but she was not smiling this time.

"What's the matter, Sarah? Sarah, what's wrong?"

My concern turned into alarm. I had never seen Sarah look like this before—pasty and sallow; the make-up running, her normally sharp eyes glassy.

"Sarah!"

Without any warning, she burst into tears and was utterly inconsolable. The band stopped playing, and her mother ran up, gibbering orders out to everyone around not to panic, while that was exactly what she proceeded to do.

"What'd you say to her?" Al demanded beside me.

"I didn't say anything."

"What did you do to her, Jack?" her mother echoed.

"Nothing!"

Sarah's face was flushed, streaked with tears, and she continued to breath uncertainly. Her eyes were half-closed.

Years later, Sarah and I both decided that we should have gone ahead and made love in the foyer when we had a chance. As it turned out, she spent our first night of official marriage in the emergency room, being treated for heat exhaustion. There was no chance for any more fun that night. Her waist, as wonderfully slim and curvy as it was, had been too restricted in the elaborate, antique family dress her mother crammed her into.

While we waited in the emergency room lobby, all of us still dressed in formal tuxedos and lavish gowns, I vented a little bit of my anger and frustration on Al, who just happened to be the closest bystander.

"Why the hell was everybody assuming it was something I did to her? You're the one who was always saying she wouldn't treat me right, and that I was too nice. Yet all Sarah has to do is swoon, and everyone in the room comes after me like I'm a common criminal or something! Even you were after me."

Before Al could open his mouth, Sarah's mother came storming over in her command-style mode and immediately invaded the personal space inches from my face.

"Jack, what the hell were you saying to her that made her cry like that?"

"I didn't say anything! She told me she wanted to leave, and when I stood to tell you, she stopped me and began crying."

More mindless exchanges ensued, during which the process of human communication in my immediate family was set back for at least a decade or two. It was inane; we were all worried; we were all frustrated. We all took it out on each other.

When my father arrived and assigned himself the role of peacemaker, things got even worse. For some reason, Sarah's mother and my father seemed to double their criticism of me when they were together. Hell, they might have even made a decent match if he'd have lived long enough to find out. They wouldn't have received very many visits from me, however.

The doctor finally let me in—after her mother had seen her. I was too tired to be insulted, or hurt, but I should have been both. I had just married Sarah. It was time for me to come first; time for "us," literally.

Sarah's smile immediately warmed me. She started crying again, but this time it was with the smile intact. It was already becoming one of those little signals that mates get to know with each other so well. If she cried with a smile, she was okay.

"Sarah, honey, you gave us all a scare." I hugged her tight, still not over the strange sensation of fright that had cropped up for the first time since I had known her. Lying here in the emergency room of the King's Daughter's Hospital, she was more fragile and vulnerable than I had ever seen her. It gave me a sour glimpse of life without her that I immediately choked down and tried to forget, forever and ever.

"I got scared today, Jack. I don't know what came over me."

"It was the heat, Sarah—"

"No, it wasn't just the heat."

I felt something besides my heart thump in my chest. It was my stomach turning over. I hated it when she made these wide open, evasive comments that could be interpreted in any of several directions—including very negatively. Was it something I had done? Was she having her doubts about me now? Doubts about marriage?

Words came back to me from a few months ago, or even just a few hours ago: "She's too good for you." "You'll always be looking over your shoulder, Jack." Even things that Sarah had said herself to me: "It's not that I don't want to hug and kiss, Jack. I just like it better when you start it." "I flirt with guys, but I don't flirt with you. With you, it's different. You're too good to flirt with."

Back in the present, Sarah still hadn't told me what it was besides the heat that had precipitated her bursting into tears at what should have been one of the happiest moments in her life. As I looked into her red-rimmed eyes, usually so milky brown and energetic, I could tell that she was trying to tell me something, but couldn't find the right words.

"What is it, Sarah? Did I do something to upset you?"

She cried a little harder. "No, Jack! I don't know how to explain it. Don't make me miserable trying to figure it out. Please just hold me."

I complied with her wish, and thus after months of hardly missing a day, we failed to make love on our wedding night. It was, indeed, one of those extreme ironies you run across in life; in fact, existence is brimming over with them.

I consoled Sarah, though there were no immediate answers for me.

OUR HONEYMOON was a startling contrast to the night in the hospital. As we drove east on Interstate-64 from Mount Sterling toward the Atlantic Ocean, we stopped the car three or four times in the middle of the faceless eastern Kentucky mountains and scrambled into the woods to make up for our lapse two nights ago. We've both thought since then how foolish it really was, with the likely possibilities of snakes, or roving State Policemen, or any other of a number of likely hazards. But the sun and clouds as only the Kentucky sky can hold them caressed us with a loving warmth that was reserved solely for that day and place in time, and neither of us will ever forget it.

We became Hokies while at Tech, but the state of Kentucky was ingrained in both of us.

We ended up at Virginia Beach, in some over-priced resort hotel, with several thousand dollars in our pockets to burn, at as reckless a pace as we wanted. It was on the waterfront that night, hand in hand along the beach, that we had one of the truly profound conversations in our sometimes stormy, always colorful history.

We were wearing matching swim suits, which had been a somewhat peculiar gift from my mother, who had an exaggerated fondness for "couples" type articles. The salty, brownish waters of the Atlantic were lapping up onto our legs, almost cool in the windy dusk of summer.

"Do you believe in true love?" Sarah asked.

I thought about it for a moment. "Yes," I answered, somewhat hesitantly. "Yes," I said, more forcefully this time. "I do believe in true love."

"Do you believe in perfect love?"

I couldn't help but laugh. "Perfect love? What's the difference?"

Her face furrowed with concern. "They are different." There were lines of sorrow marring her normally flawless cheeks, which suddenly looked almost old, and hollow. "When we were growing up, my mother and father used to tell us that they had the perfect love; that they were meant to be from the beginning of time. But they were wrong. It wasn't true love, or perfect love."

"I don't understand."

"True love is fated; it's unavoidable. Perfect love is a state that everyone can achieve if they work hard enough. One is an accident, the other is a plan. True love is what authors always try to write about; perfect love is what reality allows people to work for. Do you remember the boy and girl in 'Pale Horse, Pale Rider?'"

I shrugged, slightly confused, declining to reply. I think she was making reference to a Katherine Anne Porter story. We had never really deeply discussed our parent's divorces. As I was quickly to discover, there were some very important details that set them apart.

"My mother and father said they loved each other," she said. "They thought they had true love."

I tried to console her. "My parents used to say the same things, Sarah. Since I was an only child, I never really had anyone to discuss things with except my mother. She talked to me all the time, so I knew when I was getting a little older that some things were wrong in their relationship. For starters, their backgrounds were completely different. My father was from Appalachia, down around Cumberland, and had a completely different set of values. Mother grew up in Lexington, relatively sheltered and sophisticated. That set them apart from the beginning."

Sarah frowned deeper, if such was possible. "Is that why they got divorced?"

"There were a lot of reasons, but that was the root cause, I think. My mother wanted more out of life than hard work on a dirty, low-profit farm, and washing dishes and laundry. After all, she has a degree in teaching from U. K., just like he does. But he never let her teach."

"He didn't let her?"

"He didn't physically abuse her, but he was definitely in charge. I say, that's part of why she left."

She stopped walking and held my other hand. "You don't hold that against your father, do you?"

Sarah knew my father was a sore spot with me, and oddly enough, she was never afraid to come to his defense. I was never quite sure why that was. Sarah and her mother both seemed to gravitate toward him, both mentally, and physically when in his presence.

"I don't hold anything against him. I hate his guts sometimes, like when he tries to lecture me about the right things to do, but then I remember he's my father. I love him in spite of his flaws. Isn't that normal for most people when they get old enough to see the world as it is?"

"How old is that?"

"You know—college age, or young adult."

She nodded, as if she understood. "Do you know why my parents got divorced, Jack?"

"You've never really told me, Sarah."

She let go of one hand and resumed walking. She flipped my other hand back and forth in the air gaily, though her expression was clearly angry and bitter. "Did you notice who my father was with at the Wedding?"

"Yes, you told me it was your stepmother, Ruth. You've mentioned her several times before."

"Well, Ruth is okay in her own sorry little prissy way, but she's only one in a long line of girlfriends, sluts, and lovers. My father has had so many women in his lifetime that you'd need an accounting degree to list them. My mother, who never did anything course or unloving to him, and was completely loyal for year after year was finally forced to give up on him as a lost cause."

"She knew all along?"

"No, not at first. But she began to suspect long before the end came. The last straw was when we all returned home from a Christmas shopping trip and found him with some nameless tramp in our very own house."

"He brought her to your house?"

"He was fucking her on the living room floor, Jack."

That sentence was a slap on the face. Sarah never used that word—ever, for any reason.

We walked in silence for what seemed like an eternity. Sarah's hand was incredibly hot inside of mine, a glowering coal of anger and frustration that somehow melted away inside of my own cooling grasp. Part of me was so disturbed that I'm sure I might have killed her father right on the spot with my bare hands, had he accidentally shown up. Another part of me suddenly realized that marriage to any person would be a constant trial for Sarah.

I started to ask her which love we had, then hesitated, uncertain I wanted the answer from her.

Maybe, I reasoned, that was why she had chosen me, when there had been so many other eligible suitors to choose from. Maybe she had noticed that I seldom looked at other women (when I was around Sarah), or made jokes about the girls at the mall who wore their shorts too tight, or paid any attention to beer commercials on television. Maybe that was why she had cried on our wedding night.

The magnetic effect of Sarah was complete on me. I read into this episode a new confidence in what Sarah had been attracted to when she first met me. I was the complete opposite of her father; utterly dependable and predictable.

I expected her to make me promise that I would never do such a terrible thing to her, and was prepared to swear on my very soul that I wouldn't. But oddly enough, Sarah never once asked me to say that.

As the night grew dark around us, and the black waves crashed with exaggerated fury, she shivered. "Maybe I shouldn't have told you that, Jack. I don't want you to worry about it. I don't want you to hate my father."

I felt fiercely protective, and drew her body so close to mine that I could close my eyes and still see every inch of her. "Sarah, I'm glad you told me. I won't worry about it, because you're with me now. I don't want you to worry any more about it either. Our marriage is just "us," and we'll have to stand or fall on our own track record. We can take care of each other now."

This seemed like a logical moment for her to cry, but she didn't. Instead, she kissed me lightly on the lips and sighed.

"I love you, Jack."

She said that only infrequently, so I cherished the moment for what it was—one of her rare exhibitions of raw, unfiltered emotion.

"I love you too, Sarah."

"Promise me that we won't talk about our parents anymore on our honeymoon."

"I promise."

We resumed our walk, then finished out the evening with a bottle of champagne left over from the reception, and then some popular movie on HBO. Again, I can't remember what movie it was, and it doesn't matter. In my feeble efforts at writing, I could try to describe the early days and how I felt about Sarah over and over again, and the exercise would never be perfect—or to put it in Sarah's word, it would never be a true description.

AS WE TRAVELED back from our honeymoon on the ocean, we began to discuss for the first time our plans for the immediate future. Sarah's father had offered us the use of one his rental houses in Louisville for an indefinite period of time, and she insisted that it was okay with her to accept his help.

We laughed endlessly when we passed each spot on the Interstate where we had made a permanent indentation in the soil with our uncontrollable passions. It almost seemed as if it had never even happened, and was instead some sort of absurd fantasy, invented by a tabloid newspaper or a over-imaginative letter in a men's magazine.

At a rest stop close to home, Sarah and I got out to stretch and get some cold drinks. Thunder clouds were gathering to the west, probably forming over the Ohio River.

Sarah's latest idea was that I should go to work for a newspaper.

"You'll get to write, Jack, even if it's not fiction. A lot of famous novelists got their start that way—Hemingway, Kipling... Walt Whitman, too."

Whitman was a favorite we shared jointly. We had spent an afternoon on our way home on the Capital lawn in Richmond, taking turns reading Whitman to each other.

This was something new from Sarah. She had always suggested more conventional jobs before this—even the possibility of graduate school in political science—although her suggestions were always less than that; more like dimorphous ideas that escaped into the air. She never put any pressure on me at all.

"That would be great, but it's not that simple to get on with the big papers. I'd be lucky to even get an interview with the Courier. It's not that easy."

"It is with an entry-level position. It won't pay that much, but it'll be a start. My father can help. He's an alternate on the Board of Directors, and he was an active member until recently, so he still knows everyone."

Again I studied her face for some kind of shadow, but there was none. Sarah apparently had no compunctions about using her father's wealth or position.

I wondered about my own father. He had scrapped together a thousand dollars to give us, but that was about all he could put together even in the best of times. He had no connections. He could offer me minimum wage to bale hay.

"Okay. But don't push your father too hard. I don't want him to think that I can't do it on my own."

"Jack, my father won't give you anything. He thinks very highly of you, and even though no one can accuse him of not taking care of his girls—even after they're married—he wouldn't do something to sell your ability short."

I immediately thought of the living room floor, but Sarah was humming to the radio and enjoying the wind in her hair as she took her turn at the wheel and sped out of the rest area. She didn't seem to be making the connection with her words that I was—the connection with that one traumatic event. I couldn't separate my image of her father from that single episode.

Her father did take care of all of them. The Pontiac we were driving came directly from the showroom floor to us as a wedding gift. His ex-wife—Sarah's mother, to be specific in this case—was provided with her own car, house, and generous allowance. Sarah's other sisters, one younger and one older, were equally looked after.

It's said, though, that money can't buy love, and I wasn't sure why Sarah was oblivious to my shock at the way they all took his money and smiled at him. If I were his son, I would have cut loose all connections and never spoken to him again, and he would have felt lucky at that. I would have been thinking about that beach conversation all of the time as I went about my daily business.

But I didn't marry Sarah's father. I married her, and as we approached the Mount Sterling exit, I had no reason at all to regret it.

Chapter 3
Louisville

THE FIRST MONTH of our new life was filled with the usual ups and downs newly-weds experience. We didn't usually fight over anything, but we did have some lengthy discussions and debates over such mundane issues as where to place our limited furniture, or what to have for dinner, or where to go on the weekends. On the whole, Sarah and I concluded that we were probably doing much better than most couples.

There's no exception; no bombshell that I can throw out to make anyone else feel better about their own mishaps; no smoking gun that would give insight into later difficulties—though our happiness was doomed to be interrupted very shortly.

My father died of a heart attack the first day of August. He was fifty years old.

I was devastated in a way that no one can understand, unless they have grown up as the only son of a man who never quite reached whatever pot of gold he was searching for. I was not only sad for myself, but just as much as for him, because it seemed to me that somehow he had missed out on something important in life. It also served up a grim warning for me to contemplate—don't wait for your pot of gold, or you might blink and find out that you'll never have the chance again.

Even my mother, usually so full of vitriol hatred for the man who had ruined so many years of her life, was broken up completely, and was barely able to attend the funeral. Her reaction spoke volumes about my father's real, unfettered character, beneath the brash, simple exterior.

Most unusual, however, was Sarah's reaction. She seemed, if possible, even more overwhelmed than me by the shock. She was genuinely devastated.

As we drove to the Blanton Funeral Home in Mount Sterling to make arrangements, she alternated between quiet sobbing and complete, abject silence; barely even breathing.

Sarah, in one of her quiet, unexplainable ways, must have seen something in my father that no else did. I wanted to know what it was; I was aching to hear it—but I wasn't sure how to ask.

"Sarah, I know you're upset, but I really need to talk to you about this. I'm confused, and I'm hurt, and I'm not exactly sure what I should be feeling."

She turned to me with a harsh growl. "You should be feeling the way I feel—absolutely terrible! You've said yourself that you loved the man. Is it so hard to say it again now that he's not around?"

"I have said it," I mumbled.

"Say it!" she said again.

I pulled the car over, buried my head in the wheel and began to cry. I had not expected such an attack. I had no defense.

Anyone who has loved knows how impossible it is to see how much you care for someone who it seems you're always in conflict with, when in reality you are more alike than you can ever know. My father and I were this way. It was a horrible loss; I knew that part of me was now dead, too, forever.

She stroked my arm soothingly, while continuing to lecture me. "If you were to look at all four of our parents and compare them, Jack, I think your father would be the most honest. I think he would be the most sincere. He continued to love your mother until the very moment he died. Your father had character, whether you choose to see it or not. He worked hard, and he had ethics that he wasn't afraid to share with others. He was good to your mother in his own way."

I looked up sharply. "How do you know that?"

"I could see it in his face. He made some terrible mistakes in judgement, Jack, but he was a good man. He was good to us. He was wonderful to me. He deserved more than he got out of life. He deserved a chance at some happiness for himself."

She was right, of course, but it made me angry to be lectured about my own father. If anyone had a right to feel the way they wanted to about him, it was me. I was the only trace of my father left on the earth now, other than his neatly kept fields and a herd of Charolais cattle, and an ex-wife who had left him because his best traits were what bothered her the most about him.

But she was right.

"I loved him, Sarah. Please don't hurt me any more. I loved him and I told him so whenever I could. I'm sorry."

She hugged me fiercely, but I was as limp as a rag doll. I had nothing left in me. She had to trade places with me and drive the car.

"I loved your father," she said. "And I barely got to know him. God, why him?"

Funny. It seemed hard sometimes for her to tell me how she felt about me...My father, though, brought forth such strong pronouncements. Sarah was like that. She stood up for people in the most unlikely ways. I almost felt guilty because I had married someone like her, and in naked contrast, my father had never had anything permanent or certain.

"I'm sorry," Sarah said, as she pulled into the funeral home parking lot. "I shouldn't have jumped on you like that. I think I must be as confused and upset as you."

That was possibly true. But I was hurt and puzzled by her emotional stance, as well. My grief had shifted momentarily from my father to some part of me that felt unloved by Sarah.

BY THE EVE OF the funeral, we had both regained control of our emotions. Following her outburst in the car, Sarah held me like a child until we woke the next morning. She was exceptionally kind and gentle with me when we attended the funeral. She was loving and tender in a mother-like way that was totally out of character.

I melted into it, soaking it up for as long as I could.

Looking at my father didn't bother me as much as I thought it would. His sandy brown hair was combed more neatly than it ever had been in real life, and I wanted to hold his hands up to see if God had somehow erased the calluses just for this occasion. His arms looked as thick and strong as they had always been, ready to toss a hay bale twenty feet into the loft where it would knock over his scrawny twelve-year-old son. In Wendell Berry's words, I would keep that look as part of myself, a severe gift.

More importantly, it appeared to Sarah and I that he was at peace. He had a look frozen on his face that seemed to say that things were okay, despite all outward appearances and circumstances. This was a final gift from him that magnified his tragedy and took it away all in one feel swoop.

We both hurt terribly for many weeks, but there was a silent logic that took hold of life after a while. If anything, we both agreed that this time strengthened us in ways that could never be unraveled.

We also agreed that my father would be in us both forever. It's so strange that you can't appreciate people until they are taken away from you. Then you long deeply for one last chance to be with them, just to say how much you love them. And even if you subscribe to a version of heaven where they can look down upon your life, and know what you are feeling, it doesn't take the hurt away.

THREE WEEKS AFTER I started with the Louisville newspaper as an apprentice working the feature's copy, Al and Carla, now married, came over to our house to spend the weekend. It was a welcome break.

"God!" Al said, dragging luggage behind him, "You didn't tell me it was five-hundred and fifty miles from Richmond! You said it was one a day drive."

Carla was stretching and attempting to wake up from a car nap. They both had gained weight, but looked to be in the peak of physical and mental healthiness. I had always noticed that Carla, with her pronounced Latino features and rounded curves, had an additional magic which allowed her to gain twenty pounds and still manage to look voluptuous rather than fat.

Sarah and I jumped down from the porch and hugs were traded all around. Carla and Sarah were only passing acquaintances in school, but there was a general feeling accepted by all of us that we were going to be a successful foursome as time went by. We were all Hokies. Al and I would always be best friends.

Sarah had met Al on a number of occasions, and was not afraid to call him fat to his face, or argue about the Washington Redskins, both subjects Al could expound on at great length.

As he hugged Sarah, Al literally pulled her off her feet. "Can you tell I've been working out, Sarah?" He struck a stupid pose and flexed his arms.

"Lifting cans," Carla said, punching him.

Sarah and Carla retreated to the air conditioned indoors, leaving Al and I on the front lawn in a couple of woven chairs, with sweating beers in hand.

"Heard about your father, Jack. I'm real sorry I couldn't make the funeral."

I nodded. "That's okay. After the initial shock, we've got things patched together around here."

He guzzled and snorted, looking around at the lack of landscaping in my simple yard. "I heard you're working for the newspaper."

"That's right. Doesn't pay much, but it's good experience. You know me—still all those dreams of being a writer."

"Sarah working anywhere?"

"Yes. She's part-time in her dad's real estate business."

Al paused, shielding his eyes against the sun. "Nice neighborhood." He looked at me and suddenly grinned, as if remembering something important. "Hey, Jack, I'm dying to know something."

"Shoot."

"What's it like being married to Sarah Collins?"

"What do you mean?"

"Come on!" Al said. "You know what I'm talking about! After ignoring all my warnings and advice, you still can't give me a little report?" He winked.

I felt a little defensive. No relationship is perfect, is it? Or was he talking about sex, the topic that college boys never grew tired of?

"We're doing great," I said quickly. "Why shouldn't we be?"

"What about the, ahh, physical aspects of it?"

"They're fine."

Al shrugged with a laugh and crushed the can in his hand. "You recycle?"

I shook my head and did a double take. I was still thinking about his question. I was thinking about all of the advice, opinions, and predictions I had heard before we got married. Was I supposed to invent some fantastic story of marital infidelity, or spouse abuse, just to satisfy the raving appetites of everyone who knew us in college?

"Yes," I said absently, "the plastic container by the garage."

Al trundled over there with the can and deposited it with a loud thump. I often wondered if he and Carla were really so enamored with each other, or whether they just stuck together out of some joint agreement of convenience. It didn't seem like there was another male in the world that loved his spouse as intensely as I loved Sarah. I was beginning to get a complex, or maybe I had harbored one since I met her and was just now realizing it. Why did everyone insist that Sarah and I were headed for some kind of great tragedy? Wasn't it possible for two people to have an ordinary marriage, with no surprises?

"You and Carla doing okay?" I said.

"We're doing great," Al said, pulling another beer out of the cooler. "If I didn't have to work so doggoned much, we'd be as happy as we were the day we met."

Again, his choice of words struck me as ironic. The day I met Sarah, my life changed forever. The day Al met Carla, they both got laid. I shook my head to lose all of the free-floating nonsense.

"Let's get out of the heat, Al."

"Good idea, Jack. Don't forget the cooler."

OVER DINNER THAT night, the conversation turned back to school. Al and Carla seemed to be inordinately fascinated by the speed at which everybody changed after graduation.

"You should see Mickey," Al said. "He wears a suit and tie to work every day—it's unbelievable! And get this: he drives this old beater to work, and still lives at home. He's already socked away five thousand dollars."

"That doesn't sound like Mickey," Sarah said.

For some reason, I thought about Mickey getting Sarah drunk and trying to put the moves on her. It was a flattering thought, in one sense, because I knew how attractive Sarah was, but it was also disturbing. I could hear Al saying it again: "Jack, you'll always be looking over your shoulder." I had married the girl that everyone else in the world wanted.

Had I been looking over my shoulder? In fact, I hadn't even entertained the possibilities of such wild notions. Sarah and I were as completely happy as any two people can be in an imperfect world.

"Mickey's getting married, too," Carla said. "Get this—it's some Puerto Rican girl." She laughed heartily. "She must be good."

"Imagine that," Al said, reaching under the table and grabbing Carla's dark leg. Carla's mother was still in Puerto Rica.

"Well, everybody seems to change when they graduate," Sarah said, matter-of-factly, with the trace of a sigh. "Nobody can stay the same too long. It's impossible."

"Except for you two," Al said. "You guys don't seem to be any different at all."

I smiled, though his comment didn't really make me feel good. Across the table from me, Sarah had no readable reaction. She was playing with the pasta on the end of her fork. I guess that was a reaction.

"Maybe we're not any different," I said, playing devil's advocate.

"You guys will never change, Jack. You both look like you're about ready to settle down and have some kids. You know, do the American Dream thing..." He paused expectantly.

Al had no way of knowing it, of course, but he had just said the one thing that could ruin dinner. One of the little details about Sarah that I didn't find out until after we were married was that she was physically incapable of having any children. It was something we never talked about.

Sarah quietly excused herself into the kitchen.

"Actually, that's not us," I said quietly, "We're better off the way we are, just the two of us."

Al shrugged, then pointed to Carla. "By the way, Carla's due in seven months."

"Congratulations."

"Thanks!" Al replied, smiling broadly behind his mustache and holding his can up to salute me.

"To the Hokies," he said.

"Hokies," I agreed.

I trailed after Sarah, though she brushed aside any notion that Al's comment had upset her.

ABOUT THIS TIME I started tinkering with a new novel. I never succeeded in publishing the first one from my college days, although Sarah's father did offer to subsidize a private publication of it (which I politely declined, although this wasn't to be the end of his offers), and there was some part of me that was uneasy about my prospects of success if I ever allowed myself to take too much time off from writing fiction, which was what I really loved to write. Writing copy for the paper didn't really compare, though it had it's challenges (and had presumably given birth to those famous writers mentioned). In fact, my job at the newspaper seemed to kill some of my creativity, though I didn't share that fact with anyone else.

Sometimes at the paper—when I was on break, or when things were unusually slow—I would sneak in a few pages here and there on the new novel, and at night Sarah often encouraged me to write as well. It wasn't long before something resembling a book-length manuscript began to take shape. This was number two, in terms of books (unpublished or not), and it boosted my confidence, and gave me a sense of accomplishment.

It was early fall by this time, and it felt very strange to not be returning to the lively atmosphere at Blacksburg. Sometimes, I daydreamed about possibly teaching at the college level, but I never could pin down exactly what it was that I could teach.

Sarah was a brutal editor. She was very good for my writing. When everything was just right, we would work every night on the book for a stretch of a week or two at a time.

For some reason, I was mildly jealous of her uniquely sound insights. I almost got the feeling that she could write a better novel than me, but I'd never seen her pen so much as an ordinary letter in all the time that I knew her. I suppose she didn't want to write anything.

I was always curious, however, how she could she go for such long periods of time without expressing any serious emotions or concerns at all. The only truly serious conversation we had immediately after my father's death was a brief, but heated discussion about children following Al and Carla's visit.

"Would you ever consider adopting a child?" I had asked, as we were cleaning up the dishes from dinner.

Sarah got that look on her face that almost stole away her beauty for a moment, which I learned meant that she was irritated, even though she never admitted to it.

"It wouldn't be ours."

"But sweetheart, if we found a baby—maybe only a few months old—why in the world wouldn't it be like having our own?"

"Jack, being a mother means growing a living human being inside of you for nine months, then giving birth to it. Any medical miracles and cute little orphans aside, it wouldn't be the same. It wouldn't look like me. It wouldn't have my genetic makeup. It wouldn't be me."

"You?"

"I mean, us! You know what I'm talking about. My family; your family. I want to grow and carry my own child, the natural way."

She was referring to the advice her doctor had offered, which was that Sarah might be able to carry a child, if we artificially fertilized and created a fetus, then implanted it in her womb. Sarah would not even discuss such a possibility.

I didn't say it out loud, but I had often thought about the fact that my father wanted grandchildren. For all his outward gruffness, he had always concealed a soft spot for children. Even my mother begrudgingly admitted that he had been good with me when I was a small child.

To this point, I always told myself that I had wished for nothing more in the world than a woman like Sarah. But it bothered me that she was so hostile regarding the subject of alternatives. Why not explore the possibilities, I wondered? Life was too short to leave it unexamined.

After a long silence, during which I assumed the conversation was ended, she abruptly reopened it.

"I would love to have children, Jack. I've even daydreamed about it. But it makes me furious that I can't do it myself!"

I didn't know what to say, so I chose to say nothing.

"I don't mean that it doesn't take two people to create a child, but the woman does have to do all of the work the first nine months or so. If you want to take your Bible Beaters far enough, it's all that I was created to do. If I can't do it the natural way a woman is supposed to be able to do it, I choose not to do it. Besides...The doctor said there might be risks carrying to term."

"Nothing out of the ordinary," I reminded her. "I was there for that conversation."

"I've decided not to have children, Jack."

That was Sarah's way of controlling the problem. She made it sound like it was actually her choice not to have children, rather than a complex medical dilemma. I also noted how quickly I was removed from the decision-making process.

Later that night we were working on my book and the subject unexpectedly popped up again. She was in an exceptionally nasty editorial mood, and I was having trouble even keeping up with her rapid-fire comments, deletions, insertions, and grammatical corrections.

"Slow down, Sarah! I can only type so fast!"

"Jack, for some reason this week you've started using commas like they're going out of style. You're like an engine that's sputtering on half its cylinders."

"Okay, okay, honey, just point out which ones, because they all look fine to me."

"Am I going to get my name placed right beside yours on the cover of this thing?"

I suddenly felt the power leave my fingers. I stopped typing in mid-sentence and looked at her. She stared at me, too, waiting to see what kind of rebuttal I would make, and daring me to say something. I finally just shrugged my shoulders in exasperation.

"I really wanted to have children, Jack! My mother certainly could, with all her other flaws and conditions, and my sisters are going to—why was I singled out? What punishment do I deserve? I haven't done anything evil. My genes—screw my genes!"

I pushed the button on the monitor off and sat back in my chair. I realized at that moment that my lovely Sarah—my perfect, flawless, pretty Sarah—was brimming over with emotions that normally never quite made it to the surface of her steady existence. Marriage, I suppose, more than anything, exposes all of the nagging little flaws all of us come into the world fully equipped with, but my Sarah—my perfect Sarah—she had finally provided me with a front row seat to witness some of hers. Part of me was in shock.

Another part felt great joy, despite the tragedy of the situation. I could help her now that a few simple words had made it beyond the confines of her lips. I could help her deal with it. I could create a solution with her.

I cautiously reached for her hand, half expecting her to pull it away, but she didn't. She reached to turn the monitor back on and I stopped her.

"Sarah, I know I've told you this before, but I never thought I'd find someone just like you. If I could have drawn a blueprint up in my mind for some cosmic engineer to create another person that I would fall in love with, I would have designed you. If I could have painted a picture in my mind of someone I would die for, which I did in many private daydreams, it would have been a picture of you.

"There are a lot of minor miracles happening all the time, if you look around a little. Each one is no more likely than something ordinary, but they happen anyway. Most people don't even notice them—but you, you're not like most people. Maybe you just need to wait a little while longer and let the right thing happen."

"Jack, we're talking about a physical impossibility!"

"Nothing is impossible. I'm sitting here trying to tell you that we think we know what's going to happen every moment of every day, and yet we're constantly wrong. You're boxing yourself in, Sarah, and you shouldn't do that."

"I can't fight the impossible! Are you going to tell me now that you can walk on water, or heal the masses? Will the great J. K. Baird lay his healing hands on me and, and..."

There was a silence, then a void, and then we both stared at each other simultaneously. It was a ridiculous thing to say, but it was funny, and she hadn't said it meanly. The laughter that cautiously appeared seemed to dissipate her anger.

"Walking on water won't land you a good job these days, will it? I'd say skills like patience and faith are a little better."

"Now you are preaching, Jack, and its sickening. Close your mouth before it's too late."

She moved over and sat on my lap, pulling my arms around her.

"Maybe I missed my true calling," I said. "Reverend J. K. Baird. It's kind of got a nice ring to it. Political science; religion, psychology—where do you draw the line?"

"I think you're better off cutting commas."

"Don't rule anything out, Sarah. I've never seen anything that you couldn't do if you set your mind to it."

"Well," she sighed, "maybe you're witnessing a first. If there are such things as miracles, wishing for them always makes them go away. I don't believe in holy water or divine intervention, or happy endings coming out of tragedies. I believe you accept your lot in life, and force yourself to like who you are."

Her voice trailed off and a shadow crossed her face. I wondered if she was thinking about her father, or maybe even my father.

"Just be patient, Sarah. No one can predict what's going to happen tomorrow, and we can only dream about what might become reality."

"Now you sound like Jack Handy."

She flicked the monitor back on and we quietly resumed editing, this time at a more reasonable pace. On the outside, she seemed to be feeling a little bit better.

But inside I wondered. My perfect little Sarah was hiding a great many troubling things—mainly from herself. What else was she hiding from me?

Chapter 4
Sarah's Father

I GUESS THAT emotionless account Sarah had shared with me on the beach never really left the back of my mind. Sarah's father was always there, lending us a helping hand with this or that, never ostensibly imposing his will on any important matters.

Still, his personality troubled me somewhat. With my father gone, it might have been supposed that the senior Baird's many flaws could possibly fade and almost disappear as time went on, and his noble traits grow in strength. But with Wendell Collins, I could never pin down the real balance of his inner nature. I never really did trust him.

When my position with the paper grew into an opportunity for promotion, he suddenly entered into the new equation unexpectedly, filling in for a board member who was ill. He began making appearances in the building without warning, often seeking out my office on the pretense of official business.

It was now late in the fall, and Louisville already smelled like winter, with cold breezes blowing in off the river and knocking leaves to the ground. The Cardinals were playing preseason basketball games. On one gusty day, just before an important review with my editor, Sarah's father insisted on buying me lunch at a nearby oyster bar.

Wendell Collins was a broad man, but not unpleasantly large, and his aquiline face had about it a sense of confidence and assurance; that nothing was beyond his grasp, if he merely decided that he wanted it. I guess at the time I didn't really appreciate how successful he was in the financial sense of the word. He'd had his way with the world, you could tell. His voice was soft, but unwavering, with a steady, very Southern cadence to it. He never had to issue orders—he only made recommendations that were invariably logical and immediately followed by those around him.

He ordered for both us and smiled broadly, slapping me on the back.

"Jack, I've been meaning to tell you for a long time that I think you're a damned fine fellow."

"Thank you. I feel pretty lucky to have married Sarah. You have three great girls."

He smiled again, this time with a trace of weakness that appears on every father's face when talking about his daughters. "You're absolutely right. And I think you got the right one of the three for you. Sarah has always been the most complicated, sensitive, and adventurous of the three. You make a good match."

Our beers were pushed across the counter and we tipped the mugs at each other. I wasn't sure where the conversation was headed.

Somehow, I had always assumed that he would want Sarah to marry a wealthy lawyer, or businessman. I wasn't exactly providing Sarah with a lavish lifestyle. In fact, she made as much working part-time for her father as I made full-time at the newspaper. I believed him when he praised me, though always reluctantly. He continued to ramble pleasantly.

"Yes, I think you make a great team. And I hear your novel is almost ready to be unleashed on the world."

"Yes," I said, startled. "But I'm more caught up at the paper right now." I wasn't sure how he would know much about the novel, or why it would interest him.

"That's what I wanted to talk to you about today, in a round about way."

I would be lying if I didn't report that I had thought of his tryst on the living room floor with that soul-less tramp several times already. I found it difficult to take his tone seriously, though I have no doubt he was being completely frank. How could you take anyone serious after you knew *that* about him? Embarrassing images flashed through my head like a cheap movie.

I wondered what Sarah would think of this conversation (or, what her mother would think, for that matter.) Was this the way he talked to them when he explained why he wrecked their family?

"Jack, I want to see you be a success. You deserve it. I've seen how hard you work. I also think you deserve a chance to be a success at what you really want to do."

"That's kind of you," I said. "But I think I can tackle the position at the paper without any help."

The half-moon smile didn't waver on his face. "I'm not talking about the paper, although I'm sure you could be editor someday. I'm talking about your book."

For some reason, I thought about all the cars he bought his girls; all the clothes; the trips around the globe. When I added my book to that list, it didn't fit in at all.

"I don't want your help."

He paused, confused, his lips pursed between two wafer-like cheeks puffed out like balloons. His grin was half understanding; two thirds disbelieving.

"Jack. I know you're a hard worker. You've been raised with the belief—and rightly so—that you must earn what you receive in life. You have earned my trust, and my help because of that. I'm giving you nothing you don't already richly deserve."

Looking back on it later, I've pretty much determined that he was being completely sincere with me. But I was not of the right temperament to respond enthusiastically, so I said nothing at all. He took that as an absolute acceptance and immediately pulled two items out of his jacket: reading glasses and a check book.

"I don't want money," I started to say. But there was to be no argument.

"Jack, let's get you started in the publishing world, and let's do it the right way. Congratulations!"

Sarah edited my book; practically wrote parts of it. Her father paid for it. Exactly what role did I get to play?

From that moment on, it was as if I wasn't really writing anything at all. I was, instead, some kind of chief engineer; a manager; an overseer; someone laboring, but not really creating, or being a creator. I was the high profile corporate executive officer, leading the way on a very important project that belonged to someone else. It never did feel right.

Sarah couldn't understand why I wasn't more excited, especially when the first galleys arrived by certified mail. I didn't want to even open them. Their arrival in the mail box precipitated the first real fight we had ever had.

"You're acting like we've all done something wrong, Jack! Do you want to just curl up in a ball and clutch your computer printed rough draft to your chest for the rest of your life? 'I've written a book! But no one else can see it, because they won't understand it!' Wake up, Jack, you've finally got your break, and you won't even take it!"

"I don't want your father's help."

"Why in the world not?"

Of course Sarah wouldn't understand. She accepted every kind of material blessing in life from her father without batting an eyelash. So did her mother and sisters—it was their way of life by now. Why would this be any different?

She threw the galleys all over the house, littering the floor with them, ranting and raving the whole time about how selfish I was. I stood in one spot, rooted in place by confusion and anguish, listening and not really hearing. I was beginning to experience that strange paralysis that pacifists feel when they are in a situation that only violence will alter, and they are incapable or unwilling to use it.

I reached for a compromise. But I simply couldn't convince myself that I was wrong, and that's a terribly personal decision to betray for the sake of compromise. It's like an instinct that tells you to tense up and stick your arms out when you fall—it just happens without any conscious effort, and you can't ignore it. The more I languished, unable to respond, the more certain the conviction was inside of me that I was being violated. I refused to cave in to violence or anger.

IN AN EMOTIONAL sense, I've always been a conservative, carefully shielding myself against the winds of change with a patient exterior. For many reasons, I didn't see where things were headed; or perhaps just didn't want to see. The help from Sarah's father was just the beginning; really; just the first symptom of a disease that would grow and mutate several times. The disease distorted my ideas of love, marriage, and relationship, and created its own emotional dependence like a destructive drug..

Whatever the case, I couldn't have predicted the outcome of all the changes that were destined to shape my future, or of what effect they would have on my lovely Sarah. In particular, one change still haunts me as I stare into the reflection of my own demise. No one who loves you could do what Sarah did to me at that time.

Chapter 5
On a Dark Highway

WE WERE DRIVING east on Interstate 64 that winter, returning to Appalachia for a family reunion on my father's side, when a very strange conversation took place. It started out innocently enough, with a brief reference to Sarah's father.

We still hadn't resolved anything about the book. The galleys had been returned to the publisher— untouched by me—but carefully edited by Sarah. The first public copies were to go on sale in early January. I found myself almost hoping that it would be a monumental flop, although such a disaster could adversely affect my entire writing career.

My mother caused a commotion just before we left on the trip when she belittled my father's eastern Kentucky roots, then unexpectedly burst into tears. It was both embarrassing, and tragic, and my would-be stepfather only made it worse by reminding her that the past was truly behind her, which it wasn't, and she cried some more.

"My father's family is originally blue blood from Vermont," Sarah said in the car, beginning a conversation about relatives. "But he was born in Louisville, and he never talks about them. He's as Kentucky as anyone I know, and he never talks about old family. He doesn't want to be a Yankee."

I didn't want to talk about her father, but I nodded anyway and glanced over at her. She was dressed in a simple plaid dress my mother had given her—an article from her own early days with my father, now much too small—and despite the fact that it was worn and somewhat outdated, Sarah adopted it and made it look beautiful. Her hair, normally a rich, dark brown, was radiant in the bright, cold winter sunshine, sparkling with elusive traces of red mixed in.

"My mother's folks are blue bloods, too," I said. "Old horse money, though I can't see much of it in evidence now. She never did make a big hit with my father's family in eastern Kentucky. I guess it's obvious why." My voice was somewhat distracted, as my train of thought was still silently locked on Sarah's father. I was still angry about the money, and other things as well; things that it seemed we never discussed openly, except for a few fights. Her father silently influenced Sarah, I was convinced, more than she would ever admit. I guess that meant that he silently influenced me, too, and that really made me angry.

"My mother loved my father's family more than he ever did," Sarah said suddenly.

A reply from me almost slipped out, a tornado that I barely managed to choke off. That was a setup for a verbal swipe if I had ever heard one.

She hadn't spoken the words defensively, but they only heightened my feelings. So many angry thoughts swirled through my head.

I didn't mean to voice my thoughts out loud. I really didn't. This time I couldn't stop it.

"Your father is not without his shortcomings."

Sarah sat up straight, as if receiving an electrical shock. I belatedly realized just how well hidden my hatred of him had been kept—intentionally or not.

"My father has shown nothing but kindness and respect to you!" She peeled her sunglasses off and threw them against the dashboard. "Do you even have an ounce of appreciation? I would think that with your own father gone you would hang on a little tighter to what few elements of family you have! My father's shown more concern over you than your mother's cold-hearted lawyer!"

I let up on the accelerator when I noticed that we were flying about eighty-five. My leg was so stiff that my foot barely responded. A strange tingling was covering my body, and for a moment I wondered if something physically was wrong with me. I managed to control my panic.

The conversation, however, was already out of control. I could feel it spiraling, and like a compulsive gambler, I just couldn't stop betting. I had practiced self-control so long that a moment of weakness had finally caught up to the pace and found me.

"Your father is no substitute for mine."

I said the words icily, calculating to hurt. Sarah burst into a half-sob, half-scream. It felt as if I was suddenly releasing and relaxing muscles that were screaming with tension. There was something inside of me that had to get it out; required it to exist. I had relinquished part of it, at least.

"Not everyone can be as perfect as you, Jack. But you, of all people, should know that you can't fit everyone into the neat little cubbyholes you'd like to!"

"I can't forgive him, Sarah. It's not in me. I can't look at your mother, or his girls, and find it in my heart to just let him go Scot-Free. I can't do it! You shouldn't ask me to. That's not fair to any of us."

"You think you're so perfect..." she muttered, punching the dashboard, then wavering, as if to hit me. "You think the rest of the world should just live as righteously as you. Mister patience, and Mister calm, cool, and collected. Mister control. Mister perfect."

"Sarah, that's not fair, and you know it!"

"You've never had a sinful bone in your body, have you?"

"Sarah! Don't turn this into a fight about us. We're talking about your father, for Pete's sake."

Then there was a dreadful silence, as if the prelude to the storm had abated. I had definitely pushed some buttons. Part of me was relieved. Sarah was more human than I thought. Part of me was embarrassed, though, at my own pettiness. Minute followed minute, with the tension growing more profound.

I tried to let up again—the car was doing ninety. There was no point in having a wreck or getting a ticket. I sucked in a deep breath.

"I'm sorry I don't fit into your cubbyhole, Jack."

"Sarah, you're not being fair. Your father is the one I can't seem to find a place for. I've always known who you are."

"I'm sorry you have such high expectations."

"Sarah!"

At that moment, she looked me straight in the eyes and the world seemed to come to a complete standstill.

"Jack, I had affair last month with someone at the office."

She spoke the words so calmly, so fluently and effortlessly, that I almost didn't comprehend them. She could have been speaking Serbian, or Arabic, or Chinese. Before it could totally sink in, I locked the brakes up and sent the car fishtailing across both lanes and into the median strip, where it churned up cold mud and dead grass and came to a shuddering stop—fortunately without meeting any other vehicles.

Sarah was staring straight ahead.

"You what?"

"I had an affair. It's over now, but—"

"An affair. You slept with another man?"

"Yes. But it's not what you think. I—" Her face crinkled.

I put the car in park and released my seat belt. The warning tone bell seemed inordinately loud and angry.

"Wait, Jack. You haven't heard me out!"

I opened the door and climbed outside, turning to look at her one last time. It was a mistake. I couldn't help but grow a little weak in the knees when I looked into her eyes. I quickly glanced away.

"I don't want to hear your lame excuses, Sarah. Unless you can look me in the eye right now and swear in God's name that it will never happen again, it's over between us."

I sobbed involuntarily, shuttig the door with clenched teeth.

I carefully turned my gaze back to her, waiting tensely, but no words came out of her mouth. There was an obvious struggle on her face, as evidenced by the palsied movement of her lips, but no sound escaped. Nothing at all.

There was my answer.

"No, Jack, wait!"

I began walking down the median strip, east toward some exit near Ashland, never once looking behind me. My mind was a blank void, swirling with *nothing*, and it wasn't until much later, after many miles of angry trekking, that my thoughts finally began to catch up with my feet.

I never once looked back.

EVERYONE HAD warned me about Sarah. Even her father, within some sort of sick, twisted frame of logic, had been pointing me in this direction. I could hear all my friends telling me they had said so. I could hear my mother suddenly turning an about face, cursing the tramp who had cheated on her beloved only son.

But the shock was still complete. I had no idea what to do, really, none. No clue. I'd had no suspicion. I was sick with confusion, and at strange moments even imagined that I was dying with stress and grief. I felt my heart, to see if it was beating right, and when I suddenly would jerk up from a prone position and it raced for a moment, I would check it again. I was in danger of coming unglued mentally, and I was alone, which added a dangerous element.

I hadn't given Sarah a chance to follow me. On the Interstate, I had rushed away so quickly that she couldn't follow, torn between staying on my heels or leaving the car unattended. I angled south across the road and entered one of the countless little gullies wedged between the rounded, time-worn mountains; this particular gully was complete with a small stream, a one lane dirt road, and a couple of run down trailers that were probably inhabited, judging by the many dogs chained beside them. I knew Sarah wouldn't go that way. She would drive to the nearest exit and explore strictly on wheels. This part of the state made her nervous.

For some reason, I felt an intense, kindred spirit with the people of the hills, and probably more so now that my father was gone. He had grown up in a similar environment; another little gully hidden in Appalachia near the Tennessee border. Part of me lucidly acknowledged how angry I was, and studied it, while another part of me rejoiced that I could hide among these people—my ancestors, many still alive and aware of my existence. I rationalized that my feelings and emotions would be accepted, and understood. No one would question my right to be there and behave the way I was acting, given what my wife had done to me. Some of them would probably volunteer their shotgun for loan.

As I continued to walk along the dirt road, the idea grew in my mind that perhaps I should just stay here. I had only two ties with the outside world (other than Sarah) that fused me in a binding fashion to the rest of society. One was a Gold Master Card, luckily enough, with plenty of available credit, and I would call at the earliest opportunity and give them a new address to bill me. It was in my name only, an accidental left-over from college that suddenly was useful. The other link was my job with the paper. I would call my editor and quit sometime in the next day or so.

I thumbed a ride with a bearded teenager as far as West Liberty, then charged a cheap hotel room for the night. It smelled of vodka, probably spilled on the carpet, and was painted dull orange. As I lay in the bed, almost paralyzed with fear and anxiety, I came very close to calling my mother and explaining my situation. But she would tell Sarah, whether she wanted to or not, and I decided against it—at least for the moment. That would lead to far too many complications. Right now, what was called for was an intense, profound simplification of everything. Again, my anxieties manifested themselves in physical pains—in my chest, or my head—and I contemplated going to the hospital. Deep down, though, I knew it was the mental side of it that I needed to conquer. I took deep breathes.

I tried to argue with myself a thousand times that it just wasn't that big a deal, and that maybe I was overreacting. People have affairs all of the time, and many relationships survive it. Real life was not Doctor Zhivago. Real life was accepting things. I had probably even wondered in the deepest parts of my mind what Sarah would do if I ever did such a thing, when it was late at night, and I played little mental scenarios with myself before going to sleep.

But each time, I always came back to a brick wall. It was a big deal. I had never kept anything from Sarah, and I couldn't accept that the reverse wasn't true. It was a very big deal. It was *the* Deal.

All of the million and one little things that I had stored away and forgotten about suddenly came back; every little look that wasn't quite right; every answer that was a little bit suspicious; every gesture that seemed a little forced or awkward; everything my friends had said. Like my lawyer step-father, I started putting together a case before the trail had even been set.

I lived in hell that night. I had no idea what Sarah was doing. I didn't really care if she was worried about me. I descended into the depths, remembering vaguely something from the Bible about Jesus and his stay in hell, and I checked my wrists to make sure I wasn't trying to join him in the afterlife after being thoroughly nailed to my own cross. I had been the one who wanted Sarah so badly, hadn't I?

I didn't even trust my head and my hands to work in cooperation. I had to constantly run checks on both of them to make sure I wasn't going to try and hurt myself.

And if by some chance I had known what Sarah was doing at the same time—like writers always seem to be able to do, seeing inside the drama—it might have changed some of the monumental decisions I was about to make, and it might have changed things down the road for Sarah and I.

But another actor hadn't crossed the stage, yet; a person who would change everything for Sarah and I. I'll have to explain that person, too, before I make my final decision about the present....

Chapter 6
Eastern Kentucky

I REALIZED FROM the beginning that I couldn't keep my whereabouts secret for very long. None-the-less, I decided to begin this new phase of my life with complete disregard for as many established facts as possible. In the back of mind I figured that it wouldn't be too long before someone came along to preach advice to me, probably on the behalf of Sarah, or my mother. But until that actually happened, I wouldn't fret.

I ended up in Somerset, a quiet enough town somewhat familiar to me, close to relatives who knew me well, but far enough away from Louisville to stay a stranger. I applied for and was hired as an assistant at a Civil War gift shop near Lake Cumberland, where the battle of Mill Springs and Logan Crossroads were fought.

The curator, an aging cripple by the name of Oswald Peete, was gruff and generally suspicious of everyone, but wasted little time interviewing me. He was blind in one eye, over which he wore a greasy patch, and was constantly shuffling his body so his good eye was hard on you.

"You said you work for the Louisville paper?"

"Yes, sir—I did until yesterday."

"Why do you want to work here?"

"I want a break. I'm here for a change."

"You running from the law?"

I couldn't help laughing, which offended him greatly.

"No, sir, I'm tired of the city, and I have family around here that will vouch for me."

"You know anything about the war?"

"Yes, I do. In fact, I've published a couple of articles and—"

"Well you don't need to know anything about the war to work here. In fact, the less you talk the better. Leave all the talking about the war to me. I'm the expert in this store. Is that clear?"

I quickly found out that the primary namesake battle was a Union victory, but only if old Peete thought the customer was from north of Bluegrass. For die hard Rebels, he had a completely different version.

"As for pay, you'll only get what Uncle Sam forces me to pay you, and mind you that Uncle Sam has never been one to linger around these parts very long past dark."

"Yes, sir."

With the meager paycheck I received after the first week, I was able to rent a room above a bakery down the road a mile or so that my great uncle ran. I told him that I didn't want my wife to know I was there; that we were preparing for an ugly divorce. (That statement, not an absolute fact by any means, made me feel powerful, but also triggered depression again.) I charged a few sets of clothing on my Master Card at the local Penney's store, and tried to settle in.

At first, my existence was nothing more than bare subsistence: eat, drink, work, sleep—and constantly wondering if I should call someone to let them know I was okay. For those several weeks, I led a life devoid of all complicated decisions and duties, and functioned almost roboticly. My memories of those handful of days are not entirely without pleasant moments. I'm sure the lack of interaction with my family and friends also helped me deal with the shock. None of them could have understood, anyway. There were cousins and aunts and uncles and others within local calling distance, but I never picked up the phone. I only occasionally ran into my great uncle.

I felt better physically, and my mental strength returned. I felt power surging back into my body, and my will to write ebbed back into a daily tide. Still, I found it hard to really concentrate for long periods of time.

Instead, I was dialed in to Sarah's secret, which was never too far out of my mind. Sometimes it seemed like such a minor little thing— other times it loomed so large in my vision that I was blind, and nearly mad.

I enjoyed the work at the shop. During this same period of time, I began to tinker with an idea for a new novel, one that would belong purely to me. It was an attempt to force Sarah out of me, figuratively speaking. Working close to the history of the Civil War inspired me a great deal—what better dramatic stage to put a serious American character on, complete with all the many flaws and strengths as a nation we still had from that time? Robert Penn Warren found it a fertile setting. Jesse Stuart polished its remnants. I wanted to be the next Kentucky writer to tackle it.

I began to jot down a few ideas, and daydreamed about Morgan and the Army of Tennessee during slow hours at the shop, though my thoughts invariably returned to Sarah. It infuriated me that I couldn't write without thinking of her. Of all the kinds of dignity that could be robbed from me, my writing was the one I was least willing to sacrifice. That bothered me more than the affair in one sense.

Forgotten in the littered aftermath of this entire disaster—and unbeknownst to me at the time—the publisher proceeded with Sarah and her father's help to put my original novel on the stands in a few major cities, and one reviewer even took time out from his busy schedule to invent some new literary insults for it. I was blissfully unaware of these developments until a little later. It would only have added to my anxieties.

It's amazing to me, even today, that Sarah would have done such a thing, particularly in light of my marital exodus. It only made my anger more intense when I found out.

THE OLD MAN in the shop eventually warmed up to me a little bit. He even started making a habit of leaving me in the shop while he took Yankee tourists out to see the battlefield sites (what few had been preserved, that is, after all the commercial development). I was in the store by myself, sorting minie' balls and slug fragments, when a state trooper in traditional gray and black rang the small silver bell on the counter.

"Yes, sir. What can I do for you?"

The trooper leaned forward and looked at me closely, with an expression that made me wonder if he had been drinking. He couldn't have been much older than me, and he wasn't overtly threatening, though I immediately sensed that I was in for a hard time about something.

"I'm looking for Jack Baird."

"That's me."

He pulled out an official looking piece of paper and began reading from it: "One Jack Baird of Louisville, aged twenty-three, about six foot, with—"

"Yes, that's definitely me."

He paused, folding the paper carefully. "Were you aware, Mr. Baird, that you have been reported by your wife as missing and possibly injured? Police and FBI all over the state have been looking for you."

I didn't mean to laugh, but I did, and he grimaced with irritation.

"It's a very serious matter, Mr. Baird."

"I believe you. However, I'm not missing, and I'm not injured in any physical sense of the word. I just want to be alone."

"Yes, well I can see that now. But you should have contacted someone and let them—"

"I can't control anything my wife does, sir. If I contact or if I don't contact her, it's my own business. The police shouldn't be involved."

"You could have at least told a relative or someone where you were."

"I did. If you would have bothered to call my editor, he could have explained what was going on."

"Someone did call him, but you failed to tell him exactly where you were."

"I don't have to tell anyone where I am! And as for my wife, we are currently separated."

"Legally?"

"Yes..."

What was a 'legal' separation? I had no idea, and the technicalities, whatever they were, were completely irrelevant. I could care less if it were legal or not.

"None-the-less, Mr. Baird, all extenuating circumstances not withstanding, I'm going to need you to answer a few questions."

This was the last straw. I slowly made my way around the counter, with just enough anger to convey my irritation, but not enough to appear dangerous. The officer reached toward his hip where a revolver was holstered, then brushed lint off his pants.

"I shouldn't have to answer any questions, Officer. My wife just had an affair. I left her. It's plain and simple. There's no case for abandonment. Write that into your report."

"I have to file paper work, you understand. It's not about your marriage—it's about your whereabouts."

I didn't understand. It was as if Sarah and her father were reaching out from almost two-hundred miles away and pulling the strings all around me, even here. All I wanted was to be left alone.

"I don't have a current address."

"Where are you staying?"

I hesitated. The hole was growing deeper; the officer more and more suspicious.

"I don't want my wife to know where I am. I don't want to be harassed."

The officer sighed, then smiled lamely. "Okay, Mr. Baird, have it your way. But I have to report that I've located you so that your name can be removed from all enforcement data banks, okay?" He added in a lower voice. "Stepping out on you, huh? That's a just like a woman..."

"Will she find out about the shop?" I asked, trying to inflect more kindness in my voice. "I've taken care of everything financially—I owe no debts. Why do you need a current address? Will you tell her I was here?"

"No," he said slowly. "I'll report that it was a chance meeting in the center of town. But if there are legal questions, you'll end up seeing someone soon anyway. For today, I'll let it go, while letting everyone know that you're safe."

"Will you get in trouble?"

"No...Just a minor misunderstanding. They happen."

"Thank you," I said quietly.

"Good day, Mr. Baird, and good luck."

THAT SAME NIGHT, perhaps because of the policeman, I gave in and called my mother in Lexington.

"Jack, is that you?"

"It's me, Mom, and I'm fine, so don't worry."

"But where are you honey? I need to know! We've all been worried sick."

"I'm not that far away, and I don't want anyone coming and looking for me. I'm working and I've got a roof over my head. There's no reason to worry about me. I'm fine."

"Jack, what in the world has happened? We didn't even know if you were alive!"

"It's okay, Mom. Hasn't Sarah told you anything?"

"No. I've talked to her father, but not to her. She's been out every time I've called there. Her father has been very vague—something about you needing time to figure everything out. What did you do? What did she do?"

My hand jolted the receiver against my ear. "She's staying with her father?"

"That's what he says. But he hasn't told me much of anything else. What is going on, Jack? Start talking to me—you know I'll understand, and it won't go beyond me."

I could already sense from her voice that she would come in on my side. It was comforting, in some childish way, to know that my mother would come to my defense even before she knew the truth. That was what family was for. Part of me was worried that she might jump on the Sarah bandwagon like everyone else.

"Mom, Sarah had an affair with someone. I didn't find out until a week or so ago. That's when I left. I'm just taking some time to think about things."

"Your little Sarah, Jack? Our Sarah had an affair behind your back?"

"Yes, my Sarah—and not to get technical, but most affairs occur behind someone's back. I don't know why it happened or why I didn't find out sooner—we didn't really have too much time to talk about it. I don't want to have anything to do with her right now, so it's very important that you not tell her we talked. Nothing she can say will make it seem less drastic or dilute the magnitude of it."

"Does her father know about it?"

"Only if she told him, so I doubt it. Or maybe she told him her own version of the truth."

"My, God! The way he talks, you would think it was you who had committed some terrible crime! You needing some time...That man is a, a, well—"

"Stop, Mom. It was Sarah that did it to me, not him."

"Yes, honey, but he's not acting like there's a guilty bone in her body."

That figured. There was no telling what Sarah had told her father, or what either one was telling anyone else. Damage control, it was called in the political arena—bull crap, was what it really amounted to.

She continued to ramble, as only a mother can, for several long minutes. I found the words soothing in a vengeful way. I could listen to it and go to sleep, like hearing rain on a tin roof. I could smell her apartment on the other end, it seemed, smells of Lysol and cut flowers, and a deep pang of homesickness surged through me (though her apartment had never really been home).

"Thank God your father was not around to see this! He thought the world of that girl. How dare she do such a thing to you! Married to you less than a full year—she's sick! My God, what are we going to do? You've got to divorce her. I won't let you stay with a harlot..."

Divorce. There was an ugly word that I hadn't really thought about too much, yet. That was my mother's way of solving some of the little inconveniences in her life. That was the way Sarah's mother had eventually solved her problem. But could I actually go through with it? I had sworn that I would never do that to myself (or my spouse).

Divorce was probably at the heart of Sarah's problems; and mine, too.

"You've got to divorce her! And don't let her have anything of your father's. Do you hear me? That farm is yours, and she doesn't deserve a square inch of it!"

"Sarah doesn't need land, or money. She doesn't want the farm, and divorce is probably not my first option."

"She needs help, Jack! She's obviously sick—less than a year after her wedding vows...What will her mother think? Oh, I can't take this."

"Her mother probably understands all too well," I said mostly to myself. "That's why Sarah should be staying with her, and not her father. And I'm the one who needs help right now."

"Jack, I need to be with you. Tell me where you are, or come to see me."

"I can't, Mom. It's just too soon."

"Jack, you are my only living family left in this world. I want to see you. Do it for me, if not for yourself. Meet me somewhere in Lexington. I won't tell anyone where you are. We can just sit and sip coffee if you don't want to talk."

"Okay, okay. I'll rent a car and come up tomorrow. But I don't want anyone else to know that we're meeting."

"That's fine, Jack. I won't tell a soul."

IT WAS IN Lexington, at a Shoney's Restaurant near Interstate 64, that I saw my book for the first time.

"It really looks great, Jack. I'm very proud of you."

My mother held the book—clutched it—as if it were some precious childhood keepsake of mine; an old teddy bear or pacifier. I was a little shocked.

The cover had a colorful, cartoon-like rendition of a paper doll girl, and the back had a small picture of me, taken several months ago at Sarah's mother's house. The novel was supposed to be about a young black girl before the Civil War who, by sheer will of her incredible personality and genius, practically took over the plantation from her master and mistress....

It really was not a good novel, and part of me knew that even if I couldn't say it out loud. I was very angry and confused by the discovery that it was floating around the world against my will. Has there ever been an aspiring novelist who didn't want to be published? Perhaps, with good reason, I was the first.

"Where did you get that?"

"From Sarah. She came over to see me yesterday, but you didn't give me a number to call you back. You also didn't tell me this was so far along. She gave me this copy, and I just went to Walden Books downtown this morning and bought a copy for Alan. Don't worry, I pretended like you hadn't talked to me or anything. She doesn't know where you're staying. I tried to feel her out about things, but she was very cold and evasive."

"You didn't tell her you talked to me?" I repeated.

"Of course not! I promised, Jack."

"Walden Books, did you say?"

"Yes, Jack. Sarah said you made a deal with the Louisville, Frankfort, and Lexington stores."

I nodded slowly. I had made a deal? Sarah was certainly putting an interesting twist on things. The spin doctors at work again... The joke I had made months ago about listing her name as the author instead of mine popped into my head for a moment. Wasn't it illegal to distribute someone's book against their will?

"Are you okay, Jack?"

"Yes, I'm fine, mom. I just wish things could go back to normal for a while."

"Honey, your Sarah is not normal. I could see that much."

My mother had a talent at understatement.

THINGS WOULD never be normal. I hadn't been married a year, and already I had experienced one of the most bitter lessons in human nature that one could be forced to experience. I was devastated. The eternal optimist in me was gone, driven down a spiraling tunnel where I could barely see it as a speck, replaced with worldly cynicism and bitterness.

Was it something I did? I constantly asked myself. That was the question every victim of infidelity had to ask themselves. Were there annoying habits that I harbored which drove her to someone else? Could it somehow have been my fault? Or maybe it was all about some flaw in my personality... (I had heard of people being too nice—if possible—and driving their spouse to do terrible things. Was I too nice?)

What about marriage in general—were there people anywhere in the world that were true to each other, forever? Or, were Sarah and her father the norm? I thought about my father. He was flawed, terribly, struggling his whole life against an inner self he didn't like or fully understand, but he never once even thought about being disloyal to my mother, or to himself. I still thought that he should be the norm in that sense.

After the trip to Lexington, I spent some time around southern Kentucky visiting old family sites I had not seen in many years. It must have been some kind of crude attempt to more firmly establish my own identity. Among the first sites I visited was my grandfather's original homestead.

There was nothing left but a stone foundation now, huddled on the side of a stunted mountain, surrounded by those barren sentinels of Appalachia, wild cedars. In the narrow gulch at the bottom of the slope, a violent little stream poured its contents into a small valley, where burley tobacco was in late bloom. When you breathed deeply, you could taste the tobacco buds, and smell the iron water.

My grandfather was a lot like my father—gruff, hard-working to a fault, and driven to accomplish something that wasn't important to anyone else. Unlike my father, however, my grandfather was rewarded with enough time to finish what he started. His prize herd of Charolais cattle became my father's own valuable herd, and whenever I became so inclined, the cattle were still there waiting for me to take my turn at it. It was one of the finest herds in North America, carefully bred through seventeen bovine generations.

I climbed through waving golden rod, by now turning vivid shades of yellow, and past a bed of wild mountain shoelace (or perhaps not wild, but my great grandmother's original handiwork), and sat down among the pieces of slate and sandstone. Nearby, a large, green and black garden spider had spun a web, and now regarded me with silent caution, bouncing in the breeze and awaiting a worthy victim.

There were no other houses around, and not another soul within several miles, although I did hear a shotgun go off once in the woods across the stream. I was alone in more ways than one, for at the age of twenty-three I found myself without either of these grandparents, who had taken the reddish soil and made it into something more than survival, or my father as well, who had instilled in me the notion that there was something important about the land; the soil; the roots— something connected to the very essence of life itself. It was the sense of place that I was missing in Louisville. If Sarah wasn't there, or wasn't there for me, what was there to hold me to that place?

I had my mother, of course, and I was glad of it. But she was not from this stock of simple people on my father's side. Neither was Sarah, for that matter. She was as much like the people of the Cumberland Valley as someone from outer space. Perhaps because of what my father's side of the family represented to me, the circumstances of my own marriage embarrassed me as I sat in the ruins of the old house. I almost winced at the thought of my grandfather staring into my eyes and saying, "You should have seen what kind her type was from the beginning, J. K.. You can't trust a woman who's not brought up the right way."

"Your grandmother would never have even considered doing such a horrible thing."

It's true, she wouldn't have. But the world didn't seem to have any more women who could reach the stature of my grandmother. Perhaps it was unfair of me to say it this way, but I considered that maybe women were too liberated these days.

Down here, I knew how a lot of husbands would deal with my problem. Some of them would beat their wife senseless. Some of them would fill the unlucky lover's backside full of ought-six buckshot. Occasionally, you might find one that would kick the wife out of the house, but on the whole, that would be considered giving in to the culprit. That would be the last choice.

Any Cumberland wife who cheated on her husband would be just as likely to climb aboard a Greyhound bus and never show her face again, if she knew her husband had found out. If she did come home, she would know what to expect, and she would never stray far from the house or trailer again.

Some folks from the bluegrass part of the state liked to say that you could get away with murder in Cumberland. The truth was, you couldn't get away with it, but you could be justified in the eyes of the people, and that was the only thing that mattered most of the time here.

In this part of the state, If they knew the facts, Sarah would get funny looks when she walked down the street. The folks at church wouldn't speak to her. Ugly men from the mines, getting drunk at the bars every night, would be the only ones with something to say to her.

But I wasn't really living in Cumberland—even if I was staying there for a little while—and no one around there knew what had happened to my marriage, nor cared. Like the foundation lying empty on the side of the mountain, crumbling beneath my feet, Cumberland was an empty void outside the reach of the real world, and I couldn't use it as an excuse forever.

Later, I walked down the road to a small cemetery beside a church that was as old as the mountain. A small plaque out front informed visitors that the original structure had burnt three separate times, including once during the Civil War at the hand's of some of Morgan's men. (I wondered what old Peete would have to say about those so-called Confederate heroes?) I had been to this church before; particularly as a small child.

Both of my grandparents were buried on the side of the mountain.

I walked to their graves and was mildly surprised to see fresh flowers placed there. Who would have done that?

My mother loved to tell stories about how my grandfather gambled, drank, smoked everything legal (and sometimes illegal), and winked at every girl in town. But I knew him for almost twenty years, and I never once witnessed him as anything but sober, gruffly religious, and strangely refined for a mountain product. He did not eat food with salt, and he avoided butter like the plague. He treated my grandmother with careful respect, and never raised his voice with her over anything (although he didn't hesitate to lash his tongue out at me, or my father for that matter, if we didn't do something exactly the way he explained it).

I've pretty much concluded that my mother makes these stories up, to cover her own guilt about divorcing my father. After all, my grandparents celebrated their fiftieth anniversary before they passed away. My mother didn't make it one third of the way in comparison.

Perhaps that was why it was so easy for her to offer help to me now. If there was anything she could easily understand, it was how a marriage could go wrong. Her shoulder was always there to cry on; her understanding, based on experience. In a way, it made me angry to think of it in that light. It made me hurt for her, too.

There was a young girl in the cemetery who couldn't have been more than four years old. She was dressed in a fine white Sunday dress, complete with a down-sized parasol umbrella and matching gloves. I looked around, but didn't see who she was with.

She had a familiar look about her which I couldn't readily identify.

"Are you here with someone?"

She shook her head and skipped over to where I was standing, next to my grandfather's grave. She was bright-eyed and beautiful, with short black hair, and again I was struck by a resemblance to someone familiar.

I stumbled backwards—she had my father's forehead and eyes.

"My daddy is in there," she said, pointing to the church. "I was putting flowers on Nan-Nan's grave."

She pointed up the hill, then grabbed my hand and pulled me along. "She was very, very sick a little while ago, but now she has gone to be with God. That's what my daddy says. What do you think?"

"Yes. I'm sure she is with God."

"Have you ever met God?" she asked innocently.

I stared at the name engraved on the marble. "Stewert P. Baird."

It was my grandfather's brother and wife, which would make this little girl...My great niece?

"What's your name, sweetheart?"

"Tammy Baird. What's yours?"

"I'm Jack Baird."

Her father came out and introduced himself, and soon it was like a small family reunion outside. The father was the son of one of my dad's cousins, and thus we were all rather closely related. He knew of my father—had been at the funeral, though I couldn't recall that—and particularly knew of my grandfather, and he insisted that I come over to his place and join the rest of his family for a wonderful country dinner of fried steak smothered in white gravy, and fresh green beans.

Later that night, when my thoughts finally returned to Sarah, I felt a sick, lonely feeling in the pit of my stomach—despite the absolutely delicious meal I had been fed. In contrast to the tightly knit, down to earth people my roots were drawn from, Sarah and I were only interested in ourselves and the "right now;" physically unable to have a family of our own, and mentally unprepared to deal with the consequences of a serious relationship, or of irresponsibility in general.

We were pathetic. We used to make jokes about how primitive people lived in eastern Kentucky, and now all I wanted to do was stay with or around exactly those same kind of people. Sarah and I were a joke; no class; no common sense.

And right at that moment, I realized, Sarah was probably with her new boyfriend, or with her ignorant, arrogant father, no more enlightened now than she had been on the day she was born. There would have to be a new kind of intelligence test invented, because the standard Paiget that scored her at one-fifty was obviously flawed. There would have to be a new way to look at her beauty; or behind it.

It was tragedy. It was absolutely sickening. For one of the few times in my life, I broke down and wept. I literally cried myself to sleep and felt nothing but emptiness.

LATER IN THE week, when I was feeling a little better and had put in several hard days at the shop, I decided to give Al a call in Richmond. I had his work number, and I didn't want to talk to Carla since she might call Sarah, all good intentions not withstanding.

"Jack, is that you? Where the—hold on a second."

I heard him barking something out on the other end to someone, then the buzzing noise in the background faded away.

"Jack! Where are you?"

"I'm out in the country for a little while. Can you talk for a minute?"

"Sure, buddy, go ahead. I've got a meeting in thirty minutes, but I'm free until then. Are you doing okay? Sarah called and—"

"Sarah called you?"

"Yeah. She said you guys were having some problems."

Now there was an overstatement, a' la Sarah. Once again, she had beaten me to the punch. She had talked to everyone before me.

"She stepped out on me, Al."

He sucked his breath in. I wondered if he was smiling, grimacing, or gaping in shock. (Could a person do all three simultaneously?)

"Sarah had an affair?"

"Had, or is still having, or something like that. She told me on the way to a family reunion."

"Jeez, Jack, I'm really sorry." I could tell that he had been grimacing, for his voice had an unusually soft texture to it that I had never heard before. "I'm really, truly sorry." At this point, it was obvious that he was more upset than me. Since the night I had broken down, my feelings about the whole matter had become glazed over in stone. I was beginning to look at it from the outside.

"I want to ask you something, Al. You've known me for a long time, and you're one of my best friends. You know some of the quirks in my personality; the way I can become obsessed with something, like writing for example. Do you think it's possible that I brought it on myself?"

Al laughed, completely without humor. "You? I don't think so. You're too nice—I've told you that before. I'm sure you didn't do anything to deserve it. You're too damned nice. The frat guys never hazed you proper because you were too stinking nice and ordinary. Had you guys been fighting a lot, or spending a lot of time away from each other?"

"No. There was nothing out of the ordinary, as far as I could tell."

"Where you having sex?"

"All the time, including the very night before the trip when she told me."

Al cursed on the other end several times, obviously distraught. To his credit, however, there were no "I told you so's" in this conversation.

"Sarah doesn't know where I am, Al. I'm staying in some little rat trap, and working part time. I've got no shortage of anything I need to survive, but I'm trying to figure out what the next step is. I'm not sure if I should go ahead and contemplate a divorce."

Al sighed deeply. He was an engineer, not a lawyer, or marriage counselor. "Can I talk to Carla about this?"

"As long as she doesn't tell Sarah what we're talking about."

"She might be able to give you a little perspective on this that I can't. I mean, I'm no saint, but I can't understand why she would do this to you. I can see doing it to someone like me, but you're so damn dependable and trustworthy. It's sick, Jack. There's something wrong with her. She needs some help."

"Why don't you talk to Carla tonight, then I'll call you at work tomorrow?"

"Okay. Are you sure you're okay, Jack? I know you're not the type to go and do something stupid, but—"

"I'm fine, Al. I'm not suicidal. I just want to make sure I do the right thing."

We finished up with some small talk, and then he had to go to his meeting. I felt better after talking to him, and managed to write quite a bit on my new novel idea that evening. It was as if I had cleansed my mind for a little while.

I would call him back the next day.

BEFORE I COULD call Al, there was another incident at the Civil War shop that intruded on my would-be privacy. About ten in the morning, a thirty-ish looking woman stormed in, toting an over-sized brief case that practically held her in place like a prisoner's ball and chain every time she paused. She had short hair—very short, very black, straight as nails hair, layered underneath like some teenaged surfer type—and was wearing a blue skirt that was a little too short, and was definitely not ashamed of it. To top it off, she appeared to be my least favorite female personality type—the aggressive, commanding type.

"Can I help you?" I said.

She whipped a pair of thin-rimmed glasses up from her neck where they had been hanging, and peered at me with a far-sighted squint. "Mr. Baird?"

Old Peete heard her and popped his head out from the office, rubbing the greasy patch on his eye like he always did on mornings when he was a little hung-over (which was the majority of them). He looked at her, then looked at me.

"I need to see you about your book," she said.

"You conduct your private business on your own time," the old man warned.

"I'll take my lunch now," I fired back, glaring at him. He disappeared with a grunt. These exchanges were now a normal part of our routine, and while gruff and loud, never taken literally or seriously. He knew someone with my background would not be there forever.

My book! I looked at her again and suddenly thought that I recognized a literary agent type.

"I'm Dana Beech, with Pinto Press. We really need to talk." She slung her large attaché case onto the counter and released the latches. "And I might add that you were extremely difficult to track down. This is not standard practice for us."

"I didn't want to be found," I said, stating it rather matter of factly. I tried to look at the papers she was shuffling inside and she turned the brief case away from me so I couldn't see, glaring over the top of it with sharp eyes that were enormously large behind the thick lenses.

"It seems that there's been a little oversight, Mr. Baird."

"I hope you didn't go to all this trouble to tell me that I owe you money for something, because I don't have any to give you."

She laughed shrilly, and pushed her glasses up. "You see this agreement, Mr. Baird? It's a contract. An agreement between a publisher and author, stipulating various responsibilities and duties, etc., etc."

"I'm familiar with contracts, Ms. Beech."

"Well you aren't very familiar with this one, apparently. It very specifically prohibits distribution of your book without prior agreement of terms by both parties."

"What is your point, Ms. Beech?"

"My point is that you never signed this contract. Your wife did. Therefore, we have been working under a contract that is essentially null and void." She shrugged. "Somehow, it slipped by."

Good. For the first time in a long time, I was the one in a position to dictate to someone. Some small modicum of control was being returned to me. I tried not to smile. Instead, I did my best to look properly exasperated.

"But I've already seen the book in the stores, Ms. Beech!" (though not in Somerset, which had bothered me a little for some reason.)

"Exactly, Mr. Baird. This whole situation is most unfortunate and intolerable. You see, we have agreements with certain distributors, and they have certain agreements with their stores, and they—"

She droned on and on for several minutes about technicalities, and this, that, or another, and when she finally slowed down for a moment, it was only to shove another paper in front of me and demand immediate signature.

"No," I replied. "Not yet. I don't know what else my wife may have signed. I haven't had access to my normal mail for a while, or my writing files. We are currently separated, and she has no voice in my concerns. I don't want to sign anything yet. I'll need to think things through very carefully. I didn't really even want this book published..."

"Really..." she drawled, completely disbelieving that. "You write just for personal fulfillment?"

The prudish, lawyerly woman—at first so disorganized—suddenly smiled at me and removed her glasses. It was mirage-like change. I had to look twice, the transformation was so complete, and now she was not an agent or an editor, but a moderately attractive woman, mature perhaps, but far from middle age; charming; convincing.

"Don't be so hasty, Jack. Can I call you Jack?"

I nodded.

"Let's go grab some lunch and talk about a way we can straighten this out without anyone else being involved. And while I'm not saying that things can't be undone, I definitely am saying that things should be done right this time around."

That made sense. This time, I would dictate the terms. I could even change the galleys at my own discretion; shift percentages; discuss marketing; phase out the influence of any Collins in the affair.

Never mind that the book wasn't that good... Maybe it could make some money for me. Maybe it wasn't a bad book.

"Okay, let's go."

WE GRABBED A sack of over-cooked hot dogs from a stand near the river, then on my suggestion parked near the railroad bridge and hiked down to the water. Luckily, Ms. Beech had a pair of size five Nike walking shoes in her car, which she stuck on the end of her smallish stockinged legs.

The Cumberland, now dammed, is a hybrid river; slower, wider, deeper, greener, fuller, murkier than before. The neighboring mountains pitch down steeply, their verdant foliage (even in winter) abruptly interrupted by the tan and white starkness of the brick-brack rock at the edge of the river bank. The total impression of the environment is deceptive and shocking—one moment a road winds next to a rolling pasture field; the next, a bridge plunges across an arm of the river, emerald-green, hundreds of feet below like a brightly colored museum diorama model.

It always made an impression on me, no matter how many times I saw it, particularly when the bright summer sunshine bleached it in light, and the air smelled like some kind of fish and bird combination.

We sat down on some large rocks near the edge of the water. Occasionally, a boat roared by.

"This is wild country around here," she said, watching some birds crash into the water nearby. Her food was on her lap, untouched.

"I think that was an Osprey. You don't see them too much. I love it," I said. "This is where a lot of my family is originally from. But around Mount Sterling, where I grew up, it's a lot flatter and boring; no real mountains."

"Boring?" Ms. Beech said, smiling again. "What makes it boring—the fact that you grew up there, or the lack of real mountains?"

I felt a pang of anger pulse through me. Suddenly it was getting too personal. Maybe Ms. Beech wasn't from Kentucky. Maybe this was a stupid conversation.

"Let's talk business, Ms. Beech. I want to renegotiate everything about the book. I want to structure the deal so that it's smaller in scope. I don't think this is my best, so I want to be careful I don't blow my chances on the next one, which I've been working on. I have a plan that encompasses my long-term goals, including more, bigger and better books."

"Well, bravo, Mr. Baird. Let's hope your long range plans include Appaloosa Press, then. Because our intention is to make some money selling this book, whether you want to or not. Any future books will be a bonus."

"How many copies are you projecting?"

"Ten-thousand."

"That's more than a little optimistic, isn't it? I don't think the stores in Lexington will hold that many of all their titles combined."

"I don't think it's unrealistic. We access three-hundred retail stores and five mail outlets, and we feed through all of the on-line stores."

Our conversation settled into a soothing, almost numb professional banter, and it wasn't very long before a new deal emerged—one in which I was the creator, shaker, and mover.

I actually began to like Ms. Beech. She had dreams of her own like me. She wanted to be an editor at a major house one day.

Not that Appaloosa wasn't a big deal. It would do just fine for me.

I was two hours late coming back from lunch, and old Peete responded by chewing me out and threatening to fire me. The truth was, I didn't care now. Maybe I was a real writer after all. Did I need a minimum wage job in a tourist trap?

The trip to the river with a book editor made me feel a little bit like Jesse Stuart; Wendell Berry; or Robert Penn Warren, those immortals I daydreamed about. I was beginning to feel alive again. I started thinking of my current Civil War novel in a new light. I might be Kentucky's next poet-laureate. A second literary coming from the mountains!

MY SECOND PHONE conversation with Al brought me back to reality.

"Carla talked to Sarah, Jack. It was unavoidable."

"You said you wouldn't call her."

"Jack, I couldn't stop her. Besides, I think you'll be better off hearing what she's got to say anyway."

"What who's got to say—Sarah?"

"No, what Carla told me after she talked to Sarah."

Our conversation was a little like an Abbott and Costello routine. I was getting angry without really knowing what was upsetting me. I was losing my temper before I had even heard the facts.

But here was the control factor again. Sarah had reached out and picked up another thread of my worthless existence to pull on. Carla had not been friends with Sarah in college, but now here they were, conspiring against me, or so it seemed on first impression.

It wasn't poor Al's fault. Unlike the incident at the wedding, however, I was able to see clearly enough to avoid jumping on him unfairly.

"What did Sarah tell Carla?" I asked, forcing a calmness into my voice that really wasn't there at all. "No, wait—first tell me why Carla called Sarah. I need to know that."

Al blew a rapid sigh into the phone. "I tried to explain things to her, Jack. You know how everyone always says you need to tell your spouse everything, honesty, and all that kind of stuff? Well I told her the truth, just like you told it to me, and she went berserk. Bonkers! She waited until I wasn't looking and dialed up Sarah and left a message. When Sarah called back, I was in the garage fixing my boat. I heard Carla start screaming and I knew something was wrong."

"She was screaming?"

"Jack, she went nuts! I wish I could have taped it for you: 'you slut!, you tramp, you—'" Al paused and gave some directions to someone in the office nearby. "Well, you get the picture. She was giving her the full treatment."

"Good," I said, relieved, then almost happy. "Good. It serves Sarah right. I suppose I'd like to do the same."

"But Jack, it gets better. Then Carla starts bawling and saying how sorry she was for losing her temper, and I tried to grab the phone from her and keep screaming at Sarah. 'Why you letting her off the hook?' I said. 'Don't apologize for anything!' But she grabbed the phone back and went into the bedroom. I couldn't hear the rest of the conversation."

I shook my head. It was completely senseless. Not only was my life a complete shambles, but the most interesting details in it were becoming macabre; almost surreal bits and topics for others to converse about in private. It was a soap opera for an audience of friends and family.

"So, what did Sarah tell her, Al?"

Al paused, and at first I assumed he was talking to his secretary again. But then I heard the curious wheezing sound he made when he was confused, or upset, and I realized that he was thinking about something. I never forgot how smart he really was behind his nonchalance and machismo.

"Al, come on, tell me. It can't be that bad. I don't care what it is. You can't shelter me from anything. The truth can't hurt me any more at this point."

"Well, okay, buddy. Sarah told Carla that she wants to get back together with you, soon, and that she's thought seriously about killing herself."

At first, I wanted to laugh. Then, I actually cried out loud for a moment, a combination of a gasp and a gulp.

"That's a load of crap!" I said, my voice practically a bottled scream. "Sarah? She's not that type at all. She's just saying it to get attention. She actually said that? I've heard it all now." I started laughing again.

"Jack, Carla said she was totally serious. We almost flew over there."

"Carla's a woman, Al. You told me that years ago, and I still believe you. She looks like a woman, she acts like a woman—she's going to say what a woman's going to say, and that's just the point. Sarah would never try to kill herself. Carla is nuts."

"Now you listen," he said, his voice growing defensive, "don't start to bring Carla into this. She has nothing to do with what happened between you and Sarah! She was an accidental bystander."

My voice rose a notch to match his. "You brought her into it, Al. You said that if Carla says it true, then it must be true! Did I misunderstand you?"

"Are you calling my wife a liar, Jack? What kind of twisted vendetta are you leaving on here, now?"

For a moment we both stopped talking, and I think we simultaneously realized—even with five-hundred and fifty miles separating us—that we were about to slip into something primitive and subhuman; something without any meaning; something terrible—a conversation with no other intention than frustration, anger, and ego.

"I'm sorry, Al."

"No, I'm sorry, Jack, really. I know this isn't easy. I shouldn't be preaching to you. Damn...You're the one that has to deal with it."

There was more silence, but this time it was less uncomfortable, and we finished the conversation with a few idle pleasantries about the weather, and when we might get together sometime. Before hanging up, however, there was one last piece of business to attend to.

"Listen, Al, do me a favor; one thing, please. Tell Carla—I mean, ask Carla, please—that if Sarah calls back, please don't tell her anything about me, or where I am. You haven't given anyone this phone number, have you?"

"No."

"Good. But if Sarah does call, please let me know."

"Okay. I hope this works out, buddy. Take care, J. K."

"You too, Al. I'll call you soon."

THE THOUGHT THAT Sarah might hurt herself had never even occurred to me. In fact, if someone had suggested it to me in the first week after our separation, I probably would have applauded it. Her smug confidence, or unreadable emotions needed shaking up. That was why I had known it was the right thing to do when I walked away from the car—it had actually produced an emotional reaction in her normally unflappable exterior.

By now, however, I was painfully sober. Every new twist in the fabric of my life had its own painful pull on my insides. If Sarah really did kill herself, would I be able to live with my own part in it? It was kind of like Amantha Starr when Hamish Bond jumped off the wagon and hung himself—Robert Penn Warren knew that Amantha was guilty, even if she didn't recognize it herself. In point of fact, it didn't matter whether she knew it or not. That wasn't the point.

Sarah Collins—the cheerleader, SCA representative, straight A student, owner of model-like beauty, gifted insight, genius-like abilities in almost every area—Sarah Collins, my wife; forever; 'til death do we part,' Sarah Collins, who probably had the raw talent to be an Ernest Hemingway, but was instead wasting her time bringing along a Walter Mitty like me. Sarah Collins, whom I had only to stare in the eye to understand true love; Sarah Collins, who had...

...stabbed me; cheated on me. The girl I had only dreamed about was now my nightmare.

"DID YOU GO out to lunch again with that book lady?"

Old Peete struggled out of his office, his breath like a stale peppermint candy—only ten times stronger, in order to hide the sickly sweet whiskey smell.

I stopped pushing the rag on the counter. "Yes."

The old man's good eye twitched, then he looked away from me and changed his demeanor.

"Business has been good here, lately. Winter months are usually slow..."

He pulled out the burgundy guest book, which also served as an account sheet, and flipped it open. He pointed at the most recent week and grunted. "I've never had so many people in September before."

I started wiping the smudges off the glass cases again. "Maybe it's the weather," I suggested.

He grunted again, then slammed the book shut. I could tell by now that there was something he wanted to say, but didn't know how to. I wasn't about to make things easy on him, so I continued working, as if oblivious.

He snapped one of the cases open loudly, then simply closed it again, with childish impatience.

"Yes, business has been good," I said, smiling.

"I'm gonna give you a raise," he said quietly.

"What's that?"

"I said, I'm going to give you a raise!"

"Oh."

I tried to play it up like it wasn't any big deal, but the truth was, I was starting to like Old Peete. For all his gruffness, he had a soft side, and he had never asked me too many personal questions. I was very flattered that he thought me worthy of more than minimum wage. He also accepted that I knew a little bit about the war now, and let me take some of the guests around.

"Another thing," he said slowly. "When you leave—"

"Leave? Who said anything about leaving?"

He stared hard at me with his good eye unflinching. "I said when you leave—and I'm not a complete fool, you know, and I see what you're writing—when you leave, I want you to take some things around here with you."

I never would have guessed that Old Peete would verbally add me to his living will, but stranger things have happened. I couldn't really dispute his assertion that I wouldn't be there forever, either.

The more I reached out for old contacts and resumed normal activities, the more I started to miss the fast lane out in the real world. I couldn't stay here much longer without going stir crazy. Although dinner near the family homestead, with my distant cousins, always made me forget about Louisville and the newspaper and sometimes even Sarah for a while, I couldn't break myself of my old lifestyle that quickly. Not completely, at least.

Still, many things rooted me in place near Cumberland. It was a strain to think about leaving. It was yet another change. Peete, though, knew it was happening before I did.

Chapter 7
Man Is Born unto Trouble (The Old Testament)

I DON'T KNOW what exactly forced me into the decision to go home. But one of the reasons was probably the sound of Sarah's voice. Al called me and played the message on his answering machine. The voice seemed almost alien; disembodied; trembling and scared—it did not sound like the woman I had seen coming down the stairs at Blacksburg. It hinted at some aspect of her I had never known before; some secret place she had never disclosed.

"Al? Carla? This is Sarah Baird...I'm sorry to bother you again, but I really need to speak with Jack. Please, please! I'm getting desperate. If you know where I can get a hold of him, tell me! I know he told you not to tell me, but I need to talk to him. It's a matter of life or death. I'm desperate! Please call me back as soon as possible."

I only got to listen to the message once, so her tone of voice and the degree of seriousness in it fluctuated wildly the more I relived it in my mind, ranging from merely sarcastic to outright suicidal. It was impossible torture for me to attempt discernment of any kind of greater truth from a simple phone message, but I kept trying anyway. What could it mean? More importantly, what did it really tell me about Sarah?

It filled my head with possibilities, as I drove up the Daniel Boone highway toward Lexington, mulling about whether Sarah felt any guilt or remorse at all for her lack of devotion and self-control. She had appeared wracked with anguish when I walked away from her on the freeway, but she could always call up many unexpected emotions at will—how seriously was I to take any of them after a point?

My literary mind, always at work, thought she might feel like one of Hawthorne's puritans—driven by dark inner desires and simultaneously by a fanatical denial of the very same feelings. She also reminded me of Pearl, Hester Pyrnne's cursed daughter (of The Scarlet Letter), half possessed by evil spirits, but an elfish, angel-like little girl at the same time, sometimes alarmingly charming.

Who was Sarah? There would be no more answers for me in Cumberland. If I wanted answers about Sarah, I would have to speak with her face to face, and I dreaded that prospect, looming on the horizon as it was like the unavoidable setting or rising of the sun. How I wished I could avoid that first apology that would slide out from between her lips, like some kind of bird sharing its dead meal with the prodigal son.

Despite it all, a sharp look into the depths of my soul would have quickly revealed how much, and how deeply I still loved Sarah. You cannot feel such intense pain until you love someone so dearly. I would not treat her unfairly, even at the risk of betraying my own feelings. But neither would I reward her for her crime. There had to be a middle ground. Jack Baird's specialty was finding middle ground, stemming back to childhood when I had been the middle ground between two angry parents.

I slowly released the idea of revenge, though I remained bitter, devastated, jaded, and mentally bankrupt. I could not remain hell-bent on revenge for long, and I was not insane with jealously. The only kind of jealousy I felt was the kind experienced when I watched a young couple walking hand in hand at the rest stop, oblivious to my prying eyes—and their German Shepherd, who was taking care of bodily functions in a very orderly fashion. They had eyes only for each other; their world was the only world that mattered, and there were no other people inhabiting it. Not even the dog was there, really.

I hadn't truly felt lonely until that scene at the rest stop. It reinforced the notion that I was doing the right thing. It was time to resume communications with my wayward wife. Anger was slowly melting into a cool spring day of loneliness.

ON THE WAY through Lexington, I stopped to see my mother and her boyfriend/fiancée', Alan. If I haven't talked very much about him, it's partially because he's a lawyer, and just as importantly because he's not my father, and probably won't ever aspire to the position of step-father. Years of no-smile, stab-in-the-back, ruthless court melodrama rendered him almost without personality.

One thing going for Alan, however, was that he was nice to mom. She needed that, so I respected him somewhat. He didn't really bother me.

They shared a luxury rental condo near the Radisson Hotel downtown. I didn't really expect to find either one of them home. They usually worked during the day—he at the firm; my mother part-time at a private school.

Alan answered the door in his typical attire, silk tie with wing tips and wool slacks. His face brightened when he saw me, unusually so.

"Jack! Come on in. Honey! Jack's here!"

"Jack!" My mother appeared, also dressed in semi-professional attire, and threw her arms around me. "I had no idea you were going to be in town. Come on in. We're on lunch, but there's enough for three."

"I really can't stay long. I'm on my way home."

She drew up short of the kitchen door and stared at me curiously. Her teacher-like smile faded into a savage, angry grimace. "You're not going back to her, are you?"

Alan paused at the open bar between the dining room and kitchen, halfway finished spreading some cheese on a cracker. He saw me looking at him, then abruptly shoved the cracker into his mouth.

"I'm going to talk to her—try to figure out why, or maybe just straighten out the book mess."

She escorted me by the elbow into the kitchen. Alan's expression had turned grave (lawyer-like), his face like the marble facade on the front of the building where he worked. I halfway had been expecting what I assumed was forthcoming: a lecture about my legal options. Alan would be good at that, if necessary.

Instead, I received more motherly advice.

"Jack, I won't let my son be run over by some rich, little—" She rolled her eyes and struggled for the right words. "—self-centered, heartless snob."

"I am still married to her, Mom."

"For the moment."

Alan began spreading cheese on another cracker. He seemed to be very interested in the designs woven into the cracker.

"I understand your reaction, Mother, but I have to work some things out. It's for my own peace of mind."

She pulled out a chair for me and we both sat down.

For a while, there was no conversation. Then—somehow—the topic of Wildcat basketball came up, and we spent the better part of ten minutes arguing about that. I am a diehard Louisville Cardinal fan. It started communication back up again.

In retrospect, I see that conversation as a veiled dialogue about my marriage. By arguing on the side of Denny Crum, I was really talking about the necessity of my return to Louisville, and possible reconciliation with Sarah. Having already played the trump card of a woman's natural sympathy, and lost, I saw that it would be hard to win her back to the idea of normal relations with Sarah.

After Alan excused himself and headed back to the office, our conversation crystallized back into the real subject at hand.

"Do you really think this is a good idea, Jack?"

"I heard her voice the other day, Mom. She sounds really bad. I think I at least owe her a chance to talk to me."

She laughed lowly. "You don't owe her anything! Don't make the same mistake I made. You can't let anyone trample over your own needs and priorities. You can't save a marriage just for the sake of sanctimony, or some outdated tradition in a book. It's not worth ruining your life over."

"It's not that simple. I fell in love with Sarah. I can't deny that."

"You need to keep it simple. If you begin to feel sorry for her, that's the worst thing you can do. You can't remain objective. Pity is not love. Pity kills love."

"I'm not objective. I don't want to be."

"You have to be! This is something that has the potential to hurt you for the rest of your life. No one should have to live with that pain."

I looked at her closely. There were lines under her eyes that I'd never really noticed before. "Do you live with any pain?"

A melancholy expression wavered on her face. "Of course I live with pain. But your father was not intentionally inflicting it on me. I feel more pain now that he's gone than I ever did when he was around to remind me of all the differences we had. This isn't the same. Sarah is nothing like your father."

I found her words intensely ironic. Maybe Sarah was nothing like my father, and yet he was the one she had shown the most admiration for since I had known her. I tried to promise myself that I would never use that information against Sarah, but I already felt the evil desire building up within me. It would be a condemnation far more damning than anything else I could say about just the two of us.

"Sarah's more like her father than anyone else I know."

My mother shrugged. She didn't know about the living room scenario. She had met him at the wedding, and that was it.

"She's just like him," I said again.

I had no idea how true that statement really was.

I USED TO MAKE fun of couples who "reconciled." It seemed like such a stupid thing to do. When you're young, no one can tell you what to do—least of all a spouse, or fiancée'—and yet reconciliation is exactly that, by definition: an admission of weakness and lack of responsibility that allows one partner to get away with more than the other. There's no element of fairness in it. It's all about one partner taking, and the other giving them a chance to do it again.

A big part of me wasn't feeling nearly so positive about our reunion, and the closer I drew to Louisville, the more physically ill I became. I started imagining in vivid color and detail, my Sarah, with another man, doing the things that lovers do and I started screaming at the top of my lungs. I can describe the Cumberland River, but I can't describe those thoughts. I can tell you about famous writers and their novels, but I can't begin to describe my wife and another man, together, intimately.

On the Watterson Expressway, a policeman pulled me over, not for speeding, but for acting recklessly on the highway. He explained that he was riding two lanes over from me when I was screaming at the world in general and decided I was high, drunk, crazy, or some combination of all three. When I explained, practically in tears, he let me go with a stern warning to be careful. I hardly heard him—I was crazy with rage and pain. I was not used to feeling that way, and it frightened me. That big part of me that had taken over wanted Sarah to see these emotions, raw and unfiltered, before my better half took over again and soothed things over with sugar and spice. Getting closer and closer was physically drawing the emotions out of me.

When my parents had on occasion displayed that kind of invisible tension that almost every child recognizes as conflict, my mother sometimes appealed to my father by pointing out my steady calmness and apparent lack of emotion.

"Look at your son. Does he think that the earth is going to stop revolving if I get out of the house and do something to keep myself from going crazy? Does he look like it's that big a deal? Maybe you could learn a thing or two from him!"

I wished my father could see me now. I know that a fever pitch of emotions were often boiling inside of him, soothed only by the sparseness of the hay fields and the blind companionship of sympathetic animals, both wild and domesticated. He would no doubt be pleased to see that his son was not so completely different from him on the inside.

When I drove by Sarah's father's house, I did not stop on the first pass by. I wanted some way of verifying that he was not home before I confronted her. The driveway was empty, save for Sarah's (our) red Sunbird. There was an old pickup parked on the street, but I assumed that probably belonged to the gardener he employed part-time. I swung around a second time and pulled in behind her/our car, the crazy idea occurring to me at the last second that I should ram into the backend of the innocent Pontiac. I hit the brakes at the last second, screeching tires a little bit on the immaculate concrete.

The Collins home was a small mansion, if there really can be such a thing, a split level brick affair with elaborate, gaudy red shutters, three porches, a three car garage, and three chimneys. Did her father's compulsion with threes extend into such nebulous regions as number of simultaneous lovers?

(*I really was in a dangerous state of mind.*)

As I climbed out of the rental chariot, I heard the front door sigh open.

Sarah was as beautiful as she had ever been, with her honey brown hair cut a little bit shorter than normal above the shoulder, curled back underneath itself in almost sacrilegious sixties style, and wearing an ordinary—dare I say domestic?—blue gingham dress that hid the most interesting curves I already knew of. She had no makeup on, but the image of perfect housewife was horribly ruined beyond repair by the hellish expression on her face.

She opened her mouth to say something, then seemed to lose the courage, and instead waited there for me to make the next move.

One thing both of my parents accused me of was being melodramatic, and my newly found editor friend, Dana, had accused me of being too cliché. I decided my reaction at this critical moment could be neither. I searched for the subtle and original, and instead of screaming in outrage, or bawling like a child in despair, I finally said "hello" in a neutral tone. I didn't smile, but neither did I frown.

Then I squeezed by her without making physical contact. She followed me into the thirty foot long family room/den. She sat down in a wicker rocking chair; I chose a hideous red velvet couch.

"So," she finally said, "where do we begin?"

"Let's try the beginning."

"The beginning of what?"

I almost shouted at that point, then thought better of it. I was on the moral high ground, and I was determined to stay there. Self-control would be key.

"The beginning, Sarah. When did you first start sleeping with him, or even considering it?"

"I never considered it, Jack. It just happened." Her lips tightened. "Are we going to discuss how flawless you are again? Are we going to agree that you would have never have done such a horrible thing? Are we going to talk about what a good husband you are? You're the one who abandoned me when I needed you the most."

"Sarah, don't start that. This whole thing is about you, so let's stick to the subject. You were the one who did this, wouldn't you say?"

"Me?" A tiny cry escaped her lips. "This isn't just about me! You're the one who walked away from the car and surveyed most of Interstate sixty-four on foot. You're the one who disappeared off the face of the earth when I needed you the most desperately. This isn't just about me—it's about us."

I shook my head grimly. "Well let's get straight to the point, then. If you were me, would you stay in this marriage? What exactly would you do?"

Her eyes widened, and collapsed. I felt some inner organ that would be the outer equivalent of knees begin to buckle. Sarah could bring forth pity from me almost on command, despite my strongest protestations; despite the terrible circumstances. She looked in bad shape.

Sarah, though, quickly proved the more resilient of the two of us. She made a rapid recovery.

"Jack, what you should do is irrelevant. You didn't have an affair. You've always been devoted to me. You are not in my situation. The question is what I should do. I don't know what to do, so I'm asking for your help."

The silence was my reply. She wanted my help? That was a sorry state of affairs. I had always been the one foolishly in love, like some lost puppy. I had always been the one blind to emotional baggage. I had always been the one ready to overlook little flaws.

I was not the one to give Sarah advice at this moment in time. We were going in circles already, and we had hardly begun.

So perfect. She looked like some French fashion model. Even with tears welling in her eyes, she had grace and style—Paris in wartime... I had to remind myself that tears could be a weapon in the hands of a terrorist.

It was time for me to do a serious reality check.

"You don't need my advice, Sarah. You need a lawyer."

Her jaw drooped slightly. "Very funny, Jack. I don't expect you to be nice to me, but I do expect you to refrain from being nasty. Tell me something. I've not been worthy of you, I know, but you've always loved me. I know that. How long, though, will I have to wait until you'll be ready to admit it again? I know you still love me, and I know you've been hurt. But I can't start from scratch until you can say it to my face."

She was mocking my request from the Interstate. I made a gesture with my mouth, as if to retort, but said nothing. She was hell-bent on the impossible. Torture was the appropriate term.

It definitely wasn't the statement or attitude I had prepared for in advance. If someone admits to wrong so easily, and then asks so pleasantly and sincerely for forgiveness, what can you do? A part of me insisted that meant she wasn't really sorry. And then, on top of it, to demand a reassurance of love...What kind of response could there be to that?

"I maybe shouldn't have said it that way. We both should offer each other the easy way, instead of the hard way," she continued. "You're only human, and I'm the one who screwed up." She looked at me intensely. "And I know what you're thinking. You're thinking that I'm just like my father. Aren't you? Go ahead and say it, Jack. I know it's what you're thinking. I can see the words just dancing on the edge of your lips. Just say it and exorcise that demon right now."

I didn't say anything. I was thinking how correct that statement actually was. Sarah quietly got up and moved to sit beside me. There remained six inches of comfortable space between us, a place where the air could remain as a cool buffer zone. None-the-less, I knew I was being baited.

"I'm not my father," she said quietly, her voice cracking slightly. "And I am sorry, Jack. I'm sorry about the book; I'm sorry about everything. I screwed up big time, and I'm really confused about why I did it."

"What wasn't I providing you with?" The words burst out like a cannon shot. I could really feel the anger building like some raging animal. It had to be released. "What wasn't I giving you that you needed? Wasn't I doing my job as a husband? Wasn't I a good lover? Didn't I make enough money? What was it?"

She shook her head.

"As a friend, then—what wasn't I doing right, Sarah? What would make you go to someone else for that kind of attention? Give me something honest to work with."

The tears were inevitable, I suppose, and when they started again, they flowed freely. Some sick, twisted part of me reveled in that; took great satisfaction in seeing the celebrated Sarah Collins, the one who never showed any emotions, finally break down and cry unrepentantly. It was so foreign to her that it almost threw me. The tears almost bothered me.

A better angel inside of me said. "She's human, Jack. Allow her some room to be imperfect." Another tiny voice said, "Jack, you're losing it. You're giving in. You're about to let her take over again."

None-the-less, I stayed on the same course. "What wasn't I doing right, Sarah?"

"It wasn't you, Jack. The problem was, or is, me, I guess. I knew you were flawless, and I guess I couldn't find myself worthy of that for a lengthy period of time."

"Sarcasm will help, won't it? Come on, Sarah! I'm not flawless, so instead of playing games, just please tell me why."

"It's not you, Jack. It's all inside of me."

"So, the way to fix you would be to go out and sleep with some total stranger—then you really wouldn't deserve me, would you? That's an elegant, twisted solution—one that means nothing to me. Give me some context, Sarah!"

She stared at me for a long time. Her eyes seemed about two sizes too large, either from crying too much or from me staring at them too long after weeks without them.

Then she said, deadpan, "I tried to kill myself, Jack."

She whispered the words, and as her voice trailed off, the sudden realization struck me that she was telling the truth. Again, I fought down the urge to forgive too easily. There had to be repentance, didn't there? Even if someone had attempted suicide, did that exonerate them from their crimes? I had to feel like something had changed since the day on the Interstate. I had to know that this awful tragedy wouldn't play itself ever again.

I wanted to be stern.

The words that came out, however, said something quite different. I don't know why I spoke as I did, though the fact that I was staring at her wrists, hidden inside long sleeves, was an insight into the real images floating around in my sub-conscience. "I won't let that happen again, Sarah. I won't let that happen again, I promise."

She moved toward me slowly, too slowly, and it fell on me once again to rush into an embrace. I didn't care. All politics of marriage aside, I didn't want Sarah killing herself. Nothing was worth that.

If you haven't loved someone, then you'll never know how hard it is not to forgive them when you are staring into the same eyes that entranced you once before. That's why people getting divorced have to pay lawyers to do everything for them—they know if they deal with each other face to face, something unintended might happen (good, or bad).

Sarah and I were not getting divorced. I was becoming one of the "reconciled" masses that I had made fun of. I was like the spouse beaten black and blue, who for some unexplained, confounded reason, wouldn't walk out. There's a profound truth wrapped up in that complex feeling, if only someone could find a way to express in it words some day.

I can't explain it. I can simply report it, along with an ill-defined feeling in the back of my mind that something else was still not quite right.

Chapter 8
Louisville Again

THINGS WENT back to normal at a Southern pace. It was a process of getting to know each other again, and the person I thought was Sarah turned out to be someone altogether different—better in most ways, and worse in a few. I'm sure she felt the same way about me, and though I had never been a cold shoulder person, now I had a tendency to slip into that mode too quickly if I perceived that Sarah was doing something unfair. I caught myself using my patience and aloofness as a weapon, and had to stop.

Things did go better, though. The memory of that day on the Interstate faded into the fabric of the past, and even when we passed over the same ground on the way to a weekend retreat in Charleston, West Virginia, the awkward moment passed very quickly.

I don't have to explain about the physical side of it. It took a dozen attempts before I really started to feel intimate again. To Sarah's credit, she didn't complain, and handled it with proper tact. She was always willing to try, and just as willing to forget the attempt was a failure. For me, though, the sense of imagination that normally served me so well in creative outlets, served only to torture me when it came to our physical relationship.

She got an AIDS test right after we reconciled, and the report came in clean. Our sessions with the preacher at my father's church speeded us along, too. We did this in spite of the long drive to Mount Sterling.

We never talked about the other man. I managed to scrap together a few meager details together over time, but never anything that brought him clearly into focus as a person. It was some consolation that he didn't know Sarah was married (at the time), though it was also a strike against Sarah for not telling him. On the whole, I put details like that as far out of my mind as possible. To quote an old song, I made myself, "comfortably numb." The less I knew about him, the easier it would be to think that everything was back to some state of normalcy.

I made him a non-entity. My way of dealing with any lingering pain was to suppress it completely.

We discussed the situation regarding children again on our weekend trip to the mountains in West Virginia. It was late fall, and the leaves were blazing orange and red outside our wide cabin window. Sarah was leaning back in a plastic chair with a paper cup of wine in her hand, staring at the woods for long stretches of time. I was on the floor beside her, drinking straight from the bottle.

It had been a beautiful day, filled with invigorating hikes, sharp scenery, and the best pack lunch Sarah had ever come up with— Pastrami, Swiss and rye, olives, caviar, and French cheese on the side. It was one of those times (so common when I was in the mountains, it seemed) when your heart seemed to slow down to a barely perceptible beat, and your blood seemed to flow so slowly that time stopped, and the world promised you that it would never change, unless you fell asleep.

"We've got to stay awake," I mumbled, beginning to feel the effects of the wine.

Sarah turned inquisitively, holding her paper cup out. "What?"

"We've got to stay awake," I said again. "So the moment won't pass away."

She laughed a certain laugh, which I knew carried with it a touch of irony, and said, "Who wrote that—Robert Frost?"

"I did."

"When?"

"Just now."

We made love that evening, and for just about the first time since the separation, it was a mutual, loving, intimate event. It worked, for the most part.

Afterwards, the subject of children came up.

"I've changed my mind," she said. "I can't believe that I'm getting so old so fast, but I really have changed."

"What do you mean?" I felt signals go up; warning lights flash. Sarah was not that old, physically, or mentally.

"I mean kids, Jack. I want to have kids. This whole series of events has put things in perspective. I see what's important more clearly than I did before."

The small part inside of me that was a little bit evil immediately thought that this might be a ploy to cover up for the great sins of recent memory; a Freudian justification for being an imperfect woman, with all of the Victorian implications that accompanied it. In other words, "life is too much, therefore I will get pregnant."

"I'm not sure I follow you—do you mean adopt?"

"I mean anything, Jack. I'll go to the doctor again, if you go with me, and I'll look at all of the possibilities. Maybe they can transplant an egg or something. Maybe they can operate. Or maybe we can just adopt, like you said. But there's probably a way for me to carry a baby," she paused, rubbing her middle, "and if its medically possible, I want to do that."

She downed the last of the wine in the paper cup and stared hard at me, no trace of emotion on her face. It was that old Sarah look that was impossible to read. It should have been reassuring, a sign that normalcy was returning.

I let escape a half-laugh.

"Okay. We'll do that. But it's a big step. Are you sure we're not moving a little too fast?"

That was the wrong thing to say. A macabre shadow passed over her face.

"Too soon after what?"

I leaned over and poured more wine in her cup, and she pushed it away.

"I just mean so soon after we discussed this before. What's changed since then?"

Sarah got up slowly and walked to the inner room. In the silence that ensued, I did the typically male thing of over-analyzing what had happened and completely neglected to see the point.

It was still too soon. Whether we were having sex or not couldn't change the outline of what had happened. Everything had changed. Every serious conversation we tried to have somehow came back to what had happened, and it would for the foreseeable future. I was foolish to think otherwise.

We both hid from each other, metaphorically, for a few days. The mood passed, and once more the subject came up at an ordinary dinner back in Louisville.

I was pouring over some notes on my latest novel idea (the Civil War story), while Sarah absently slipped into some kind of nebulous housewife mode and served me tomato and basil pasta. She was so quiet it caused me to glance up. Her barometer brown eyes were rising.

"I think I'm ready," she stated again, as if clarifying a conversation that had happened only moments ago, not several days.

"Okay. I'll call and make an appointment with your doctor."

"No, Jack. You don't have to shield me, or protect me anymore. I'll call myself and make the appointment."

I pursed my lips and shrugged. "Okay—do you mind if I go with you?"

She glided down into the chair beside me and placed a mother-like hand on my shoulder. I blinked to make sure it was Sarah.

"I want you to be with me, Jack. We have to do this together."

I couldn't help it—I laughed. Not a sarcastic sound, or even anything that could be construed as rude, but more like a muted sound of surprise. Sarah was putting me on. She was acting so nineteen-fifty-ish that I wanted to cry out and talk about my grandparents.

"Are you feeling okay, Sarah?"

"I've never felt better, Jack."

She smiled, perhaps a little blandly, though genuine enough if gauged correctly. She continued to smile at me. Her hand was still on my shoulder.

"Are you going to eat something?" I finally asked.

She sighed and looked at the pasta, as if it were nothing more than a inconvenience that we had to eat at all. She had poured a glass of beer for me, and coffee for herself.

"Yes. I suppose since I made this myself, I should try some."

We ate in silence for a while, though it certainly was not abject silence, the void instead being filled with many smiles, nods, grins and gestures.

Something was definitely wrong with her. The thought crossed my mind that maybe seeing the pastor every now and then definitely was not enough in the counseling department. It seemed to me that she had snapped. Something had stretched too far, and Sarah Collins Baird had metamorphosed into June Cleaver. I had to force myself to concentrate on eating. Aliens might burst forth at any moment.

When Sarah noticed my lingering stares, she scolded me lightly: "Go over your notes, Jack. I don't want you to slow down. You've got a lot done today. I want you to read it back to me later, before I go to sleep."

It had been a long time since Sarah had volunteered to read or listen to me read my own writing. I stared at her back returning to the kitchen, momentarily distracted by a sight I hadn't let myself look at very much since the affair. Sarah certainly had me by the scruff of my neck, so to speak; still.

The notes in my hand fell out onto the table, dipping into a piece of strawberry pie. I collected them back up and stared at them.

Something was wrong with her. It was not like Sarah to act so servant-like. She was always polite, but never like a personal attendant.

I tried to concentrate on the notes.

The agent from Appaloosa Press was scheduled to meet with me soon about this new novel. A recent encounter between Sarah and

Dana Beech had nearly ended in a cat fight. Not over me, of course, but over the book. Sarah Jane Collins would never fight over a man—it was beneath her ante-bellum dignity. My writing was like her own child (at least the first book, which was selling only slowly, despite my rearrangement of the contract), and she was now showing signs of adopting this one.

"Would you like another beer, honey?"

Before I could reply, a shapeless form entered the room and approached me, saying, "Sure, thanks!" over its shoulder.

It was Al.

I jumped up and clapped him on the shoulders. He was a little heavier than I remembered, and sported a thick mustache. In the kitchen, I heard Carla and Sarah exchanging similar greetings.

"What are you doing here?" I asked, whispering, as if part of a conspiracy. The last time I had talked to Al, the "crisis" was still going strong.

"Aren't you glad to see me, or something?" he said, feigning as if hurt.

"Of course. I'm just a little surprised."

"I'm in town for a conference—you know, boring stuff about structural stresses on Interstate bridges and stuff like that. We just stopped by to say hello."

An unexpected sound issued forth from the kitchen. It sounded strangely like a baby crying. Al's face lit up and he gestured for me to go with him.

The baby was beautiful, and Carla and Al had a wonderful and serene easiness about them that seemed to promise that there would be more babies in the future. The transition from college student to spouse and parent had been a very small step for them, it seemed, whereas Sarah and I appeared to be regressing into juvenile pettiness and outdated stereotypes.

Sarah was fascinated with the baby. There was a twinkle in her brown eyes that I had never seen before, which sparkled every time the baby made a sound or turned to the light. Sarah's dainty, smooth and narrow fingers dwarfed the baby's hands as she held it.

"So, how about you guys?" Al said to me, sipping his beer.

Carla glared at him, without Sarah noticing, and he quickly guided me back into the dining room. He lowered his voice.

"What about it—you guys going to have kids?"

I knew better than to think Al would ask me a question that loaded. I was wary, none-the-less. The "crisis" had turned me cynical.

"We've talked about it, but there are some medical issues."

"I know, Sarah told Carla a little. So does that mean a definite no?"

For some reason, this information really irritated me. What else, I wondered, had Sarah told her? I was always the last one to know about everything.

"Not definitely," I said slowly.

Al was oblivious to my nerves, maybe by choice. He didn't seem to be following the effects of the conversation. I set my beer can on the table hard enough that Al's gaze diverted from the baby in the kitched back to me.

"What else has Sarah told Carla?" I said in a low voice. "Anything about me?"

Al crunched his can and laughed. "Take it easy, Jack. It's not like that. They're buddies—almost like you and me. They talk about everything, but no one or no thing has been compromised."

I hadn't really thought Sarah was that close with Carla. "Sorry," I said, though I didn't really mean it. There was no telling what Sarah had told Carla.

I had to kick myself. I was falling back into my Cumberland mode, and it would only lead to trouble. It was irresistible, though, and so seductive that I was falling right into it.

"Don't sweat it, chief. You've been through some class four rapids in the last six months."

Even as I opened my mouth to reply, I realized that everyone—including Al—was completely wrapped up in the baby. No one was listening to me, let alone reading my body language. I was the only one experiencing a moment of supreme drama.

I went to the fridge for another beer.

LATER, ALONE ON the front porch, our conversation finally drifted back to something I wanted to talk about.

"So," he said, "is Sarah different now? Does she act sorry all the time, or is she more submissive, or anything?"

"She is different. She's much more quiet most of the time, and she's more domestic."

"Domestic?" Al giggled, as if he couldn't believe it.

"Yes, she still works at her dad's place, and of course you knew that I got my job back at the paper, but when we're home she dotes on me. She brings me my dinner; she cleans up after me; she hovers over me..."

"That is not Sarah Collins," Al said, blinking.

"I'm telling you, Al, I don't know what to make of it. It's more than just a fad, too. It's been going on for weeks."

"Are you sure she's sincere about it?"

"Yes. As far as I can tell."

Al's lower lip protruded and he gave a short, satisfied, very macho nod. "I guess you shouldn't complain. Why fuss about it, huh? Woman's place, and all..."

"It's just not like her. She doesn't have the same spunk, or vitality about her."

Al sighed and leaned back in the wicker chair he was in, causing it to creak dangerously. "I still wouldn't complain. Isn't that the way a wife is supposed to be? I mean, do you want to be married to some hot babe that's full of spunk all of the time?"

"I guess not..." I said, really not convinced either way.

He shook his head. "I still, for the life of me, can't figure out why she even did it to begin with."

"Family history..." I said, forgetting that no one knew about the living room except for me, outside of Sarah's family. Al, of course, did not know about Sarah's father, or the divorce, or any of it. But he could probably guess. There was a wife alone in a big house with a fancy car in the driveway and three beautiful daughters with every material want provided for. Why else wouldn't the father be there to complete the perfect picture?

"That's not an excuse," Al said, speaking from ignorance, but probably telling the truth.

"I know. Just don't start saying that you warned me about Sarah."

"But I did, Jack."

We both laughed, although the joke was a little thin at this point; a little uneasy. There was too much cold truth in the humor now to consider it a joke. It was a feeling and a phrase that I was even telling myself.

"She does want to have kids," I said, referring back to our earlier discussion.

"So what's wrong with that? It's the best thing that ever happened to Carla and me. Hey, even Mickey's even got a kid now."

"He's married?"

"Of course not."

We both laughed again. This time more real, and genuine.

Carla and Al were the perfect picture of an American couple. They were national stereotypes—slightly overweight, but attractive;

educated and working; smart, but willing to engage in the more base forms of fun. They had on matching Washington Redskins sweatshirts, and drove a Malibu. Now they had a kid.

"You said Sarah has medical problems?"

"Yes. As a matter of fact, we're going to see her doctor tomorrow. She may be able to supply an egg, and then they'll have to implant it after they impregnate it in the lab."

Al shrugged. "Lots of people do that these days."

"I know, but Sarah's also become a lot more sensitive lately. She's very stressed by the fact that she can't do it naturally."

"Why? My great-grandparents didn't have antibiotics. Does that mean I should let a sinus infection kill me because I pine for the good old days?"

"No..."

"It's the nineties, Jack—she's healthy. She'll be fine."

"I guess so. I've told you, though, I'm not sure we're ready as a couple for this. She's so different now. What if she goes back to being the old Sarah and doesn't want the baby?"

"Give her a chance, Jack. You're the one I could barely convince that she was serious about hurting herself. You still don't think she's human like the rest of us, do you? Even after all of this... Give her a chance."

"So you think she's okay? None of these domestic changes bother you?"

"I didn't say they didn't bother me. I'm saying I don't think they're that important. She's still recovering from the trauma of everything. Just give her a chance. Having a baby might help her recover."

Of course. How silly of me. Once again, it was Sarah that was the victim of her own affair. It reminded me of the wedding when she had swooned, and everyone had blamed me instead of the heat.

I looked for another beer and shut out the rest of what Al was talking about.

Al was my friend, but he was dead wrong.

THE NEXT DAY, Sarah and I went to her doctor. There had already been tests run on her before our marriage (which I didn't know about until now), and drawing largely on that information and a comprehensive family history, the physician lectured us quietly on the situation. He was a tall, stately man, whom hair would have leant less credibility to. His hands were carefully manicured, and his voice like velvet, and in some abstract way, I found myself lulled into a warm sleepy, carefree state as he went on.

Sarah sat rigid and completely subdued. I tried to hold her hand and found it clammy and shaky. After a while, she seemed to notice the effort, and looked at me with a forced smile. She was dressed in a plain blue jumper that my mother had given her, and for all the world she looked like she was in her thirties, and heading downhill quickly.

"There's not anything wrong with you," the doctor said to her. "The condition we're talking about is almost as common as a cold, or a twisted ankle. All it means is that it takes an additional step or two for you to conceive. Once you are pregnant, you should be able to carry full term and give birth normally like any other woman."

"What do we have to do?" I asked.

"Well," the doctor said, lowering his face and sticking his chin out at me, "you'll need to provide a sperm specimen. We'll run some routine tests on it to make sure it's normal. I'm sure it is. And Sarah, of course, will have to go through a couple of simple lab procedures to provide healthy eggs. Once that is done, we'll plant a fertilized egg and she'll be pregnant like any other woman."

I squeezed Sarah around the shoulders in response to his doctor smile, but she felt like a rag doll.

"You okay?" I whispered.

She nodded listlessly.

Something about the whole process was still bothering her. She seemed to be losing her courage. The doctor, though—erstwhile master of human nature that he was—chuckled and patted Sarah on the shoulder, as if she had just finished some great athletic event.

"You'll be fine," he said, turning to leave the room. "The mental stress is getting you down, but you've got the physical side of it licked. Don't worry about anything—you're doing fine."

The doctor left us alone for along time, and I wasn't sure why. I figured that maybe he expected me to perk her up and lift her spirits a little bit. It was a harder job than he probably imagined.

Sarah was a limp sack of bones, her normally shapely female body hunched into a collection of twists that seemed to be more like a gnarled tree than a human body. Her face was turned inward on herself, and I had to pry her chin up to see it at all. Her arms stayed stiff at her sides, even as her neck resisted my effort at contact.

"Sarah, I think I know what's bugging you."

"It's not natural," she said, beating me to the punch. "I can't get over that barrier. Everything's easy for you, because you're so talented and busy all of the time. You can go into a room with a dirty magazine and provide everything they need. This is something that has nothing to do with talent at all. I'm handicapped. There's something physically wrong with me, and if I were some religious freak, I might even interpret this to mean that I shouldn't have children."

Religion was a topic we hadn't discussed in a while. "Religious freak," was a term Sarah readily applied to anyone in the church of my parents before they divorced (a rather conservative Brothers of Christ denomination peculiar to the mountains of Kentucky, that sometimes had been known to believe in such talents as snake-taming and radical spiritual healing). I didn't see any sideways purpose in her remark, so I let it go at face value.

"Since you're not a 'religious freak,' let's be more mainstreamed about this. God has enabled many people to have children through unorthodox means—look at the immaculate conception."

I smiled, but Sarah frowned deeply. "That's not funny. Don't mock God, or the Bible."

"I'm not mocking anything. I'm being serious." I pried a hand away from her side and tried to rub it. Greenish veins were prominent on it that I'd never noticed in college. Could it be that Sarah was aging that rapidly? I looked at her face to be sure, and was relieved to see that Sarah was still, indeed, Sarah—and beautiful, too, even with a lower lip sticking out.

"If you think you understand me," she said, "then keep explaining what you think I must be feeling."

This was a loaded question, to be sure, and also an opportunity I couldn't resist.

"I think you're a perfectionist Sarah. You didn't show it at first, but now I see it more completely. You demand so much of yourself that the smallest little fault is magnified one-thousand fold, and the tiniest of defects or what you perceive to be a defect, becomes an earth-shattering melodrama and test of your character."

I paused and she stared with hollow eyes at me. "Go on," she said. "That can't possibly be all."

"It's not just you, Sarah. There are tens of thousands of women who suffer from the same condition. There are thousands of men who are impotent. For all we know, there may be a problem with me when they start running the tests. This isn't the kind of thing that should come between two people, and it certainly shouldn't stop them from having a family."

"Yes," she said, squinting as if in pain. "That still doesn't deal with me, does it? I'm not a number or a statistic. I'm a woman, and I want to conceive the way a woman was created to conceive."

"But that's just it, Sarah! If you bring God into it, your argument falls flat. God never said it had to be just one way. God has permitted women a variety of ways to have a family."

She sat in stony silence, still clutching my hand like a walking cane, or a guardrail above a precipice. I couldn't tell if she was accepting what I had to say, or mulling over the possible counter-attacks.

The bald doctor chose that moment to reappear, a slight trace of bored humor glinting in his eye.

"Everything okay?"

"Yes," I said slowly.

"Yes!" Sarah said jumping up. Her hand suddenly slid away from me. She walked over to the doctor and stood inches away from him, her diminutive stature contrasted with his bony height.

"I'm ready," she said in a stern voice. "I want to start now."

"And this is okay?" the doctor said, peering around her shoulder at me.

I nodded my assent, and the doctor bobbed his chin.

I DIDN'T THINK I would mind providing my part of the bargain, but I discovered midway through the process some of what Sarah had been trying so hard to explain to me. It felt very unnatural sitting in a darkened room, which was not soundproofed and permitted the muffled conversations from the receptionist's desk to filter in, trying to concentrate on a task that was normally so effortless.

For Sarah, the process would involve no stimulation what-so-ever. Removing the eggs from her ovaries would be more of a surgical procedure. Ours would not be an immaculate conception as much as it would be a sterile, technological conception.

When she went in for her portion of the plan the next day, I still felt strange about my sample. It was sitting somewhere in a lab with a code on it, instead of where nature had really intended it to be. I tried to talk to Sarah about it, reasoning that it would comfort her to know that I had discovered these feelings.

"I understand you better, now," I said as we waited in the front room. I reached for her hand, and Sarah smiled lamely.

"What do you mean?"

"I mean about nature, and the way things are supposed to be."

"Oh. You really didn't enjoy that yesterday, did you?"

"No. It didn't seem right. I wanted to go home and make love. That would have felt right, but even then it still wouldn't be the same."

She stared at me emotionlessly, then cocked her head slightly. "I'm resigned to this, Jack, and believe me, it's worse for me than what you're describing."

"I'm sure it is," I said carefully. Sarah had worn more ubiquitous clothes, moving more and more towards a nineteen fifties poster housewife. Today it was plain tan slacks and a white cotton blouse.

I shook my head and wondered if maybe I was the one with a problem. If I couldn't forgive Sarah for her mistake, then I shouldn't be having children with her—naturally or otherwise.

"Are you still open to adoption, even if we have kids of our own?" I said.

Sarah's face unexpectedly brightened. "Yes. I'm glad you remembered saying that to me so long ago. Yes, I am still interested. Let's see how this whole thing goes, and keep it in mind."

"I'll probably need a better job..."

"My father can help," she said, forgetting herself momentarily.

"I don't want his help."

Sarah tilted her head in readiness to reply, just as the doctor intervened. Mister Stick-man, as I now thought of him, was not dressed in his snappy sterile whites today. He looked ready to golf in his polo shirt and tennis shorts.

"Let's go make a baby," he said.

Sarah laughed gaily, while I grimaced and no one noticed. Sarah was more right about my situation than she could ever know. Something about the whole process really didn't suit me. It wasn't natural, and I concluded that there was something to be said for the old ways; the original ways; the true ways.

Chapter 9
Deliverance

AFTER SARAH was officially pregnant, her mother and sisters started to visit our humble abode more frequently. I did my best to provide good entertainment, but the cloud of Sarah's affair often swirled around the room like a ghost, and conversation quickly grew awkward; the mood, more somber and restrained. I tried to stay late at the paper more, and I was there around dinner one evening when an unexpected visitor showed up at my cramped cubicle.

It was Dana Beech, editor and agent. She was dressed in her usual perky attire, much more apropos in New York than Louisville. This time it was a pair of blue power slacks, and a men's cut dress shirt with a sharp, thin blue tie. Her glasses were fashionably thicker and the frames a silky brown swirl that matched the overall outfit. She was carrying a leather coat in her arm.

"Mr. Baird. You are a hard man to track down."

"Ms. Beech. How are sales?"

I asked the question with more than a trace of sarcasm and irritation, since the last royalty check I had cashed was less than two-hundred dollars, and according to our contract, I would still need to sell two-thousand copies to insure that I didn't owe Appaloosa Press money. I couldn't say I was pleased. It was an absolute disaster.

Dana Beech knew this, and seemed to be reading my thoughts. "It's not your fault, Jack." She set her briefcase down beside my cubby divider and helped herself to nearby coffee. "I was probably overly optimistic to think that we could solve all of our problems with that restructuring. We had to try, though."

"When you talked to me in Somerset, you made me feel like the next John Grisham."

She sat down across from me and crossed her thin legs smartly. "It's a little like marriage," she explained. "You see, I tried like hell to make mine work, but the harder I worked at it, the worse it got. There comes a time when you have to cut your losses. The art is in recognizing the time. By the way, I hear your new Civil War novel is almost done. What's the scoop?"

I still was smarting from the marriage analogy. Somehow, with what Sarah had done, I didn't want to compare my book to any part of anyone's marriage. "Wait a second, Ms. Beech. If my book is like your marriage, are you saying it can't be worked out?"

She shrugged and pushed her glasses up onto a button nose that mothers across America would say was cute. "Yes, I got divorced, Jack. You missed the point. What I'm saying is that the incident with Sarah making business arrangements soured things with the book deal from the beginning. There's nothing wrong with the book itself. It's the deal that's botched, and the strange circumstances that messed it up. What I'm saying is that maybe it's not worth it now on that one."

I laughed contemptuously. "Not worth it? You guys are the ones who offered me the contract! Either it's a good book, or it's not. What does structure or a deal have to do with it? And by the way, did you come here to make me feel like crap?"

Her expression changed to a more compassionate, more feminine one, and she turned to the briefcase. "No, I'm sorry. Actually, in the briefcase you will see the latest marketing plan we've come up with that I need you to sign off on. We have not given up, and I am sure that you will meet your quota and actually clear some money, but I still want to talk about the future. There are much bigger things on your horizon. We want your next book."

I grumbled a bit, but didn't overtly object.

"The problem is Sarah."

When she said the words, they didn't sink in for a couple of seconds. When they did penetrate my outer layer of cognizance, I felt blood boil up into my face. I stood up, spilling coffee on my keyboard. It wasn't the comment I had expected; or perhaps, wanted to hear.

"What in the hell is that supposed to mean?"

She slowly removed her glasses and stood to face me. Her height was significantly less than Sarah's, and I was forced to look down on her as if she were an adolescent. It lent a bizarre sense of comedy to the scene, even though her face was as stern and combative as ever.

"Are you going to listen to me, or not?" she said slowly, pronouncing each word carefully.

Incredibly, Sarah's father chose that moment of any millions of potential ones to poke his ruddy face into the cubicle. I couldn't tell if he had been listening. His smile seemed genuine enough. Then again, the smile on his face had probably been genuine enough when Sarah and her sisters had walked in on him years ago in the living room. How could I know?

"Jack!" he said, beaming. "We've got to do our oyster lunch

again." His gaze traveled to a nonplussed Dana Beech. His eyes roved up and down the lines of her back and slacks like a horse breeder. "And who is this? Someone I should know?"

"Dana Beech," I said slowly. "Appaloosa Press."

Mr. Collins' eyes lit up. "Of course! I talked to you on the phone when we initially set everything up. I guess I've never met you face to face." He boisterously grabbed her hand and shook it, his tie dangling around like some other part of his anatomy.

"Yes..." she said slowly, failing to rise from her seat. "That would be me. And I guess I met your secretary, not you."

"We're all real proud of Jack," he said, still smiling stupidly. "I knew Sarah had done right when she came home with him."

Dana Beech laughed so limply that Mr. Collins would have to be insulted, but somehow he was not. He continued with empty platitudes.

"Yes, he and my Sarah make quite a team. She does a lot of his editing, you know. I think Sarah could be quite a writer herself, if she wanted to be. But she seems content with being Jack's editor."

"Actually," Dana Beech said, "I'm his editor."

But she said it so low, that he didn't hear her.

"Well, I'll run on and let you finish your business. Jack, if there's anything I can do, from financing to just plain old advice, you just let me know. I fully support your writing career, and I know you're going to be a big success. I'm always available."

"Thank you," I said. "Everything's smooth right now."

He winked and nodded at me, then winked in a different sort of way at Dana Beech, then waved to both of us and disappeared around the corner.

"Your father-in-law works here?" she asked quietly.

"No, he doesn't, technically. He's on the board of trustees that make some of the operating decisions. He's very seldom here. It's purely coincidence."

She peered around the cubicle warily. "We need to go somewhere where we can finish this conversation in private."

"By the way," I said, grabbing my rain jacket off the chair, "Sarah's pregnant."

"Oh! Oh..."

I waited for the perfunctory congratulations, or the stereotypical squeal and exclamation of excitement, and nothing came forth. There was remarkable indifference on her face as she poured her coffee into the trash can.

"She's very excited about it."

"I'm glad. Congratulations to both of you."
I nodded my head slowly.

WE ENDED UP at the oyster bar, precisely, I'm sure, because Sarah's father had planted the germ of the idea in Dana Beech's head. There was something more to it, as well, some kind of perverse revenge against him for looking at her that way—now she was in control of my fate; now she was having that oyster lunch (or dinner) with me; now she would make me into a real writer.

We sat down at the bar and waited for a table to open up. Dana Beech swivelled on the stool like a little girl, her normally pale face suddenly flush from the heat of the frying vats and ovens nearby. She smiled and opened her mouth to say something, then thought better of it; then said something else.

"Shouldn't you call Sarah and let her know you're going to be late?"

I shrugged. "She doesn't care. I told her that I was working late tonight, and her mother is there anyway."

"You don't get along with your mother-in-law?"

"She's fine, as far as it goes. She's just over-protective of Sarah, and she always blames me when something goes wrong. Last week, she stopped the toilet up with her own make-up wipes, and she even blamed me for that."

"So, how long until the baby is due?"

"We just got started—a full eight months to go. They say Sarah is perfectly normal beyond the issue of getting pregnant."

Dana Beech sipped carefully on her Mint Julep and peered at me over the rim. I sensed that she had more she wanted to say on the subject of Sarah.

I know Sarah had created a tremendous amount of heartache for me in the last year, but I was strangely defensive about it. Somehow, when you get married, you end up defending the worst traits in your spouse. It's a war that comes with the territory. Sarah had been wrong about many things, but she was my wife, and my first true love.

"Let's talk business," she said, sucking the last of her drink from the bottom of the glass. "Let's talk about your new book."

"What about my first book?"

She recklessly slung her briefcase onto her lap and snapped it open, producing several papers and an expensive Cross pen. "Sign there, keep the white copy, and keep the pen, too. You are agreeing to one more marketing attempt on our part to promote the book in several major chains we haven't already worked with. It's not an ideal situation, but if your book gets hot in these stores on the left coast, the first group will probably want to reorder again. As it stands, though, we can't get the first group of stores to buy any more stock based on the current performance."

I signed on the line, not really caring what I was agreeing to. I felt that someone was responsible for ruining what could have been a decent—granted, not great—but a respectable book. I was not willing to completely hold Dana Beech, or Sarah and her father responsible. Nor could I say that it was my fault. It had simply happened.

"Now," she said, much more cheerfully, "let's talk about the new book." She placed a light hand on my knee just as the waiter arrived to show us our table. "I'm excited about what I've heard."

Reluctantly at first, then with more spirit as I felt the satisfaction of a captive audience, I rambled about the ideas and plotting I had done so far. It was to be another Civil War novel, though this time with a more serious theme. The flavor would be a little more macabre, and the outcome a little less happy; the language a little more mature and developed; the characters a little more tragic and compelling. It was set in Kentucky, of course, which I increasingly saw as my stage for many things I would write.

"So what do you think?" I finally said.

She popped an oyster, then licked her fingers. It was that kind of restaurant.

"I think it's great. But what makes a book really great is how you promote it and market it. I could make a trashy romance number one if I handled it the right way. Your book will great, but it's the deal I'm worried about."

I shook my head, slightly disappointed. It wasn't the response I had hoped for. It sounded like a clever subterfuge to me.

Dana Beech, though, was one step in front of me. "You've got to understand, Jack, I believe in your writing ability without question. It's the business side of it I want to help you on. Your writing speaks for itself."

She said it as she was sliding another oyster down; almost as an afterthought. But I definitely heard what I wanted to hear. It had taken two hours of conversation, and some barely-cooked shellfish. I smiled a little, then looked down at my own plate, full of oysters grown cold.

Yes, Dana Beech's stock was going up, slowly, and in fits.

"Now," she said suddenly, breaking the moment's gold. "Let's get back to Sarah."

I felt my face tighten. "What about Sarah?"

"It's what I wanted to talk to you about originally. I know she's your wife, and I would never say anything negative about her. But your father-in-law and Sarah seem to have taken a great deal of interest in your writing career. You told me yourself back in Somerset that many things in the first deal were done without your permission. You even implied that your signature had been forged, a charge my boss was forced to take very, very seriously."

"Yes, I remember..."

"I'm sorry to bring it up, but we need to make sure we get this one just the way you want it. The emphasis is on *you*, Jack Baird."

She said the word "you" differently than I had heard it said in a while, and I kicked myself for reading too much into it. Granted, my sex-life had been far from stellar since the incident (I don't like to call it an affair—it sounds too much like a cold-war spy story), but not completely empty and void. I took a mental deep breath and nodded. She was absolutely right about the first deal, and there was no way to argue about it this time around. She had a way of making a book deal sound sexy.

"I will let Sarah be a part of these negotiations, but only on your terms. That's what we need to discuss."

"We're talking about the new book?"

"Yes, of course."

"Sarah doesn't have to be involved. I just don't want to imply that she is, well, that she is—"

Dana Beech raised a thick, black eyebrow. "—not important?"

"Yes. I couldn't do this without her; I just don't want her to be involved in all the messy business decisions this time around. I don't want to hurt her in any way."

She smiled deeply. "See, that wasn't hard, was it? We're in complete agreement. This is going so much smoother already. That's all I want, too."

I nodded my head and ate a cold oyster. This time, I would make my own bed and sleep in it. This book would be what I had dreamed about—signings, talk shows, and yes, royalty checks. I would be able to read reviews written by people with more education and talent than myself. I would be able to see literary accomplishment.

Sarah's father wouldn't have to be listed in the jacket sleeve.

"Does this place serve champagne?" she asked.

I started to flag down a waitress, and she caught my arm in a light pinch.

"I'm only kidding, Jack. Let's not pull the cork yet. There's a lot of work to be done. The first thing I'd like to do is see some Chapters and outlines."

"How soon?"

"How about tomorrow night?"

"Okay. Why don't you come over for dinner, and I'll hand deliver them."

She flashed her teeth in a cautious smile then presented a mock frown. "Remember, we don't want to hurt Sarah's feelings."

"It won't hurt her feelings. If we're going to do this the right way, she needs to be comfortable with our working relationship. Let her see us in action. She needs to be around you—that's the way she finds it easiest to trust people. Ask her to talk about the book, but don't really take any notes, if you know what I mean."

She clapped her wrists together and shrugged her hands. "If you think that will work, then I'm fine with it. I'll do whatever you want, as long as you and I are ultimately calling the shots."

"Good. Tomorrow night, then."

"Good, then."

SARAH HAD NO readable reaction when I told her about the dinner invitation. In fact, she was somewhat domestic in her reply:

"What do you think I should make?"

"Well, you don't have to make anything. I can go get some Chinese, or something like a pizza, and a little wine, and save you the trouble."

She tilted her head. "Jack, I'm only at the agency one day a week now. It's not like I'm doing anything around here. I'll cook something. I can cook—remember? What do you want?"

"How about some of your stuffed peppers, then?"

"Those aren't fancy enough for company."

I tried not to sound exasperated. "Sarah, it's not like real company. She's my editor, and she's here just to socialize with us for a little bit and pick up some chapters. It's no big deal. Just make something simple, and it'll be fine. She doesn't want a big fuss."

"Well, alright. But I want her to think that I'm a good cook."

"Why?"

"Because I am! And...I didn't like her the first time I met her."

"Sarah, you are a good cook. And this is a person I have to have a professional relationship with. I'm asking you to try, for me, please." I walked over and kissed her on the forehead, but clearly she was in one of those almost creepy moods where nothing pleased her, and her beautiful complexion and exterior appearance remained calm and placid on the outside while some interior war raged on unabated. It was vintage Sarah since the incident.

I wondered if she were jealous, though that was a stretch, and I couldn't really believe it. She had nothing to be jealous about. Dana Beech was pretty in a proletariat sort of way—meaning she would merge into the crowd if a group of woman were together talking, though she was not unpleasing to look at. Sarah, on the other hand, was still the stuff all my college buddies dreamed about. Maybe she was jealous, though. Her eyes belied some kind of fire.

"By the way," she said, as I retreated into the kitchen for a beer, "Al called earlier. I said you'd call him back."

Strangely enough, I didn't feel like talking to Al. There was some emerging truth in events that I was afraid he would recognize, and force me to face up to. I didn't really want to do that. And speaking of jealousy, Al's picture-perfect (even if a little boring) lifestyle seemed to make me look pretty poor in comparison. Carla might gain twenty pounds by the time she turned thirty and had a couple of kids, but at least she would remain faithful.

I didn't call Al back.

DINNER STARTED out very unpleasantly. Sarah had dressed rather plainly or "politely" as she stated it, wearing a simple pair of jeans and a very conservative white cotton sweater so big that it hid her figure. Dana Beech arrived in heels and a low-cut red dress. There was quite a contrast between the two. Sarah had wrapped her hair up in a short ponytail and for once did look more like a college student than housewife. Dana Beech was much shorter than Sarah, but the effect of her dress was such that her legs looked much longer than before. Her black hair was clearly prepared for the occasion, as well, showing several swirls around the forehead and ears, as well as an unusual glossy sheen.

Sarah looked her up and down with unabashed contempt. Dana Beech, in return, ignored her and smiled deeply.

"Let's eat," I said, taking Dana's coat. I gently placed a hand on Sarah's shoulder to guide her back into the dining room.

"You told me to dress casual," she said, almost hissing the words like a cat.

"We are casual," I said.

Things went no better during dinner. Sarah had, indeed, gone ahead with the stuffed peppers. The red wine was perfect, and the fresh bread her mother had baked literally melted in your mouth.

Still, Dana Beech did not say the right thing.

"This is very good," she said. "In fact, it's excellent."

"Thank you," Sarah replied coldly. "It's my mother's recipe."

"No, I mean the wine." Then, quickly: "The peppers are delicious, too!"

Silence covered the table. Neither female would look at the other, or at me. I set my fork down and stood up. Still, neither would look at me.

"I'm going to get my book and read some from it." I said the words loudly and slowly, like Caesar issuing a proclamation. "Maybe it will help everyone get into the spirit of things. I'll be right back."

I don't know what happened while I was gone. I ran as fast as I could, grabbing a pile of papers off the top of my desk, hoping they were in some semblance of order, then skipping back into the dining room.

There had been no change. In fact, I don't think either one of them had done anything apart from breathing since I left. I cleared my throat and sat back down. Oddly, they both looked at me, carefully, without turning too far, so they could see me without catching too much of the other.

"I think this is the third chapter. It's when he enters battle for the first time as a Major in charge of his company. He's already married, of course, and he doesn't know that she's sick and that he's seen her for the last time..."

I stared at them. They didn't seem to be alive. They were looking at me with vacant expressions of emptiness. Then Dana Beech suddenly smiled.

"Yes, you said it was scarlet fever."

Sarah suddenly shook to life and pursed her lips in agitation. "It's not scarlet fever. That's what his mother dies from."

"Actually," I said, all too careful to word it correctly, "they both contract scarlet fever. Why don't I go ahead and read for a bit?" I poured them each a generous portion of the wine, emptying the bottle, then cleared space for my papers.

NONE OF THEM had experienced battle. None of them had any idea what it would sound like; smell like; feel like; look like. They had a foolish combination of excitement and resignation. They did not yet have fear, the one ingredient that might help them survive the coming maelstrom.

 Morgan saw this, and noted it, fully aware that he himself was as vulnerable as the men he was selected to lead. He tried to focus on thoughts far removed from the army; thoughts of home, and a wife he had only spent two months with. The snort of his horse, and the sounds of marching men intruded, however, and forced reality upon him.

 Sarah and Dana both listened without interrupting, although their body language was very different. Sarah was slouching, almost pouting. Dana was forward on her seat, her chin resting on her palm, her eyes locked with mine.

 I realized I was about to lose important territory with my wife. I issued orders for a hasty retreat.

 "Why don't you take this with you and finish it?" I said, handing Dana the papers. "I think I should clean up the dishes."

 Sarah seemed to take this as her cue, and she joined me near the dishwasher with a load from the table.

 "Are you enjoying this?" she asked quietly.

 "Not really," I said truthfully.

 "Tell the truth," she insisted.

 "I'm not enjoying it!" I said a little too loudly.

 She looked carefully at me to gauge the genuineness, and it seemed to pass muster after the second attempt.

 "Well, I'm not either. Please find a way to gracefully end the evening."

 I nodded, and went back to the table.

 "Dana," I said, "I'm not feeling too hot. If you don't mind—"

 She jumped up and squeezed my hand and with a half-grin. "I understand completely. I'll talk to you tomorrow."

 She and Sarah managed, somehow, to exchange the requisite pleasantries for good-byes, and the nightmare suddenly was over.

 Or so I thought.

THAT NIGHT IN bed, Sarah tossed and turned as I was reading. Finally, she draped her chin over my shoulder and stared at me until I looked up from the book.

 "Are you attracted to that woman?"

 "What? Of course not. If I had a sister, that's who she would remind me of. I like her—but not that way."

 "You're sure?"

 "Yes. How could I compare her with you?'

She let her head bob back and forth, as if considering whether that qualified as a compliment, then turned back over with a sigh. She suddenly guided my hand over to her stomach, and the book fell off the bed.

"Do you feel anything?"

"No," I said. "It's too soon, Sarah."

"I know. But you never can tell. When will you be able to feel something?"

"You've got that book—what does it say?"

"It says two months before you begin to show—maybe even longer. You won't be able to feel anything until almost six months. You're not like everyone else, though. I just figured you might be able to tell sooner."

That was a funny comment, I thought. It was my turn to wonder if I had just been complimented.

I felt her stomach, which was as flat and creamy smooth as it had always been. It was not the stomach of a pregnant woman, yet. But I didn't say that.

"Yes, Sarah. I feel something there. It's not kicking yet, but I can feel it."

"Good," she said, turning over. "Don't forget where your real treasures are—right in there."

I leaned over and picked the book up off the floor, and I thought about what she said. Treasure was a funny word for it. For some reason, the word treasure made me think of the other man. It was the first time I had thought about Sarah's affair in at least several days, and I had to drown my anger out in Umberto Eco and cold coffee.

I TOOK UP gardening during this time. I'm not sure what the allure was, since I had grown up on a farm and sworn I would never pull weeds again. Something in the act of growing, though, appealed to me and I recklessly stepped into a big project. Maybe it was because Sarah was growing something and I wasn't.

It was still winter, of course, so my enthusiasm translated into the construction of a small frame and plastic greenhouse in the backyard. The sun was out enough to sufficiently warm it on all but the coldest of days. The greenhouse had room for a folding chair, and now I had a place that would double as a retreat from the tensions indoors, when that was necessary.

I started with some simple tomato plants and other salad vegetables, figuring the best thing to grow was something you could quickly show off in the kitchen. I knew enough to get the seedbeds started, and how to arrange the shelves so watering would be easy.

At some later point, when the tomatoes died, I would realize just how hard growing things is—inside or outside the body. What starts off healthy and green, can mysteriously end up shriveled and brown.

Growing up on a farm doesn't automatically make you a green thumb. Being a woman doesn't automatically make you a good mother and wife.

The greenhouse, though, quickly became a secret retreat. Many of the thoughts that inhabited my head since the affair were strangers to me, and I sat in the folding chair, beside the barren, soil-filled trays, trying to get to know them better. Eventually, trying to come to terms with them. Maybe forget them.

AFTER THE DINNER fiasco, Sarah fell into some of her old habits. Her housewife facade faded away, revealing an angry woman; worse, really, an angry, pregnant woman.

The fight that ensued was like one of our old ones. Sarah would suddenly rage with anger, as if her outward calmness had been a cover-up while she stored up the lurid emotions of the past for months and months until it was forced to pour forth in an explosion. I would play the part of the calm observer, the superior male who knew he was right, and pitied the animal emotions in his partner.

We played our parts well. Sarah showed remarkable stamina, maintaining her angst for at least thirty minutes without repose. At one point, I tried to shove a bite of my uneaten dinner into my mouth, and nearly found the fork jammed down my throat for the trouble.

I didn't usually get enraged myself, though somehow on this occasion Sarah seemed to pass the normal bounds of reason and decency, and I found my wells and reserves of patience suddenly dry, sapped of every last drop of sympathy. Maybe it was the fork—I really did almost ingest it. It probably could have killed me.

"And this bitch—Beech—woman. Whatever her name is! You spend more time with her than you do with your own pregnant wife. Is there something more about this I should know about?"

Sarah knew who she was, so the name game was ultimately just a poor effort at irony, or humor. It had the effect, though, of sending me over the top.

I threw the fork on the table with such unintended force that it ricocheted into the nearby living room with a muffled clang.

"Where did that come from, Sarah? She happens to be my

publisher and editor. And what in the world does my writing have to do with this at all? You knew I was going to have to work with someone. Why not her?"

"I'm not talking about your writing!" she shrieked. "I'm talking about that woman. She, she, she—"

I threw my hands up. "This is not the Sarah Collins I met on those dorm stairs all those years ago. That Sarah Collins would not have been threatened by someone like this. You would have scoffed at the notion of being jealous of Dana Beech. Think back, Sarah. Remember who you were when I met you. Were you the jealous, raving woman I see now?"

"Jealous? Do you think I'm jealous?"

"Yes. I should know by now. You can't spend years—"

"It hasn't been years!" she snapped.

"It's been over two and a half years. When I met you, I felt like I was out of my league. I wondered if you would even grant me an audience. Now you doubt my fidelity? What has happened to you? You never once doubted me. Now, because I work with a woman instead of a man, you give me the third degree? Why, I have to ask. Is it because..."

"No," she said quickly, looking at me with a twisted, pained expression. She abruptly left the room. To my surprise, she reappeared with the fork. She sat it down carefully; with exaggerated properness.

I wasn't sure what she thought I was going to say. I wasn't sure I knew.

"And if you had told me then," she said, "that I would see a day when Jack Baird would get so mad that he'd put a fork through the wall, I would have said you were crazy. Are you going to pretend this is all about me?"

"That is not fair, Sarah."

"None of this is fair, Jack. I don't want you working with her. I don't want her setting foot in this house again. She's got you in her clutches, I can see it. I can feel it. I'm more sensitive right now..."

"She doesn't have to come back into this house, Sarah. But I do need to work with her occasionally, and what does that mean exactly— in her clutches?"

"I don't want you working with her."

"I don't have any choice. And actually, she's good at what she does. Don't you want my book to do well?"

She glared at me defiantly. She didn't say "no," though her expression was clearly one of sympathy for that position. I shook my head in disbelief and threw the fork again.

"You can have a baby, but I can't have a book?"

"We," she said. "We are having a baby." Sarah burst into tears and ran from the room.

I NOTICED numerous occasions where it seemed more and more like the luster had faded off of life. Things just didn't seem as exciting as they used to be. In the greenhouse, I often sat with books that I never read. I became one of those type of people I hate—those who carry books around they are pretending to read, and never really finish. I couldn't stand when people did that. What greater insult could you issue to Ernest Hemingway than to carry him around for months and never read the first sentence?

I recognized the danger signals, but was unable to muster a response. Sarah's fits were breaking me down, slowly, steadily; and the pressure of working on the book and staying full-time at the paper was adding its weight, as well. The worries didn't even end there: I also worried about the baby, and paying the bills without handouts from Sarah's father.

I missed my own father more during these days, and on a morning when the winter sunshine was unusually warm, I felt the irresistible urge to return to the Mount Sterling farm. I hadn't inherited any money with his passing, though my father had left me the farm. His meager pension payment served to pay an old hand who had been there for years. The house was rented out to his family.

Sarah and I had briefly discussed living there. At the time, however, there was no compelling reason for us to do so. We were happy newlyweds, and the prospect of being so far away from the glittering lights and conveniences of the city was not seriously considered.

Since Sarah's affair, my perspective had changed. My time spent in Somerset, and around the rest of Cumberland territory had changed me, too. The glittering lights were not as appealing as they once were. I was beginning to associate Louisville with Sarah and her family, and predictably, the feelings were not always positive. I was starting to associate Mount Sterling with simplicity and family.

The drive to the farm was a somber one. I've always prided myself on being the eternal optimist, so it was unusual and disturbing that I felt that low. I wasn't thinking about doing anything stupid—it was just a feeling that I had totally lost control and was drowning in a sea of conflict. The closer I got to Mount Sterling, the more I thought about my father. He really was a tragic figure in my life.

Sarah was with her sisters. I invited them to join me later in the day for a winter picnic, indoors of course, and they were going to call the family renting the house to let me know if they were coming or not.

I pulled the old Ford Escort, which served as our second vehicle, into the cedar-lined driveway, and slowed down to traverse the bumpy potholes and dips. The driveway was beautiful, even in that salt-less winter season, lined with older maples and oaks planted by my grandfather, with younger trees planted by my father in-between. Charolais cattle grazed peacefully amongst the bare shadows of the trees. It was really like a picture out of an old painting. Over the rise of the hill, the comfortable white farmhouse slowly came into view.

This was the house where I had grown up. It was where the only memories of my mother and father together originated. It was a place filled with mainly happy memories.

It also made me feel a little uneasy. Sarah and her family did not see the value in such a place. Sarah hadn't said anything, but her mother and father both had suggested that we sell the place and use the money to make things more comfortable in Louisville. I found it ironic that her father would give us anything we asked for, then turn around and ask me to give up the one thing left by my father in world. What would Sarah's father leave behind when his time came? Money. And that little scene in the living room. My father had at least left behind something with more intrinsic value than simply money, or some other secular attachment.

The family renting the house was poor. They had worked for my father before his death, and I didn't charge them much to live there. The house appeared to be in good upkeep, and the lawn was actually looking better than it had before—obviously the result of a late fall seeding. My father had grown a large, prize-winning garden, then neglected things like flowers or shrubs. My mother had handled that side of things before she left.

The screen door slammed at the back of the house as I got out of the car, and a man appeared, gaunt, tanned, and somber.

"Mr. Baird," he said, reclining his head slightly.

"Call me Jack," I said. "Things haven't changed that much, Bill."

Bill Hawkins breathed deeply and shook my hand, then tilted his head toward the house.

"Come on in. It's still a little chilly out here today. Sally has some food ready."

There were a lot of smells that assaulted me, familiar reminders of farm life in Kentucky: the pungent smell of a barn in need of scrapping; the smell of the old border collie that boarded beneath the back porch; the liquor-like smell of the silo, growing more empty day by day.

"How are the cattle?" I said as we went in the kitchen at the back of the house.

"They're doing well. We don't have any pasture to speak of, but the hay is holding up well. We're down to the last five bays in the silo, since it didn't start out full. We'll be alright, though. The weather is supposed to be mild around here the rest of the winter."

A woman appeared, his wife, a woman in her late forties or early fifties who actually appeared much older than that. Her life of poverty had obviously taken its toll, although she managed somehow to make more of whatever she had. The food she presented was simple and delicious—homemade bread and jam. There was a color in her complexion that hadn't been there before, now that she was living in the farmhouse instead of the tenant shack they had inhabited for many years.

"Your wife called, Mr. Baird."

"Call me Jack, Sally."

"She said that she was sorry, but she and her sisters are going to go shopping in Lexington for the baby, and she doesn't think she'll make it tonight."

"Oh."

I don't know why I was surprised. It was a logical conclusion. I thought I had prepared myself for that contingency. Somehow, though, it still bit a small hole inside of me.

"Have more bread," Sally said, smiling kindly.

I took a piece, then followed Bill out to tour the farm.

AFTER A LONG afternoon of walking around and inspecting the cattle, as well as the general state of the high-tensile fences, the barns, the tractors, and everything else, I returned to the warmth of the house.

Sally had hot coffee waiting.

After some small talk, I retired to my father's study, which Sally and Bill had quickly agreed should remain free for me to use whenever I visited. There was a computer on the desk, so I toyed with working on my book for a while.

Strangely enough, I felt better now. Sitting in my father's chair, and typing at his computer, and looking around at his momentos on the wall, and smelling his musty pipe smell, all of this actually made me feel like I was with him again. I relaxed and typed almost six pages on the new book. I had more or less claimed that it was done when I spoke to Dana Beech, though I secretly knew that many pages needed reworked, and several sections completely rewritten from scratch.

Outside, the light quickly faded. While I was staring at the screen, I heard the faint tinkle of a phone ringing somewhere out in the house. Then there was a quiet knock on the door.

"Mr. Baird, your wife is on the phone."

I took the portable phone from her hand, and she quickly left me alone.

"Hello?"

"Jack. How are you?"

"I'm fine. What's going on?"

"Just checking on you. We got some wonderful things for the baby, and I also picked out some things for the room. You said you would take my little room and turn it into a nursery—remember?"

"Yes."

"Are you doing okay?"

"Yes, why wouldn't I be? Everything's fine."

"Well, I just worried, since it's so soon after... I mean I didn't want you to be by yourself, but you know how Beth and Paige are."

"Yes, I know."

"So, everything's okay, honey?"

"Yes, Sarah, everything is okay."

"Well, be careful. I'll meet you at home. You're not staying overnight are you?"

"No, I'll come home."

"Good. Be careful. I love you."

"I love you, too. Good-bye, Sarah."

Did I mean those words? Did she mean those words? We said that we loved each other, because we were expected to. But was it really the truth?

Suddenly, I realized that my father wasn't in this room. He would never be in this room again—ever. It was a terrible, devastating discovery that crushed the breath out of me.

I laid my head down on the desk and cried. It was a long two hour drive back to Louisville, and I didn't really want to go. I didn't want to stay in the farmhouse, either. I didn't know what I wanted.

BETH AND PAIGE, as I've stated, began to spend more and more time at our house in Louisville. They were there when I got home from

Mount Sterling, even though Sarah was sound asleep.

"We promised her we'd wait up to make sure you got in," Beth explained, the younger sister. "She was worried about you."

Beth looked a little like Sarah, although she was really a carbon copy of her father, with sterling silver eyes and that waxy smile that wooed you and offended you at the same time. She was nineteen, a sophomore at the University of Louisville, and every bit the débutante her father enabled her to be. She tended to flaunt her attractiveness in an absent-minded way.

Paige, the older sister, was more conservative, with her dirty blond hair tied up in a prudish bun. She took after Sarah's mother, with the upturned lip and haughty tinge of superiority. Paige was pretty, though not nearly as attractive as Beth, who would easily be the poster girl for any big fraternity. Paige was married to a future doctor, and wanted her own baby now that Sarah was having one.

"We told her we'd wait up for you. She's very tired..."

I nodded and purposely waited for them to say something else.

"Was the farm okay?" Paige finally said, after an awkward moment. "The cows still there?"

"Oh, yes. Everything was fine. All the cattle were there. I was hoping you guys would make it over to see everything. I don't think you and Beth have ever been there, have you?"

They looked at each other and lamely shook their heads.

"It's a great place. We'll go there some time together. So... How about your trip—did you get a lot of great stuff for the baby?"

They livened up a bit. "Yes," Beth said quickly, "You should see the wallpaper Sarah picked out. It is so cute; it has little rabbits all over it. I can't wait until you put it up."

I smiled, somewhat falsely, I'm sure, and replied, "I can't wait, either. It's late, you'd better get going."

Rabbits—that would be slightly offensive, since Sarah and I couldn't exactly imitate that level of natural propagation. It took some medical intervention for us to procreate. We were more like rare, hard-to-breed Panda bears, than rabbits.

They left without any sort of hug or good-bye—just cautious nods and quick breaths. I'm not sure why I make them nervous; likewise, I don't know why they bother me so much. For what they are, good or bad, there's no crime or mystery or about it, and there's nothing less human about them than what's inside of everyone else. They have been trained well for the lives they are leading. Still, there was an unspoken sense shared in common that we would never really get along, particularly when Sarah was not mediating for us.

When they were gone, I undressed and joined Sarah in bed. Since the pregnancy, it seemed like Sarah was sleeping more deeply. She did not stir. I laid awake for a long time, yearning to talk about my return to the homestead. I did not wake her, though, and it was adequately comforting to stare at her slightly flush complexion, relaxed in sleep, not angry or sad, for just a few minutes wearing that "glow" that accompanies many mothers-to-be.

For some strange reason, I said a prayer for both of us. It was not like me to be religious, but is seemed like the right thing to do.

I WAS IN THE greenhouse the next morning, nursing a cup of coffee and reading snatches from Michael Shaara's "Killer Angels," when a series of what I considered profound thoughts struck me.

Just as writers plot their stories; give them a beginning, an end, and eventually a life beyond the beginning and end; just as life consists of birth and death, with all of the minor details stuck in-between—I began to see all of the events of the past several years from the top of a mountain like the one where Sarah and I had rediscovered ourselves. Everything suddenly made sense, and I could see where we were heading.

I was not loving Sarah. I was still fighting all of the anger about what had happened. I was looking for excuses to be away from her. I was locking out her family from my personal feelings. I was isolating myself, and distracting myself with mindless activities. I was using my writing as a crutch; a crooked walking stick to navigate the maze. I was feeling somewhat sorry for myself. I was still in deep anguish over my father. I was not giving my job all of the attention that I needed to for advancement.

The worst part of this realization was that the writer in me saw what type of future followed logically from this. It would be depression, failure, and possibly divorce. It would be messy; there would be a least one child involved. It would be costly, mentally and financially.

It would be a complete disaster.

Sarah was in the house cooking something innocuous for lunch when I entered through the back door. She looked at me without recognizing the change that had overtaken me.

"How are the plants doing?"

"They're fine."

Something in my voice caused her to turn to me. When she did, I imagined for the first time I could see the gentle swell in her stomach where our child was growing. She adopted her mothering tone and stance, holding her hands out.

"What's wrong, Jack?"

"Sarah, you'd better sit down for what I'm about to say."

The level of concern in her normally placid brown eyes quickly grew. The pot on the stove boiled over, without so much as a flinch on her part, and she sat down in one of the kitchen chairs.

"Sarah, I am sorry for the last few months or more. I have been feeling sorry for myself, and I have been angry. Worse, though, I have tried to hide it from you. I've tried to pretend like nothing was wrong. I have been mean-spirited to your family. I've been unfair to you, holding the guilt over your head in silent terms of dominance. I've not told you all of my true feelings. I'm sorry."

"Jack," she said quietly, her voice quivering, and tears appearing in the now sad brown eyes, "you don't have to do this. What I did was wrong."

"Yes, Sarah, I know that. But we all make mistakes, and when I think back to your childhood, and the broken family scenario we both grew up with, what happened to you doesn't seem so outlandish. What kind of role models have we had for this type of relationship?"

Sarah started crying, but blissfully nodded in complete agreement.

"You married me, Sarah, because you thought I was kind, patient, understanding, forgiving, and intelligent."

"Don't speak too highly of yourself," she said, laughing between sniffles, in a gentle attempt at humor.

"No, I'm serious, Sarah. Those are the things I see in myself, and I'm sure you saw them, too. They've all been woefully absent since your affair."

She cried again when I said "the word," but I felt a tremendous sense of release as the word came out.

"Yes, Sarah, you had an affair. And since then, the meanness I've felt has probably equaled or succeeded your guilt. I am sorry for that, terribly sorry. I've ruined what I thought was best about me."

"That's not true, Jack."

The fire alarm went off, piercing the kitchen with shrill beeps, and I quickly turned the stove off and ripped the cover off the detector, silencing it.

"It is true, Sarah, and I'm sorry. I'm angry at myself now, not you."

"So you think it's that easy—just like that, you can really forgive me?

"Yes, Sarah, I'm ready to forget about it—completely."

She stood up and started pacing, an odd departure from her usual economy of movement. She was obviously not good at it—she was too graceful to be a true pacer.

"You can't ever forget about it completely," she said slowly. Her eyes glazed over and she stopped in the kitchen doorway, staring at all of the family portraits over the mantle in the living room. "It's impossible. People can't forget. Can they?" She turned and looked at me.

"I think I can. I don't want to remember it anymore."

"That's the point, Jack! Do you think I want to remember what happened to my parents? Do you think I want to remember that day we found him in the living room? Do you think my mother can forget? Do you think my sisters and I can forget?"

"We're not the same, Sarah. We have the benefit of their experiences, as well as our own. What we have is different. We're not like your parents, or mine for that matter. We are us, and we can decide what we want or don't want to do. I choose to forget."

"It's that simple?"

"I say it is."

She nodded slowly, as if considering it, then meandered in my direction until she ended up in my arms.

"Jack, how did I ever get so lucky?"

"That's what I always ask myself, Sarah."

"Even now?"

"Even now."

She gently directed my hand to her stomach, where she softly rubbed it in a circular motion. "Feel that? That's your son."

"It's a boy?"

She nodded affirmatively. "I can tell. I want to name him after your father, and you."

I smiled, and for the first time in a long time, I felt that Sarah cared about me deeply, and wasn't just going through the motions. A tremendous weight suddenly slipped from my shoulders, and my spirit leaped free.

Chapter 10
Dana Beech

THINGS SEEMED to go better after this, not just at home, but in all
phases of my life. Life at the newspaper was a little more pleasant; I
wasn't quite so willing to stay late anymore, and the quality of my
writing improved. In return, I was assigned better projects. My boss
was happier, and I even got a small raise.

Life at home was better, too. Sarah smiled more, and she did
begin to show the presence of a third family member as the months
turned closer to spring. There was a healthiness about her that she
hadn't exhibited since her college days; a kind of thickness (in a good
sense) about her cheeks that made her facial expressions more adult
and attractive. She continued to work one day a week, and at home she
took up some tax work for her father to make extra money. She stayed
busy, and remained a remarkably efficient housekeeper and hostess.

The plants in the greenhouse were bursting out of their trays,
ready for transplanting, and the air had warmed enough for me to
borrow a neighbors' tiller and churn up part of our tiny urban
backyard. I went through the ritual of covering sensitive plants on cold
nights. I watched them slowly take hold.

I continued to refine and rewrite the new Civil War novel. It had a
flow to it like nothing I had ever written before, and a small voice
inside of me kept telling me that it was something special, perhaps the
novel I had meant to write when the concept of being a writer first
appeared out of the mists and hazes of youth.

Everything seemed fine. The itching thoughts that had nagged me
so long about my own actions in response to Sarah's mistakes faded
into the background.

A couple of strange things did occur. The first involved my
editor, Ms. Beech.

Dana Beech and I spent more time together as the book plans
progressed, and our conversation grew progressively more intimate. On
one particular day, it led to some territory that I didn't necessarily want
to travel to.

We were at a greasy burger place on Bardstown Road after work,
discussing some chapter revisions. In-between french fries, she pushed

her hair out of her eyes (which she was letting grow long, for some reason), then scribbled furiously with a pencil in the margins of the paper.

"What are you doing?" I said, my mouth full of onions and hamburger.

"I don't like this scene," she said, "or this chapter, for that matter."

"Which chapter?"

"Twenty-three, where he comes home and finds everyone gone and everything on the farm destroyed by raiders."

"What's wrong with it? That's what happened to a lot of people in the war. You're not from the South, so you might not understand."

She looked up, annoyed. "Indiana is not that far removed from Kentucky, Jack. In fact, you and I grew up within two hours of one another. How does that make you a Rebel, and me a Yankee?"

"It makes a difference," I insisted.

She shrugged. "It's the Ohio River, Jack, not some cosmic intellectual or political barrier. That's not my point, anyway. My point has to do with this pseudo-suicide scene that evolves shortly thereafter. I mean, come on, Jack, this guy is a rock all through the book, and now all of the sudden he's sniffling and crying? Does that really fit?"

"Yes it fits. Everyone has their moments of doubt."

"Of course they do in real life. But this isn't reality—it's fiction. How does it make your character more attractive? Should Ian Fleming have James Bond fart because we all do that, too? Should Shakespeare have Juliet time-out to deal with her period?"

I felt my face turn a little bit red. "That's not what I mean..."

"Uh, oh," she said sarcastically. "I recognize the hurt artist look. Maybe we should save this conversation for some other time."

"No," I said, angry by now. "Let's finish with it. Is fiction allowed to deal with suicide or not?"

"Of course it is. No subject is barred. That's censorship. As your editor—and unofficial agent, too, I might add—it's my job to worry about selling your book, not turning it into a self-help, Maslow-like actualization manual."

"He doesn't kill himself, Dana. Why can't he think about it?"

"Because..."

Suddenly, her words slowed down. Her tone took on a timbre that I had never heard before—quite and low.

"Because, Jack, suicide is not a light matter. Either you deal with it seriously, or you shouldn't deal with it at all."

I heard something else in her voice now—perhaps a tinge of experience, or first-hand knowledge?

"Okay," I said, backing off. "I'm listening. Suicide is serious. Suicide sucks. Lost a good friend in high school that way. Why can't I let my character flirt with it?"

"Because, suicide is not a girl, Jack. You don't flirt with her. If you go to the dance with her, it changes you forever, whether you actually follow through with it or not. It's a permanent scar."

A tear had appeared at the corner of her left eye, smearing her mascara. Two greasy french fries had congealed between her fingers. Her tiny upper lip was defiant and refused to quiver.

"What have I done?" I said quietly.

"You haven't done anything. To make a long story short, my first husband did some very bad things to me. Not that he was bad person, necessarily, but he did do some terrible things—to me, and to himself. Before I went through with the court-ordered divorce proceedings, I tried to kill myself. If I had had any common sense about it, I would have succeeded."

"I'm glad you didn't."

"Thanks. But the point is this: those feelings still hang around the edges of my sub-conscience, and I can't get rid of them. They'll be with me forever. I don't get any sense of that from your character. All I see is some macho man feeling sorry for himself. That's not great literature. It's probably you trying to make up for..." her voice trailed off.

Ouch. That hurt. We weren't just talking about a scene, now, we talking about an entire novel built around this character. We were talking about me. I felt despair creeping up again, like it did in some of those helpless fights Sarah and I had endured right after the affair. I also was embarrassed about discovering this private part of Dana Beech I never knew about.

"How close did you come?" I said.

"What?"

"To hurting yourself—how close was it?"

It's funny the expressions you discover in people. I had known Ms. Beech for almost a year, and now this expression arose on her face, like a ship's captain warily approaching a rocky inlet where he had left a vessel wrecked once before. There was fear there, and also an unusual sadness. There was none of her bubbly exterior now.

"That's kind of personal, isn't it Mr. Baird?"

"Fair is fair," I replied. "You know everything about my colorful marriage, and you've seen me in some places and situations I'd rather you hadn't. You don't have to tell me, of course."

"Why do you want to know?"

"You're editing my book; a creation I've labored my whole life to produce, if you want to stretch it just a little bit. I want to be able to trust you and trust all of the changes your making. I want to understand what you're saying. I need to trust you."

She huffed and pointed a red fingernail at herself. "Me? Jack, you don't trust me, by now?"

"Professionally, yes. Personal trust takes a little more."

For a moment, I got a funny feeling that I was digging a hole to climb into. Then, it seemed okay.

"Well, then. I ask for a couple of things in return."

"Negotiation?" I said. "You mean a deal—like a book deal."

"Yes, Jack. Isn't that why we're together? Everything between us is a deal."

"Okay. I'm listening."

"I'll tell you about suicide. In return, I want to know more about Sarah."

"Sarah?"

When I said it, I didn't realize how loud I was. People at surrounding tables stopped in mid-bite and stared at us. I smiled at them, and nodded politely, then focused on Dana Beech again. There was an intensity in her oval face that squared all of the round edges.

"Okay...I'll tell you about Sarah. But you go first."

She nodded assent, then said, "Agreed. Not here, though. Let's go someplace quieter; someplace that serves alcohol. I need a drink."

WE ENDED UP in a shady dance place; one of those outfits run by New Yorkers who come into Louisville and make a big fuss about the big city and the big lights. Louisville, I'm afraid, will always disappoint them in that sense. As for laundering their money, however, Louisville couldn't be a better, less suspicious, place. Nightclubs like the one we went into come and go like the seasons. They are usually bought and sold, closed and opened, burnt down and rebuilt, all in the same week; always by the same people.

We choose a booth in the corner far removed from the dancing, or the waiters dashing in and out of the kitchen with expensive entrees. Dana Beech ordered a tall mint julep, then removed her lime green pumps (that matched her lime green dress) and tucked her feet underneath herself on the bench across from me. I ordered a beer.

"All right," I said, after a few minutes passed and no conversation was forthcoming. "You said you would go first. Tell me about suicide."

"It's not that simple. For me to tell you about it, I have to tell you about me, and that's much too complicated to get into."

"So you're reneging?"

She stared off into the distance. "I need a cigarette," she finally said.

"Spoken like a true ex-smoker," I observed.

"How did you know?"

"It's your voice. You said the word cigarette the way Sarah says the word chocolate."

Surprisingly, she burst out laughing. I laughed, too.

"So you're reneging?" I said again. Our drinks arrived before she could answer, and she immediately drank deeply from the heavy crystal goblet, pulling down at least half the entire contents.

"No," she finally replied. "I'll go first." Her gaze traveled over the lines of my face, as if reassessing who exactly I was, that she should share this information with me. There were dark lines beneath her eyes that were normally not present. "First of all, Jack, let me tell you something. I'm not going to pull any punches. Men suck, plain and simple. Women would be better off without them. I'm not singling you out as an exception, either. All men suck."

She drained the remainder of the mint julep and started scanning for a waiter.

"Well, I guess I'll try not to take that personally."

"Don't," she continued. "Men like to feel sorry for themselves—they're experts at it. And the kicker is that when they feel bad, they make sure you feel bad, too."

"Can we get back to the subject?" I asked gently.

"This *is* the subject! I'm trying to explain it to you, and you're just as dense as the rest of them...Another one," she said to the waiter, who hesitated. "Please," she added when he pouted, and he immediately went away.

"See? Even some little piss-ant male waiter gives that sorry crap to you, if you're a woman. But if a man says please to his waitress, it's because he wants to screw her."

I shook my head, a little unnerved, and a little confused. This was not what I had expected from her, and I was fighting hard not to be offended myself.

"And your Sarah," she said, her voice toneless and even, "I'll bet she's the perfect wife now, isn't she? But let a man make that mistake, and everyone turns the other way. He can come home when he feels like it."

"Don't bring Sarah into this," I said threateningly, still trying to figure out what the hell she was talking about. "I come home when I want to."

Dana Beech jabbed a finger at me. "That's your half of the bargain, buster. Your turn is next. Let me continue."

"Fine. You finish."

Her drink arrived and she slugged down a good portion of it immediately. I looked into my own warm beer, which I hadn't even sipped from yet. I pushed it aside, figuring I was probably going to end up driving her home at the rate she was going.

Before we could resume, a small bell tinkled on my belt. I plucked the pager and stared at it. Sarah was calling.

"Newspaper?" Dana Beech asked.

"No," I said, offering nothing else. Hell, she would know it was Sarah, anyway, but I was feeling combative.

At the pay phone, I listened to the phone ring and stared across the lobby at Dana Beech. She was hunched over, her feet still tucked beneath her like a little girl's, her (longer now) straight, jet-black hair falling forward so I couldn't see her eyes. I sensed some kind of tragedy in the air, and assumed it was waiting in the rest of her story about suicide. I thought about my own character in the book; the officer returning home from the war—was this really going to help me fix that?

Then I thought a strange thing. I wondered what character I was playing in my own life story.

"Hello?" a sleepy voice said on the other end.

"Sarah? It's me."

"Where are you, Jack?"

"I'm at Rudi's, on Bardstown Road. I worked late, and I met Dana here to figure out a problem with chapter twenty-three."

"You're with Dana Beech?"

"Yes, I didn't want to come home and bother you. It sounds like you've been sleeping."

"I have been. But you still could have come here. I'd rather have you working here, where you can be close by."

"Well, we can come there if you like, but we're almost done. What do you want me to do?"

There was a deep sigh on the other end of the line. "I know I can trust you, Jack, but I do get a little bit jealous. I haven't seen you all day."

"I know, Sarah. I promise I'll be home soon. Okay?"

"Okay. Just be careful. Rudi's is a bad place to hang out."

I returned to the table, and found that Dana Beech had straightened herself up. Her face had on fresh make-up, her eyes were brighter, and there was a cup of steaming coffee where the mint julep had been.

She laughed shyly. "I don't hold my liquor very well. I'd better stop."

"We can continue this some other time."

"No, no, I'll stop drinking. We can keep talking, can't we?"

"Sure..."

"Let me try again, Jack, without all the venom. I married a man I met in college, a pre-law student, and things were normal for a long time. Down the road a couple of years, I found out he had been cheating on me with someone in his law office. It was probably an issue we could have worked out, but things started to go wrong. He wouldn't talk to me, and when I tried to talk to him, he started getting physical. I guess I thought I loved him or something, because for a long time I put up with it, even as it got progressively worse."

"Why was he so angry?"

"I don't know. I guess he felt guilty or something. When he passed the bar, he started holding that over my head. He threatened me with going to court, if you can believe that, when he was the one who had been guilty of infidelity."

"Why did you take it—why didn't you leave?"

"I would, now. I was just a kid then, with all of these dreams and idealisms, and the optimist in me couldn't accept the plain cold fact that things were getting so bad. At one point, my parents found me at home dazed, bruised, black-eye and all, and they forced me to contact another lawyer."

"So you got divorced?"

"Yes, it ended up clean and complete. I haven't heard from him since."

"So where does suicide fit into this picture?"

"Jack, use your writer's imagination for a moment. You only know me now; the sum total of what I've become. Go back in time a little, and put yourself in the shoe's of a terrified woman, a little girl, physically unable to defend herself, afraid to even call the police because of the intellectual pseudo-legal bullying her husband slaps her with—belittled, dazed, forced against her will to have sex, bruised, and insignificant. I used to look in the mirror and cry, because I couldn't see myself. There was something else there, something ugly and used up, and it made me feel like I wanted to die."

I didn't want to say the wrong thing, so I said nothing. She stared off into space for a long time, then smiled wryly. "Maybe I will have another drink," she whispered. "I need it."

"You don't need it, Ms. Beech, but I'll gladly drive you home if you would like another one anyway."

"What the hell," she flagged the waiter down and ordered a beer. "So," she continued, "I can't explain what that feeling is inside. It's a feeling of being so worthless, so unimportant, so frustrated and helpless, that even the fantasy of watching your own blood flow from your wrists makes you feel good. It makes you feel like you're atoning for something. It's the only thing you can control that might get somebody's attention. It's the only way you can make up for everything."

"But you didn't do anything wrong."

"Maybe not. In fact, I'm sure I didn't. Back then, though, you couldn't have convinced me of that. I was sure that I had mortally sinned, and that I was being punished for something that was bad inside of me. I was angry about people who were blessed with happy relationships, and I wanted all the world to experience what I was going through. I'm afraid I put my mother through hell for a year or two. I'm lucky she was such a good person."

"So how close did you come?"

"I never actually came that close. But, oh, it felt close. I cut my wrists, and idiot that I was, I slit them the wrong way. If you want to bleed to death, you have to cut this way—" She abruptly demonstrated, making a vertical slash down her wrist that sent a chill through me. Her wrists were so thin, so vulnerable. "But I cut horizontally, across, and all it did was make a big mess. I also tried to drink myself to death, but as I told you, I have zero tolerance. I'm about wasted right now after two little drinks."

"Two big drinks," I said quietly.

"I don't think I really wanted to do it. But I was so desperate. I would've sold my soul to get rid of that unhappiness, and there was never a minute of the day or night when I could escape the dread and aching pain."

"How did you get over it?"

She smiled, a drunken, playful grin: "Who says I'm over it?"

"You're drunk, now, Ms. Beech."

"Good."

"Come on," I suggested cautiously. "I'll take you home, and I'll tell you about Sarah on the way. Wasn't that my half of the bargain? We can get your rental car in the morning." I flipped some money on the table and waited. When she just smiled at me lethargically, I reached down and bodily picked her up and set her on her feet. I was surprised at how light she was. She smiled as I did it.

"Does this help you now with your suicide scene?" she said.

"My character doesn't have a suicide scene like you've described. It's not like your story. It's supposed to be more dramatic; more Shakespearean or something. You know, like Hamlet: 'To be, or not to be..'"

"Shakespeare was never beaten and raped, Jack."

"Well, when you're feeling a little more straight, you can give me some suggestions."

In the car, I thought she was sleeping beside me. Her head had slumped over onto my shoulder. At a stoplight, however, I twisted my eye sideways and was startled to see she was wide awake. Suddenly, it was an awkward moment.

"Let me tell you about Sarah," I said. "That's my half of the bargain."

There was no immediate response.

"You do still want to hear about it, don't you?" I said.

Still no response. I started, anyway.

"Sarah and I met in college. I was a geek-like kid with dreams of being a famous writer; she was the perfect sorority girl that every guy wanted to go out with. I never thought I had a chance with her, so I had nothing to lose when I asked her out. She said yes, and we started going out. After a while, though, we both noticed that we weren't dating other people, and it seemed to become more serious."

"My roommate, Al, and all of my frat buddies warned me away from her. They said she was too good for me. They said I didn't stand a chance. Al even said that I would be looking over my shoulder forever, and I guess now he can say he told me so."

I looked over to see if she was asleep yet, though if anything, she was more sober than she had been all night. I had her attention.

"So why do you think Sarah cheated on you?" she asked, finally breaking her long silence.

"I'm not to that part, yet. Sarah told me some things about her childhood that were very creepy. Her perfect life hadn't been as normal as it appeared to be. We had a couple of rough moments early in our marriage that stemmed from that. Ironically, it was me that ended them by reassuring her of my dependability. Sometimes, I think she married me because I was safe."

Dana Beech unexpectedly laughed, and a little bit of anger flashed into my voice. "What's so funny?"

"It's not you, Jack. It's just what you said. Think about what happened to me. Do you know how damned hard I tried to be a good wife to that idiot? Can you conceive of how hard I attempted to make the whole thing work? I would have killed for someone 'safe.' But we always end up marrying people who know how to hurt us. It's as if we don't want to be happy."

"You're right about that—Sarah and I know exactly how to push each other to the limit. It goes against human nature somehow to let yourself be so vulnerable. In prehistoric times, cavemen didn't survive if they left themselves vulnerable. Today, we seek it out in relationships. It's counter-evolutionary."

"Take it easy," she warned, "I'm not that sober. Don't go all intellectual on me."

I continued the story. "So, things seemed to be going reasonably well when another bombshell struck. Sarah informed me that she couldn't have any children, and sort of apologized for not telling me ahead of time. I didn't take it too well, although I managed to cover up my feelings to a certain extent, and it eventually led to more tension, anyway, so it was just one more thing. It seemed like she always kept secrets from me.

"Then, in the middle of all of this growing up and building relationships, Sarah and I are driving down the Interstate and she tells me she's been sleeping with someone else. I got out of the car and started walking, and I didn't stop until I got to Somerset, where you and I met initially. I have no idea where her affair came from. Left field, whatever that cliché means. I still don't know."

"Were you having sex?"

Something in Dana's voice made the question sound personal, which pushed her a little further into a category beyond just literary agent and publishing confidant. It immediately made me nervous.

"Yes," I said quickly—probably too defensively, no doubt. "We had plenty of it. And it was good. It was great."

"For her, too?"

"Yes, dammit. Do you have to make me feel like I'm being cross-examined by a lawyer?"

"I just want to understand."

"Well how can you understand, when I can't even explain it myself?"

She pushed her finger into my shoulder and said, "Touché! Now you know exactly what I was talking about earlier. It took us six hours, but now you know what your scene in the book needs."

"That's it?" I said. "This is all about the book? This is all so I can rewrite a chapter for the fifteen millionth time, and finally say I've gotten it right?"

I stopped the car in the middle of the street, which was okay because there was no traffic, and examined her carefully. There was no anger or overt emotion in her face—only a vague sadness, and a hint of puffiness around her eyes that gave away the fact she had cried several times tonight. She returned my stare unflinchingly, and it made me look away because I thought of how it had felt earlier with her head on my shoulder; when I had looked over and seen that she was awake the whole time.

"I'm sorry," I said. "I didn't mean it that way. It's just that this Sarah thing is ongoing—I'm in the middle of it, and I don't know where it's headed. Everything seems fine now, but I just don't know. Things seem to change so quickly. We go from lovers to mortal enemies in the space it takes to suck in one breath."

"I'm sorry, Jack. I shouldn't say anything. I don't want to steer you wrong about marriage. Just because mine ended in disaster doesn't mean everyone else's needs to."

We arrived at the hotel where she was staying—living, sort of, while she worked on my book, and looked into relocating—and I swung into a parking space in front of her door. For several minutes we sat there, staring out the windshield at the lights of the city, and then finally I remembered that I'd promised Sarah I wouldn't be long.

I turned to say goodnight to Dana, and this time she really was asleep. I climbed out the driver side and walked around to open her door. I intentionally was loud about it, and the noise roused her from momentary slumber. She stumbled out of the door, and I caught her by the arm to steady her.

"I think it's night-night time," I said.

"See you, Jack. I have to fly back to Cincinnati tomorrow to meet with my boss. He thinks I've been spending too much time down here."

"I'll work on chapter twenty-three."

"You do that. I'll call you in a day or two. He's going to want to see your manuscript when I come back again."

"Okay."

"Okay, then. Good night."

She walked slowly to her door, fumbled with keys, then said good night again, and disappeared inside.

I drove home and did not realize how late it really was.

WHEN I WAS home in bed with Sarah (who did not wake when I came in, but instinctively wrapped her arms around me and smiled) I could not sleep. I thought for a long time about the story Dana Beech had told me. I tried to imagine the things her husband had done. As vicious, terrible images filled my head, I winced and wriggled uncomfortably between the sheets. Sleep would not come.

There was nothing that could possibly be construed as offensive about her. She was good looking, and while on the small and short side, she was wonderfully curved, and she was certainly smart enough. She maintained a reasonable sense of humor, and balanced it with a normal sense of responsibility. I had never seen her display an emotional tirade, or blow up over nothing. What would make a man do those terrible things to her?

Was I capable of such things? I wondered. I had never raised my hand in anger against anyone, short of boyhood brawls and play fighting around the farm, let alone threatened someone who was physically unable to stop me. Sarah and I had experienced our moments, to be sure, and I could feel that anger in the back of my throat—it was a taste that was never very far removed in our confrontations. But I had never once thought about hitting her.

Then I remembered the fork. Throwing the fork was not the same as striking someone, and yet it was still unlike me. Was I capable of more? What had happened to Jack Baird since he met Sarah Collins?

As I lay there, unable to sleep, I almost woke Sarah up to talk about it. The more I thought, though, the less I decided she would be able to relate to it. Her father had never raised a hand against his girls. He'd basically slept with anyone and everyone he wanted to, and openly displayed it. He had never been physically abusive. Sarah's mother was the most gentle person in the world.

A strange thought followed all of this. It was actually Dana Beech that I wanted to talk to, and I wrestled with that realization the rest of the night, wriggling and turning to the point that I did wake up a grumpy Sarah.

I ended up on the couch.

"SO," SARAH SAID gaily, "did you and Dana get a lot done last night?"

I looked up over the newspaper to see if she was kidding, and was mildly surprised to see that she wasn't. She pecked me on the mouth with a kiss before I could answer, and placed a steaming mug of coffee in front of me.

"Yes," I said slowly. "We got a lot done."

"What do you think?" she said suddenly, twirling around so that her sideways profile was pointed at me. "Does it show, yet? Be honest."

Sarah had her long wavy, honey-brown hair tied up in a pony-tail, and was wearing one of those over-sized white aprons that French chefs don all the time. She still had on her pink-striped pajamas underneath it. She was actually incredibly cute. There was no doubt in every male cell in my body that Sarah was mine.

She was definitely showing. "Yes," I blurted out, smiling the whole time. "Go look in the mirror if you don't believe me."

She ran into the other room, then reappeared a moment later, still smiling. She carefully slid into the chair next to me and laid her legs across mine. I winked at her, and she winked back at me.

"Is there something I'm missing here?" I said.

"No, nothing at all. I just feel good this morning. Sometimes I just get in these crazy moods and I feel good. I've been in them more lately. I think I felt the baby last night, too. I forgot to tell you that on the phone."

"Did you also forget about me waking you up in the middle of the night?"

"Just about."

"You felt the baby. That's incredible. Let me see..."

She twisted in her chair until I could snake my hand through the apron and under the pajama top to her stomach, which was only slightly puffy; perhaps not puffy at all by some standards. I held it there for a while, noting what seemed to be unusual warmth. There was no movement, however.

"Nothing?" she asked.

"No, not now."

"He must be sleeping."

I laughed and shook my head. She really was in a silly mood. "Are you still standing by that prediction?"

"It's not a prediction, Jack. We're going to name him after your father—remember?"

"Okay. I hope you're right."

"Of course I'm right." She kissed me on the forehead and poured more coffee in a travel mug, which she held out to with me an expression that clearly said I was late to work. "Why don't I meet you for lunch?"

"Sounds good to me."

"Let's go to that oyster bar that my father likes."

"See you there."

"Don't forget about dinner tonight!"

"Oh, yeah."

Yes, how could I forget? Her entire family was coming, including her father. It was a little bit of an experiment. A big experiment.

She kissed me again and I ran out the door. In the car on the way to the paper, I wondered if maybe Dana Beech was wrong, after all, about marriage. She had made an unfortunate choice, and it didn't have to be that way for everyone. I didn't have to love my in-laws for my marriage to be a success. All I had to do was love Sarah.

Sarah was holding her own regardless.

AT WORK, SOMETHING reminded me of Al, and I remembered that I had left his call unanswered for quite some time. I dialed his work number in Richmond, hoping to catch him in.

"Al, it's Jack. Do you have a minute?"

"Yeah, sure. How you been, Jack? You must have been busy."

"Yes, I'm sorry I took so long to get back to you. How's the baby doing?"

"She's great, man. She's getting bigger every day. What about you guys? Carla said the medical stuff went okay."

I was a little bit irritated again, or perhaps I was feeling guilty because Sarah had called Carla when I should've been calling Al. "Yes, it did. I had to go into a dark room with some magazines and provide a sample for the procedure."

"That's my boy! So how long will it be?"

"We're probably about three months along, now."

"Wow, that's great. I can't wait to see you as a father. It'll change you, Jack, trust me. It will change you for the better."

"That's what I hear."

"Hey listen, Hoss. The reason I called you was because the Orioles will be at Riverfront this May. Do you think you can get us some tickets?"

"Yes, sure."

"I figured you and I can go hop some bars in the Queen City for a couple of days while Carla and Maria visit with Sarah. What do you think?"

"That'll be great. I'll call and get tickets. Is that what you called about?"

I didn't intend for the question to sound funny, though it came out that way. I had thought for a long time that Al had called to share some new great truth about Sarah, or how to save my marriage. Not about baseball.

Al was nonplussed. "Yeah, that's why I called. Got to run, Jack. I've got a meeting."

"I'll get the tickets, Al, I promise—I'll call right now. It sounds like a great idea."

"I knew you'd agree. Talk to you soon."

I hung the phone up and stroked my chin, staring for a long time at the receiver. Why did I constantly have to read so much into everything? There was nothing wrong with Al. There was nothing wrong with me, either. Paranoia was a lingering side-effect of Sarah's mistake, and I just would have to get over it.

The strange conversation with Dana about suicide, and the dangerous feelings that I had experienced would have to be buried.

AT LUNCH, I couldn't help myself. I started asking questions that I probably shouldn't have. For some reason, the whole thing was bugging me with Al and Carla.

"Have you talked to Carla lately?" I asked.

Sarah didn't bother looking up. She was devouring a plate of fried oysters; a rare diversion from her normally ultra-healthy diet for the last three months. "I guess it's been a couple of weeks...Did you ever call Al back?"

"Yes, today, in fact."

"So what's going on with them?"

"The baby's fine. Al wants me to get some ball tickets for May, so they'll be over then." I hesitated. "Do you and Carla ever talk about—" Then I chickened out, leaving the dangerous question lingering in the air like hazy smoke.

Sarah, to her credit, continued to be in an amazingly graceful mood. "Talk about what, Jack—Sex? Life? Religion? What?"

"The incident."

The merest of clouds briefly passed over her face before

completely evaporating. "Yes, we have. Does that bother you?"

I decided to go for the truth, and set myself free, metaphorically speaking. "I don't think so. But sometimes Al lectures me about you, and it kind of makes me feel like I'm out of the loop or something. I don't want to have any secrets between us."

"Al lectures you—about me?" she pointed at her chest. "Me?"

"Yes, he tries to tell me how to treat you right. He tries to tell me how to be a good husband, or I guess that's what it is."

Her porcelain face broke into a wide grin. "Well, that's so sweet of him! I wouldn't have thought he had it in him. Damn... And here I thought he was just a beer-guzzling, macho, pretzel-eating, football-watching 'man.' What kind of advice has he given you?"

I shrugged.

"Come on, Jack, tell me. You brought this up."

"Honestly, Sarah, he's just been concerned that I'm taking good care of you."

"Are you?" she asked, arching her eyebrows.

"I think so. I'm trying. Is there something I'm not providing you with?"

She laughed again. "Is that what marriage is about—providing for me? My father provides for me, but I don't think you want me to make that comparison, do you?"

She made her shoulders bunch up and flexed her arms comically.

"Okay, Macho woman," I said, "I get the point. I just don't want you to think that I don't take good care of you."

"Of course not," she said, slipping her hand over mine. With the other hand, she reached for shrimp. "Look at the way you're feeding me—I'm stuffed. We're stuffed. You always take good care of me."

"I'm trying very hard. Remember, though, to help me be calm tonight."

"Don't worry. Everything will be fine tonight."

She leaned over and gave me a shrimp kiss, and once again, the healing process progressed. Her wavy brown hair was so beautiful; her face, flush with expected motherhood. I smiled back and trusted her.

Damn, Sarah could turn the charm on.

THAT AFTERNOON, I did something I hadn't in a long time: I sent flowers to Sarah, two dozen long-stem roses. I knew she would be home after our lunch because she was preparing the big dinner. I purposely avoided taking any calls the rest of the day, because I wanted to see the expression on her face in person.

Things were finally starting to look so good. My second novel was just about ready for publication, and Sarah and I were settling into a very relaxed, comfortable routine. Work was beginning to seem like a place with some rewards (and my name was actually appearing in by-lines from time to time). Cursory analysis showed the Baird curve on the upswing.

When I pulled into the driveway, I noticed with a little dismay that her mother was already here. I had hoped to catch Sarah before anyone else arrived. Unfortunately, it was her mother who popped out the front door to greet me.

"Nice flowers, Jack. They're beautiful!"

"Thanks," I said, trying not to sound wilted.

"Sarah's lucky to have a guy like you!"

I nodded my head, but inside I wondered when she said things like that—did she really mean them? It was hard to convince me. Memories of the occasions like our wedding reception tended to make a skeptic of me.

"Come on," she said, pulling me in the door, "let's give Sarah a hand."

So much for romance. The reality is in-laws. Romance is only fantasy for those who live real life.

Chapter 11
Dinner

SARAH OUTDID herself for dinner. She fixed a massive series of somewhat exotic dishes that ranged from oyster stew to chicken cacciatore, and then arranged them carefully so they looked even more exotic than they really were. She served each item one at a time, garnished lavishly, while her family sat agape, shocked that this wasn't catered or ordered out.

"Sarah," her mother exclaimed, "I didn't know you had it in you! I didn't teach you how to cook like this..."

"She certainly didn't," Mr. Collins whispered in my ear. Sarah had placed herself on one side, and me on the other, hoping to keep him isolated from the rest of the girls. He had taken it upon himself—perhaps to relieve the stress, if he really felt any—to share every passing thought that crossed his mind with me, like an old drinking partner.

This family, as I've said before, has a very strange working arrangement. There are no formal splits. Yes, they are divorced, but I mean that no one has stopped associating with anyone. They still try to act like a family. It's made more strange by the fact that no one will admit to anything. Mr. Collins will never talk about anything wrong he has done. Neither will Sarah's mother. If I didn't know the story about the living room, and a few other minor things, I would be in complete bafflement as to why they weren't still together.

The girls, Beth and Paige, complicated the picture, too. They worshiped their father as if he were a god, despite knowing what he was. They took his money; his paternal handouts; his probably genuine affections; his influence. The same thing applied to Mrs. Collins. She lived in the big family house and carried on paternal business as if everything was normal. She had never worked a day in her life.

My parents both worked (or tried to); my parents were loyal to each other in their peculiar way, though never too loyal to talk about the other's faults when they came up. If my father had done what Mr. Collins did, my mother would have shot him. That was the mountain way of doing things, even if she was from Lexington rather than Hazard. Instead, they got divorced because they knew each other too well, and could clearly see the things about each other that would drive them crazy. Or did drive them crazy.

It was hard for me to respect any of Sarah's family members. Of course, I was married to one of their own, though it was different with Sarah, since she was the black sheep in the bunch. While her sisters were protective of her, there was an upper-crust gleam in their eyes that I never once found in Sarah's. They wore clothes that Sarah only glanced in passing at in catalogues. Sarah had also stopped (more or less) taking her father's wealth since our marriage. She had, as of late, also domesticated herself to a incredible extent for a Collins, and this was a constant source of amazement to them all.

I watched Sarah carefully as they reacted to the surroundings and the meal.

"Fantastic!" her mother said again, devouring a second helping of the chicken.

"Is this house big enough for you?" her father said with grave concern.

"These napkins look like ours—the floral pattern," Beth said. "Where did you get them?"

"How do you slave in the hot kitchen, pregnant, Sarah?" Paige said.

Sarah was overwhelmed. She didn't know which query to respond to first, and naturally chose her mother.

"Thank you, mother, it's one of Jack's mother's recipes."

"Oh!" Mrs. Collins said, turning to me for one of the few times during the meal. She really could have been an attractive for a woman in her mid-fifties, yet some small invisible element was missing, and if I didn't know the history behind her marriage, I probably would have liked her. She placed a wrinkle-free hand over Sarah's and smiled at me with ivory teeth. "I'll bet your mother is a great cook, too."

"Yes, she is," I agreed. "I don't go over there enough."

"Well you should have invited her over tonight."

"Mom," Beth said, in a voice that was annoyingly teenage-like, "please pass the wine."

"One glass there, little lady," Mr. Collins said abruptly. "You've still got a few months to go to become legal." As if to flaunt his patriarchal authority, he poured himself a generous slug, and sipped mightily.

Mrs. Collins caught her breath, as if to argue the point then acquiesced and told Beth the exact same thing.

"I'm not a baby anymore," Beth said, grumbling.

Paige tried to hide a smile.

"So," Mr. Collins said to me, obviously trying to change the subject, "how is that new book of yours doing? Is there anything I can do to help at this point?"

"No, sir. I mean, yes, it's coming along well." I happened to glance at Sarah and I saw a warning signal in her facial muscles. I tried to cut the discussion short. "You met Dana Beech—she's doing a great job of handling the business end of it. So, things are fine. She's great."

Mr. Collins didn't meet my eyes, and said: "I'm sure she is. But I still feel like maybe you should be going for a bigger publisher this time."

Sarah dropped her fork with a clatter. "Daddy..."

Mr. Collins shrugged. "I'm just voicing my opinion, Sarah. Since when can't I do that around here?"

There was silence for a moment. I tried to step back in and set everything straight. Jack—the great mediator; the one for compromise.

"It is a small press, Mr. Collins. This isn't my last book, though, so bigger things may be on the horizon."

There was silence again, with Beth and Paige glaring at me as if they were vaguely aware I was challenging him, but neither was so sure of it that they would dare speak.

Sarah, who still hadn't picked up her fork, stumbled into the breach without warning. Her words came spilling out.

"She really is good, father. I know you'd like her. She's a better editor than even me." She tried to squeak out a laugh. "And I know she'll be able to sell it."

"I find it hard to believe she's better than you," he said gravely, "but I have met her, and I must say she is impressive."

The way Mr. Collins said "impressive" carried with it a great many connotations. I couldn't believe no one else heard it the way I did. None of the others reacted at all. None of them apparently read anything into it. It was a defining moment for all four women, in my eyes; a reflection of some small piece of dignity he had permanently taken away from them, and was now flaunting in their face. None of them recognized it, or perhaps to be more fair, acknowledged it.

He continued to stare at me, as if awaiting a response of agreement. I was a little bit jealous. Dana Beech and I had no relationship outside of the book, but actually I was damned jealous at that moment. The way he said "impressive" was obscene. The thought of him with her turned my guts inside out. I flipped my napkin on the table and excused myself.

Sarah jumped up after me and twirled me around by the shoulders in the kitchen. She thought she knew why I was upset. She didn't really come close to the mark.

It was a whispered fight. I hate them, because you can't really say the words the way they are meant to be said: shouted, blurted, cursed, lisped, or whatever—it's just a mouse conversation about dynamite. It can't end in anything but an explosion.

"Why are you doing this to him?" she said.

"Doing what?"

"You practically ignored him for no reason and just—went out!"

"I didn't just go out. I politely excused myself from the table. No one paid any attention to me at all. He left the topic immediately—do you hear him chortling away in there now?"

As if to back my conclusion, laughter drifted in from the dining room. It was her father leading, but all of them were definitely laughing about something. I hoped it wasn't us.

I pointed my eyes toward the dining room. "See? There's nothing wrong. Let it go, Sarah. I'm trying my best."

Sarah pouted for a moment, then left me and rejoined her family. I remained there in the kitchen for a while, mentally catching my breath, contemplating my next move. Sarah had seen my reaction to his comment, and she was astute enough to interpret it correctly. She might know what I had really felt.

No, that wasn't likely. She was too wrapped up in everything going well with the dinner. Besides....

How was I to interpret it for myself?

I was jealous. It was a messy, gooey feeling that clung to the edge of my mind, even when I didn't want it to. I remembered it well, since it had dogged me for many months after Sarah's affair. It had dogged me in college when we were dating. I never met the man she slept with—I still don't know the first thing about him, and I don't want to know—so I understood jealousy then, and I was definitely feeling it now.

Sarah's father had no clue what he had triggered in me, I'm sure. To him, Dana Beech was one of a race of millions of interchangeable parts; another example of a woman—nothing more, literally.

The bastard showed his pudgy face in the kitchen doorway and smiled at me lubriciously.

"Any more wine, Jack? We're running a little bit low..."

How strange. I was certain he was going to tell me about how I needed to not take things so seriously; how I needed to get into the spirit of things and enjoy myself.

He wanted more alcohol.

"I'll bring some with me. I just need to get a glass of water first."

"Everything okay, Jack?"

"Couldn't be better."

Yes, Sarah is smart, I reminded myself. It was killing me wondering what she was thinking right now. As I carried the wine into the dining room, she met my eyes, and all I got was the public version of events: a broad smile, a wink, and a thank you. Who knows how sincere it was.

At the earliest acceptable time, I excused myself from the party on the pretense of work and peeled out to the office.

The tragedy: the roses were forgotten. It had started out as such a great romantic idea; a tiny attempt to resurrect the old Jack.

IN MY TINY office cubicle, I shoved some Mozart into the CDROM bay and dimmed the lights. I kicked back in my swivel chair and tried to do some self-analysis.

The dinner had been okay, I supposed. There had been no major disasters. Sarah's storm had quickly passed. It might even become one of those incidents that were completely forgotten.

There was, however, an ill-defined premonition in my head that something else was wrong. I tried to focus inward on positive thoughts. I was going to be a father soon, and the idea of that creased a smile across my face. In my first novel, the main character (named Polly) had seen having a baby as her salvation during one phase of her life. It did, in fact, change things for her, and I was certain it would change things for Sarah and I, too. We were both intense people—Sarah, increasingly in an outward fashion; and myself, always more internally. A child would force us to communicate more, and work more as a team. It would have to be a good thing.

I also had my next book coming out. This one was so much better than the first that I couldn't help but feel that some kind of success was looming on the horizon.

I also had Sarah. Thinking back to the college dorm days, with pimples and literature books two-thousand pages thick, and greasy cafeteria food and cold, autumn football games, the idea of Sarah Collins suddenly thrilled me again. The girl I could never have was mine. Mostly, mine... There was still some small part of Sarah I didn't possess. Yet I had won the major victory, and the thrill of that could still fill me with joy when I thought about it long enough.

There were also some worrisome memories that suddenly sprang out—for example, how I had always been the one to initiate physical contact; how I was the one always saying "I love you;" how I was the one always planning out dates and getaways. All of those old insecurities.

I also couldn't escape the affair. I was still very hurt and upset about what Sarah had done. I wasn't over it by any stretch of imagination.

In the quietness of the office I could hear the confessions pouring out of me, even without my lips moving. If it's possible, I was acting as my own therapist, spilling out everything so it could be examined clinically and reacted to with new insight.

Then anger swept into me. It was her damned father who was most responsible for all of their problems. Her whole family was messed up. The fall of America was somewhere in their habits, and the father was at the center of it. Was he what a real man was all about? If a woman sleeps around, she's called a slut. If a man sleeps around, everyone winks or shakes their head and lets it go, chalking it up to human nature. People did a lot of winking or shaking their heads with him.

Historically, men have been able to get away with it, because they always made the rules and they always enforced them. The corollary that followed from male domination was that men could break the rules; even their own. If you make the rules, then you can change the rules. If you're powerful enough, you can do that whenever you want to. Perhaps men have been too powerful.

So Sarah's mother never whimpered a word of protest. She held her hand out for money and winked, or shook her head in disgust—it doesn't really matter which it was, because the end result was the same.

My father, fool that he was in some ways, was at least the kind of man that would follow his own rules, even if they didn't make any sense. He did not use his maleness as a way to circumvent morals. Granted, his out-dated ideas about the role of the woman in the family ultimately led to the demise of his marriage. But his convictions were just that—ideas that he held to, for himself as well as others. There are women I've seen who are perfectly willing to accept traditional roles in the family who would have been happy to stay forever with a man like my father. My mother was not that type, and in the long run my father recognized that. That was why my mother still fought to protect him whenever I said anything negative about him, even though she could turn around and say something nasty herself when she remembered the old battles she had survived. She knew, too, that he had a nobility about him even when he was dead wrong.

There was no nobility that I could see in Mr. Collins. There was none of the sympathy or spunk that Sarah had that I could try to imagine in part of Mrs. Collins' personality. So where did that leave Sarah? She was the black sheep, I supposed; the diamond in the rough. She was the exception to the rule.

As I mulled over this, the phone beside my computer monitor blinked and beeped. I hesitated to answer, thinking it was probably Sarah, calling to debrief me on the dinner details—in other words, everything I had done to upset her sisters and parents. My therapy had jumped up and bit me, making me feel worse instead of better. I picked the phone up anyway, nervous, almost sliding again into the mood for a little confrontation.

"Hello."

"Jack, it's me."

"Dana. How did you know I was here?"

"Sarah gave me the number."

I arranged myself more comfortably in the chair and pressed the phone closer to my ear. Sarah had given her the number?

"Is something wrong, Dana?"

There was not an immediate reply.

I repeated my question.

"Can we get together and talk?" she said in reply. "I don't want to have to do this over the phone."

"Just tell me, are you okay?"

"I'll be fine."

"What's that mean?"

"Just meet me at my hotel. I don't have a car."

I grabbed my jacket and flew out the door.

A MILLION DIFFERENT possibilities flew through my head as I drove over there. Most of them had to do with her former husband—the things she had told me he did; the element of uncertainty in her voice as she shared them with me. I thought of all the bad things that can happen to women, and I thought about the fact that usually men are at the bottom of them. The suicide conversation also fluttered up from the depths of my brain.

When I got there, she was standing in the half-open door of her room, smoking a cigarette. She was dressed in a pair of jeans with holes in the knees, and a T-shirt that advertised some long-gone book

that Appaloosa Press had put out years ago. She was barefoot, and
there was an open beer in her other hand.

"Has somebody hurt you?" I said, more menace in my voice than
I intended.

"No, Jack. I didn't tell you all of that stuff the other night so I
could adopt you as a bodyguard. Come on in—have a beer if you want
one."

My feelings were a little hurt. Her voice made it clear, however,
that she was flattered by my concern—just not impressed, though the
subtlety involved almost escaped me. I let it go for the moment,
consoling myself with the idea that macho heroism might find an
opening or usefulness later. It was no damsel in distress waiting for me.

She closed the door behind us and sat down in one of the flowery
chairs that cheap hotels everywhere have. I had never actually been in
the room before. It was dingier inside than I expected, with cracks in
the plaster and deep bare spots in the orange carpet. The bed had a
lump in it. There was a musty smell vaguely reminiscent of a street
hours after the parade is gone.

"This place is a dump,"

"Yes," she agreed, stubbing the cigarette out in a glass ashtray
shaped like a racehorse. "They do most of their business during Derby
Week. The rest of the year, it's mainly kids renting by the hour."

"I thought you had to go back to Cincinnati."

"I went back, Jack. I had a long talk with my boss. I no longer
work for Appaloosa Press."

At first, I didn't see the problem. "Well, why don't you look for
work here in town? There are a couple of medium-size publishers here,
bigger than Appaloosa, and you have good experience."

She looked at me blankly. "Jack, you're not getting it yet. Your
book is not going to be published."

"What? I signed—I mean, we signed—a contract! What are you
talking about?" I sat up on the edge of the bed where I had plopped
down. "They can't do that. We have a legal agreement."

She sighed and continued to stare at me unflinchingly. "It's in the
fine print, Jack. If I leave the company, all of the contracts I negotiated
are void. Sometimes they'll renegotiate, but often it's just an excuse
to..."

"To what?" I demanded.

She looked away from me and fumbled with her cigarettes. "To
get rid of books when they over-publish."

"Get rid of my book!" I stood up slowly. "My book still belongs to me, Dana, contract or not. Where are my drafts and galleys? I want them back."

"I don't have that stuff, Jack. I just got canned. I don't even have my personal effects. I hopped a Greyhound and came here, hoping we could talk about this and come up with a plan."

I shook my head, incredulous. "I can't believe this happened. My first book got screwed up, and now my second won't even get a chance? What exactly is going on at that place? Were they going to screw up the second one, too?"

"That's part of the problem," she said. "My boss doesn't like to keep authors around who don't make money."

"That's not my Goddamned fault, Dana! Sarah and her father made that first deal without my consent—you know that. All of you—including mainly your boss—screwed that up. Your boss even admitted he made a mistake."

"You can hire a lawyer..."

"That's what you came here to tell me? That I can hire a lawyer and sue over a book that's a failure and another one that hasn't even come out yet? Who am I going to sue—my own wife and father-in-law? Or maybe I can sue your boss—is that what you want me to do? Maybe I could sue you."

"Jack, that's not why I came here."

"Why did you come here? I've poured my guts out on this project, and it's a damned good novel. You've told me so yourself over and over again. Did you really mean all of that, Dana, or were you thinking like your boss all the time?"

"That's not fair, Jack! I've been an advocate for you the whole way through this process. Do you think you can stand there and talk about your 'goddamned' book like it's the end of the world, and conveniently forget the fact that I just got fired? I don't have a whole lot of money. I've spent over five-thousand dollars on this crummy little hotel room in past four months. Now I have nothing. I don't even have my stuff. A lot of it is still in my office."

"Well, go and get it."

"I don't want to go back there, Jack."

"It's your stuff. He can't stop you from getting it."

Her voice suddenly cracked again, like it had the night she was drunk and reliving her marriage. "You don't understand, Jack. I can't go back. I won't go back in that building, or anywhere near it."

"Why the hell not?"

"I'll tell you 'why the hell not.' He told me I had to sleep with

him if I wanted to keep my job and keep your book on the fast track."
She reluctantly let one sob escape, then continued. "I don't care how
badly you want your 'goddamned' book published, I can't do that."

"Dana," I said, suddenly at a loss. "I wouldn't dream of you doing
that. And that's definitely stuff for lawyers."

"I thought about it," she sobbed. "God, I actually thought about it.
Your book is a good book, and I worked so hard on it, too."

"I know that." I reached across the space between us and grasped
her hand. The cigarette in it tumbled to the floor, unlit.

"But I couldn't sleep with him, Jack. I couldn't do it."

"Of course not. Is that what you think of me—that I'd have you
sleep with your boss so that I could get ahead? What kind of person
would that make me?"

"No, Jack," she said quietly. "That's not what I think of you. The
fact that I would even consider it..." her voice trailed off, and she
shook her head. Tears trailed down her puffy cheeks.

Suddenly the implications roared up to me, and washed over me,
wrecking me on the rocks of reality. I shook my head, unwilling to
accept responsibility for the situation. My knees buckled, and I tumbled
back onto the bed and covered my face with my hand.

"I'm sorry, Jack. It's my fault."

"It's not your fault." I said. "It's no one's fault. I just can't
believe all of this happening."

Actually, she did have to bear some responsibility. I was feeling a
peculiar brand of male anxiety that was just like what happened when
Sarah made me feel certain uncomfortable ways—sometimes in love;
sometimes out of it; sometimes angry; sometimes incredibly blessed.
It's something that women can do. It made me feel helpless.

"You need a place to stay," I said quietly. "And you need to get
your things."

"I'm not going back there, Jack."

"How about your parents—don't they still live in Cincinnati?"

"Jack, I'm thirty years old—I can't move back in with my
parents. I have a little bit of money, and a little bit of pride, too. The
Dana they know is the one that survived that story I told you about. I'm
not that person anymore, despite my obvious weaknesses. But my
parents have seen enough of my dramas."

I mulled over if for a moment. Then an idea struck me. It was a
dubious idea, but I was feeling desperate.

"Okay, Dana. I want you to listen to me."

Her eyes flashed. "What's that tone about? You're not my father,

Jack, and you're not my husband, either, so don't go bullying me around."

I waited for her tantrum to settle, then continued. "I want you to take all of your things here and pack them up, then check out. I'll take you to my father's house in Mount Sterling. It's a big old farm house with plenty of rooms. An older couple live there as caretakers, but the house belongs to me. There's an office with a computer, modem, phone—everything a small business needs. You can stay there as long as you need to, and the rent will be part of your fee when I publish my book."

"Jack, I can't do that. What's Sarah going to think? I'm not your mistress, or secret lover..." her voice trailed off again and she looked away.

"Listen to me, Dana. Do you really believe in my book, or not?"

"Yes," she said, still not meeting my eyes. "You know that I do."

"Then act as my agent and work out of the farmhouse."

"Jack, I don't want to feel like I owe you anything."

Still, her eyes were cast down. I waited patiently until they came back up, and then her brown eyes finally met mine.

"Dana, neither of us are in debt. Why can't we do something for each other just out of kindness? Are you going to help me with the book, or not?"

"I can do that."

"Good." I stood up. "Start packing your things."

She held her arms up, frustrated. "Most of my stuff isn't here. I left my suitcases in the office."

"I know. I'll go to Cincinnati tomorrow and pick them up."

"Jack!" she said, anger creeping back in. "You can't do that. I already told you I don't need a keeper. I'll figure something out."

I looked at her sternly. "Dana, I'm going there anyway to have a serious conversation with your boss about my galleys and files. You can't stop me from doing that. I have the right to do that. I might as well get your things while I'm there."

I turned around and went out the door to get some fresh air. She appeared behind me, meek-looking, reaching for a cigarette. I didn't want to be like all of those male stereotypes I had just thought so much about earlier, but I couldn't help myself. I calmly reached out and took the cigarettes from her hand and crushed them, then dumped them on the pavement.

I saw the flame jumping into her expression again, and held my hand up. "Part of the deal," I said. "You can't smoke in that old house, and you shouldn't do it anyway." The truth was, I hadn't seen her smoke before our night out at the club. My guess was that she hadn't smoked since that time she had talked about: the bad days with her old husband.

"Jack," she said, her voice steady. "I don't like feeling like I'm not someone's equal; like I can't make my own decisions. I'll smoke if I want to smoke."

I didn't flinch. "Dana, I don't like the idea of not being able to help someone I care about."

"I'll smoke if I want to."

"What if I don't want you to?"

She tried to say something, then couldn't. Finally, she turned on her heels and went back into the room. Inside, I could hear the sounds of things being packed, and I knew that I had convinced her.

WHEN I RETURNED to the house, Sarah was not asleep. It was uncustomary for her to wait up for me, so I immediately knew that something was wrong. She was sitting in the kitchen at the small table with a glass of warm milk in front of her. She was wearing a huge cotton nightgown that was probably three sizes two big.

She smiled lamely as I walked in. My first theory was that it had something to do with the dinner.

"I'm glad you're alright," she said quietly. "I called the office about three hours ago and you weren't there. Since Dana Beech called here and I gave her your number, I must assume that—"

"I was with her," I said, quickly growing weary of the game. "She got fired, and my book is not going to be published."

"What?" genuine concern crept into her voice. "What are you talking about?"

I sat down with her at the table, sliding my jacket behind the chair.

"When she got fired, my book went with her."

"Why or how could that happen?"

I hesitated for a moment, wondering if the truth was really necessary. Perhaps it is some male weakness, but when part of your brain tells you that the truth will get you out of trouble, you usually do it, regardless of the consequences. So I told the truth.

"She wouldn't sleep with her boss."

A look of great consternation crossed Sarah's face in heavy waves. My brain had been correct. She was struggling with a series of reactions which left her mute to the issue of my lateness. It was probably cruel of me to do it, yet some part of me realized it, and didn't refrain.

"So," I continued, "he fired her, and nuked my book, too, since she was the acting agent for it."

Suddenly Sarah grew alert. "Well, I'll act as your agent. Call the idiot up and I'll talk to him. Or better yet, let me talk to my father—"

I held my hand up, and realized with a jerk that it was the identical gesture I had used with Dana Beech only a few moments ago over the cigarettes. "Don't get your father involved. We'll handle this. I sent Dana—" I stumbled, suddenly blundering. "—to a friendly place; a friend's place; a safe place to stay...She borrowed my car temporarily."

Sarah looked at me quizzically, then moved on. "So, is she still involved with your book, or not?"

"Yes. She's going to act as my agent while she gets herself another job or sets up her own agency. I feel bad for her. It's really not going to be easy."

"Do you think she can really help you with your book now?"

"Yes, I do."

"I could be your agent, really, Jack. It's something I'd like to explore."

"You would be great, Sarah. But Dana's not pregnant and she's not married. It'll be easier for her."

Sarah mulled over that, pushing the hair out of her eyes several times as she leaned forward, dipping her body rhythmically. "Well..." she said, then lapsed into silence. Then she said, "Well..." again.

"Can we go to bed, Sarah? I just found out my book is in trouble, and I'm dead tired. I have to go to Cincinnati tomorrow to get the galleys and files. I really need to rest. I'm still in a state of shock. Can you please give me a little bit of a break?"

She abruptly jumped up and came over and stroked the top of my head. "Come on, then, let's go." She pulled me up and we made our way to the bedroom. "Have you called the newspaper about tomorrow yet?"

"No. He won't care. My work for the Sunday issue is already downstairs."

"Well, be careful. I'll fax it to the office for you. I hate it when you go away on trips, though. Your son needs you around to talk to him."

I gently rubbed her growing stomach. A million thoughts swirled in my head as she turned the light off. How far distant that family dinner from six hours ago seemed! I fell asleep with her stroking my hair, but it was a restless, uneasy, disturbed slumber I clambered into.

There were strange visions in my dreams; things that I didn't understand, though that nagging part of my mind that recognized all of the other things probably understood the dreams as well, and just wasn't loud enough for me to hear.

I did something else unusual. I mumbled a prayer for all of us before unconsciousness took over.

Chapter 12
Cincinnati

APPALOOSA PRESS was housed in a modern two-story glass office building. The second floor jutted out over the first, creating the impression of an upside down cake, and making you feel that when you walked close to the door it was probably going to tumble on top of you. The building was situated on the side of a hill a few blocks north of downtown, and faced the high-rises and Ohio River. That intensified the strange architectural effects. There were a variety of smaller businesses housed inside.

The directory showed Appaloosa Press on the second floor in suite number two-sixty. I climbed into the elevator and stepped within a pile of boxes. A man in a green moving suit smiled, partially toothless, and said, "Pardon it buddy, but it's moving day."

I nodded and felt the elevator move down instead of up. I discovered that the boxes were headed to the basement where the parking garage was. I stood patiently while another green friend joined him and trolleyed the boxes off the elevator one by one. A few minutes later, the elevator finally lurched up to the second floor.

When I stepped off, there were more boxes. I stepped around them, and looked for door number two-sixty. I found it at the end of the hallway. Inside the suite entrance were more boxes. A pretty girl in red shorts was sitting on one of the boxes. She looked at me—I was wearing an expensive suit and tie, carrying a small briefcase. I guess I looked a little incongruous.

"Do you work here?" I asked.

"Yes, sir. What can I do for you?"

"I need to see Joseph Lambert."

"Are you from the IRS?" she said very slowly, edging off the box.

"No. My name is Jack Baird."

"Jack Baird? The writer?"

"Yes, that's me."

She smiled and hopped over to me to shake my hand. "I read 'Polly's Ransom.' I loved it! Great book!"

"Thank you. Can I see Mr. Lambert?"

"Yes. He's right around here—come on."

I followed her through a maze of boxes. In the very back of the suite, Lambert's office was tucked away by itself, complete with a full glass view of downtown. His mahogany desk was all that was left—everything else was packed. Lambert himself was hovering over an open box, dressed in shorts and a baby blue polo shirt. He was a course man, consisting of more hard features than soft ones, starting with his wiry hair and ending with a long, sharp nose.

He turned when we entered and smiled, then frowned. The secretary quickly shook her head 'no,' and he smiled again.

"What can I do for you?"

"I'm Jack Baird."

A puzzled look crossed his face for the barest of moments, and then the plastic smile returned. He was balding, which isn't so bad normally (and I'll be there myself someday), but his recession was the type that does offend. It looks unnatural. You only noticed it when he dipped forward. His baldness made him appear phony, and accented the wildness of the hair that remained.

"Jack Baird! Well...I'd invite you to have a seat, except there isn't one." He laughed at his own joke, then looked at the secretary, who immediately scurried away. "What's on your mind?"

"For starters, I'd like to know why the contract I signed on my second book is not going to be honored."

"Oh..." He sat down on a box and said it again. "Oh! That's strictly a business policy. It's in your contract"

"I work in the publishing industry, too, Mr. Lambert. It's my experience that authors don't get fired just because their editors get fired. A contract is a legal, binding document."

"Yes it is, Mr. Baird, and if you examine yours, you'll find that the marriage clause is included in the language. It was written into your first contract, as well."

"Marriage clause?"

"Yes. If the editor leaves, the author may leave, too."

"Even if it's John Grisham?"

"It is a legal agreement, Mr. Baird."

"Like the one you let my wife sign without my permission?"

A small grunt escaped his mouth on the heels of a sigh. "Yes, I mean, no. Your wife was the one who made the mistake. We covered our end of the deal."

"My lawyer has said something a little different than that." I lied.

"I'm sure."

I started pacing around the room, looking down at the boxes. "Getting ready to go somewhere, I see."

"Yes, we've been bought out. Part of the deal was that we would downsize our editorial staff; clean up our titles."

"So, Dana Beech didn't leave—she was fired."

"She was laid off. It's not against the law. It happens all the time. Lot's of people are laid off. You said you know the publishing business—you should know that, too. People leave; people get promoted; people get laid off."

"Laid off?"

Dana's version of events suddenly came to mind. His choice of words was a little bit funny. There was no expression now on his face.

"Mr. Baird, if there's nothing else, I have a lot of work to do. I'm sorry your first book didn't do better. You could have stayed with us after the takeover if things had been different."

What a great good-bye he came up with up. Things were that simple to him. However, I wasn't through with him.

"Dana told me why she was released."

Lambert looked at me curiously. "Oh, really. I can imagine...What kind of twisted tale was it?"

"She told me that she was going to get laid...off, but she politely declined."

Lambert stared at me, and the blankness turned into redness. "What exactly are you implying?"

"I'm not implying anything—I'm telling you I know exactly what happened."

"Good day, Mr. Baird."

"My manuscripts and files, please."

"They'll be returned. They're already packed, Mr. Baird. Good day."

"I'm not leaving without them. Shall I call my lawyer, or should I just go open every box until I find them?"

Mr. Baird! I've had about—"

The secretary popped her head in the door, cutting Lambert off.

"What is it?" he snapped.

"Those men are here," she said quietly.

"Dammit!" he said, and wheeled around the desk.

I continued on the offensive. "I'll start looking," I said to him as he left, "in Dana's office."

"Go with him!" he ordered the secretary. "Make sure he doesn't take anything that doesn't belong to him—nothing!"

Dana's office was a cubicle smaller than mine at the newspaper. There was room for her desk, a bookshelf, and little else. The computer was gone, leaving a dusty imprint on the wood, but all of her personal effects were still on the desk. There were two small suitcases in the corner.

"I'm getting these for Dana," I said. "Mr. Lambert looked like he might throw them away."

The secretary didn't say anything. No doubt she had a good working relationship with him. No doubt she was willing to do whatever it took to get ahead.

I began packing ordinary things like pencils and erasers, computer disks and White-Out. Eventually I came to more personal items. The first one was a picture of her parents. They were smiling urbanites standing beside their large recreational vehicle. Their house was a modest middle class Cape Cod. No doubt he was retired from the Hudepohl brewery, and she was a former Montgomery school teacher. They looked happy, and I would have guessed that Dana had a fairly stable upbringing.

There was also a picture of Sarah and I pinned to the wall. It was from the night she had come over to dinner. It gave me a pause. In fact, it made me feel ashamed for no good reason.

"You and Dana close?" the secretary asked, handing me an empty box.

I thought about that for a moment. The obvious answer might not be the correct answer around here.

"I feel really bad about how she's been treated," I said.

The secretary nodded and looked out the door to see if anyone was listening. "I heard what you said to Mr. Lambert. I know what happened, because I've had the same thing happen to me. I'm really glad you said what did."

I looked at her carefully. I couldn't tell how sincere she was being. "I don't think it's fair to use your position or your sex to bully someone." I said.

She nodded eagerly in agreement.

"Tell Dana I miss her," she said. Then she pointed to the bottom desk drawer. "I think all of your papers and manuscripts are in that drawer."

"Thank you," I said to her, and I meant it. "Don't let him bully you around."

"I won't," she said, and left smiling.

When everything was together, I borrowed one of the dollies I saw sitting around, and wheeled the boxes and suitcases down to my rental car. My association with Appaloosa Press had come to an abrupt close.

I did not see Mr. Lambert again. It's probably best that I didn't, since I would have been rude, and he seemed very awfully concerned about his other visitors from the IRS

Hopefully, I would graduate to a bigger and more professional publisher. Maybe Lambert, with any luck, would end up in jail.

I MADE TWO phone calls from the airport. The first was to Sarah.

"I'm done, honey." I said. "My plane boards in ten minutes."

"Any problems?"

"No, I got all the stuff. It wasn't as much as I thought it would be. I got it all on the plane."

"Doesn't she have an apartment up there or something?"

"I don't know. She didn't say anything about it."

"You know, Jack, I love you dearly, but sometimes you are too nice. Do you know that?"

"I came up here to get my book, Sarah."

"I know. Just don't let her take too much advantage of you—or us, for that matter. I like Dana, but we can't adopt her. We've got our own child on the way. You are very sweet, but sometimes you have to back away a little."

"It's all about my book, Sarah."

"Yes, but is your book the biggest priority in your life?"

"Of course not."

"I just don't want you to miss out on the important things right now."

"Don't worry, Sarah. I won't give away too much of your compassion without your approval."

"Very funny, Mister Liberal. Just be careful, Jack. I want you home, safe and sound."

"Okay, I'll see you in an hour or two."

The second call was to Dana Beech. I only had four minutes left until boarding started, and on commuter flights, it usually closed quickly.

"Jack, this is a fabulous house!"

"Are you enjoying yourself?"

"Yes, this is great. I still don't understand, though. Why don't you guys move out here?"

I didn't tell her again that Sarah didn't like it. That didn't seem appropriate. I made something else up. "It's too far away from the paper," I said. "And where Sarah works, too. It'd be one hellaceous commute."

"This room is full of your dad's stuff, and some of yours, too. This is a great room."

"Uh, Dana, I've got to go. My plane is boarding. I got your suitcases. Did you have anything else—an apartment or storage unit or anything?"

"No, I have a bunch of stuff at my parents. The suitcases were the main thing."

"Well, I've got to go now..."

"Jack, are you sure you don't mind me staying here? The Hawkins are cooking for me, and I really don't feel right just acting like a prima donna or something. I feel like I'm on vacation or something. Did you know your father was a basketball star in high school? I saw his trophies and—"

"Yes, Dana. I really do have to go now..."

"When can I get my stuff? I'm out of underwear."

"I'm sorry about that, truly—I'll get it to you soon. Good-bye, Dana."

I'm not sure if she heard me. I hung the phone up and didn't know whether to laugh or not. My father's house was nice, but it couldn't possibly be that much fun. I grew up there, so I should have known.

I ran up the ramp and grabbed one of the last seats. As the strip malls and suburbs of Northern Kentucky receded below me, I thought about my father's study.

There was some cool stuff in there. It made me think about him in a way that I hadn't been able to in a long time. He was a good man, in spite of his flaws.

THERE WAS SOME fallout from the Cincinnati trip that I did not anticipate. Sarah's father got wind that I had parted ways with Appaloosa Press, and he showed up at the newspaper the very next day. Sarah insisted she hadn't told him, but I can't think of any other way he could have known so quickly.

He ambushed me on my lunch break, as I was trying to have a phone conversation with my long-lost mother, who had just returned from a trip to New York City.

"Jack," he said rudely, "I've got to talk to you for a second. How long are you going to be?"

The little things in life, like manners and politeness, never seemed to get in the way of Mr. Collins' agenda. He was completely stuck in the rut of having his own will carried out immediately.

"Mom, hold on just a second." I cupped the phone in my hands. "Can I call you in just a little bit?" I asked him.

He straightened his gray suit over his belly and made a duck-like expression. "I'll hang around here and do a couple of things. I'll be back in ten minutes."

"I've got ten minutes," I said into the phone, sarcastically.

"What's wrong, Jack?"

"Nothing, Mom. The book deal went sour on the new novel, and I'll tell you about it when we get together."

We exchanged a few more generalities, and even though it had only been about three minutes, Mr. Collins suddenly appeared at the exact moment I hung the phone up.

"Jack," he said, inviting himself into my cubicle, which immediately caused a problem with personal space—as in, there was none. I had been sitting on the outer side of my desk, so as to spread my lunch "out" (my co-workers joked about not leaving the office) and relax a little bit. I quickly retreated to the other side, behind the computer monitor.

"We have got to talk," he said again.

"Yes?"

"I heard through the grapevine that Appaloosa Press went under."

"Went under? I thought they were bought out."

"No, no," he said, grinning as if he enjoyed delivering grim economic news. "They were supposed to be bought out. But something went wrong. There was a rumor of tax problems, and if that's true, that explains why the takeover soured."

"So they declared bankruptcy?"

"They sure did. I called this morning to verify it. That's real bad news for your book."

I shoved the monitor to one side. "What do you mean?"

"I mean, that if your first book is still under contract, any new royalties you generate through another publisher might be garnished to pay off debts with Appaloosa. Your second one could be the same way."

"What?" I stood up, suddenly all ears.

"Now, don't panic," he said, smiling that damn smile again. "I've consulted my attorney, and he thinks we're okay on this—at least for the second book. I want you to come over and talk to him after lunch."

"After lunch—I do have a job here, Mr. Collins..."

"I know, I know. I talked to your supervisor already. Frank and I go way back. He said you're free until tomorrow if necessary."

Part of me was outraged at the way he was interfering—again. Part of me was terrified that I wouldn't be able to handle the new situation without his help. I was torn in two. Here was the book again, like Sarah had implied, taking over my life.

Part of my mind, miraculously, did function, though, and I remembered some very important information from my journey to Cincinnati.

"Mr. Collins, Dana Beech was fired a few days ago."

"Really? What on earth for?"

"She refused to sleep with her boss."

It was a sneaky ambush, but the moment was too perfect. Oh, how I relished that brief victory.

Mr. Collins disappointed me, however, and didn't skip a beat.

"Bully for Ms. Beech. I knew there was some spunk in her."

"Yes, but more to the point, her boss told me that when they fire editors, they often dump their books and authors, too. Essentially, he led me to believe that my legal relationship with Appaloosa was severed when Dana Beech lost her job."

"Hmmm..." he said, rolling his bulk in the tiny cloth chair opposite me. "I think we should get Dana Beech into this discussion, too. Maybe we can add our names to the growing list of people who say that Appaloosa owes them something."

I held my hand up. "I don't want anything from them. Dana and I are in agreement that we can sell this new book somewhere else. I want to completely cut myself off from them."

"Maybe that's best," he said. "Where's Dana Beech? If she's in Cincinnati, we should call her and get her down here."

"Actually, she's over in Mount Sterling at my father's place. She didn't have a place to stay. She's been working on the book. I got all of the original manuscripts and files back when I went up to Cincinnati yesterday. Do you want me to call her?"

"That's just as far as Cincinnati," he groused, "and they don't have a real airport, either."

"They have commuter service. Do you want me to call her?"

"No," he finally said, "let's you and I go ahead and we can call her if we need to."

Against part of my better judgement, I went to see the lawyer. Mr. Collins' concern had partially convinced me it was necessary. The memory of those IRS officers was also disturbing. I was knee-deep in the whole affair, even though I hadn't done anything.

Every writer fears something will happen to their book. The house will burn down consuming the only copy; someone else will steal it and sell it; the computer disk will pass near a magnet—or your publisher will screw you. Sometimes you even think you might die with only one page to go. It was a constant paranoia. I've often wondered if even famous writers occasionally experience a twinge of it.

It was fear that drove my decision on that particular day.

THE LAWYER immediately reminded me of my parent's divorce. Maybe all lawyers are alike; or maybe the half-dozen I had met were all cousins or something. Particularly in Kentucky, if you've heard the joke, it was a possibility.

When my mother left, and things started getting rocky, a man in a cheap suit had shown up at the farm and wanted to ask me a bunch of stupid questions. He wanted to know if my father beat me. My father actually almost beat him when he literally kicked him out. I ended up going to his office later and telling him everything I knew, which wasn't much. Eventually, both parents began to see the lawyers more as the enemy than each other, and an equitable parting was quickly and quietly arranged without the aide of legal professionals. The lawyers did collect their checks, though, even if my parents did come up with the solution themselves. That's the way lawyers work—you pay them even if they don't do anything.

The questions on this occasion seemed like questions I had answered before:

"Jack, when did you first enter into this relationship?"

"When I was born," had been my response back during the divorce. This time, I said, "When I signed my first book contract, about a year ago."

"What can you tell me about the nature of the conflict?"

"They're acting like children," had been my response. Today, I said, "They fired my editor, for a very dubious reason, and I was told that nullified my contract. Now that they are filing for bankruptcy, I want to make sure I still own my book, and have complete control over it."

Actually, it was a very useful conversation. It reminded me how much I hated the business side of writing; how much I hated lawyers. Good old Dana Beech had done a wonderful job of sheltering me from much of it, and I owed her one for that. This was why Sarah couldn't act as my agent.

Mr. Collins then got involved, since it was his lawyer (and his son-in-law, whether I liked it or not), and it soon became clear that there would be no great crime committed over my book without a firm legal battle. As I sat there, I began to feel like I was in a New York City cab that had been driving for hours with the meter running—I began to sweat. Naturally, Sarah's father would pay for this, but I usually put up a token resistance about that kind of thing, and this lawyer was not wearing a cheap suit.

I didn't feel that "spunk" today, however. I didn't talk as much as usual. When we left the office, even Mr. Collins seemed to notice.

"Are you okay with all of this, Jack?"

It was an unusual question for him to ask. He was definitely not the sensitive type.

"Yes, sir."

"Don't start 'sirring' me. Is there something still bothering you about the demise of Appaloosa?"

"No," I said, not really anxious to be drawn into serious conversation about my artistic fears.

"Well, you'd better give Ms. Beech a call and let her know what Ken said about contacting editors, if she's the one who's going to be doing it."

"Yes," I said slowly. "I'll do that."

WHEN I ARRIVED home, Sarah was on the couch watching television. Odd, since it was on the History Channel. I walked over and kissed her on the forehead. She smiled, then craned her neck to see the TV.

"You ready to eat dinner?" I said, stowing my jacket in the coat closet.

"Sure—what are we eating?"

I turned, thinking the question was a sarcastic one. When I saw her, however, eyes still glued to the squawk box, I realized she was completely serious. I had grown so used to her domestic slant, that it gave me a mild shock to remember that the original Sarah didn't really care for cooking. The original Sarah would have never watched the History Channel, for that matter.

"You should have called me," I said, keeping my tone neutral, "I could have picked something up."

"I did call you. Your boss said you went out with my father."

She still wasn't looking at me, and when I glanced at the television and saw that the show was something about medieval weapons, I realized that this wasn't an ordinary situation. Something was definitely wrong. Even within the broad category of history, that was a subject that never would have piqued Sarah's interest.

I had no idea what was wrong, so I started fishing.

"I talked to your dad's lawyer about my book. Your dad was worried when he saw the Wall Street Journal, or something like that, and it said Appaloosa Press was being targeted by the IRS for investigation. Didn't Frank tell you that was where I was?"

"No, he didn't."

"I'm not that late, Sarah. It's only five-thirty. I can still go get something if you want me to. It's not like I'm that late, and I don't think taking the afternoon off to protect my literary rights is a big deal, is it?"

"Of course not."

I searched for the remote, then clicked the show off. Sarah looked like she was ready to find her own battleaxe to use on me. When her eyes meet mine for the first time, it was clearly anger I saw in them.

Something was wrong; something I was responsible for.

"What did I do this time, Sarah?"

"You really don't know?"

"I don't have a clue."

"Stop and think about if for a minute. Remember all of the discussions we've had since our incident?"

I stumbled backwards. For the first time, I felt some blood surge into my own face. "It wasn't our incident, Sarah, it was your incident. I was an unwilling participant in an adventure that I could not have predicted in advance."

"It was my accident—it was our incident."

"Spare me the semantics, Sarah. You're too clever for that. Just talk straight and tell me: What did I do? Or what happened to you? Or what did I supposedly do?"

"Let me try again," she said, huffing and crossing her arms. "Uninterrupted this time. I repeat, do you remember all of the discussions we had about truth and honesty after the...after what happened?"

I didn't, really, but I decided to play the game anyway. She still couldn't say the ugly "A" word, I noted.

"Sure. I remember them."

"Did they mean anything to you? Or where you just looking for a way to heap more guilt on me?"

"I still don't get it, Sarah. Can't you just come out and say what the problem is?"

Evidently the willpower was not in her, for she stormed out of the room (as much as a pregnant woman's altered gait can be described as such), and muttered and mumbled from the confines of the kitchen. As I stepped in to follow her, I saw that the table was set, and food was there, too. So she had cooked. Something was terribly wrong.

"You asked me what we were eating," I reminded her. "Why didn't you tell me you had fixed something? Why are you deceiving me?"

It was a low blow, but too openly invited to pass on.

"The truth seems to be in short supply," she snapped. "A lie doesn't become a lie until the truth changes anyway."

"What the hell is that supposed to mean? I come home thirty minutes later than normal, and now my wife is acting like a lunatic. Tell me what's going on, Sarah."

Still no answer.

The phone rang out of the blue, and I grabbed at it greedily, desperate for some break in the current gridlock.

"Hello?"

"Jack, is that you? I think there's a problem."

It was Dana Beech. Suddenly, something in Dana's voice gave it all away to me, or enough of it for me to make an immediate, instinctual decision about what was wrong. Sarah's problem had something to do with Dana Beech. I could hear it in Dana's voice.

I hadn't even spoken to Dana that afternoon, let alone seen her.

I couldn't let Sarah know it was her on the phone. I could already see out of the corner of my eye that she was glaring at me, dying to see who it was. Probably wondering if it was Dana.

"Listen," I said, cupping my hand around the receiver, and looking warily at Sarah, with planned (but probably genuine) nervousness, "this is not a good time. Can I call you back?"

On the other end, Dana Beech seemed put out. "No, Jack! We've got to do something. I'm at a rest stop near Frankfort and—"

Sarah was really glaring at me now.

"Come on, Frank," I continued, "I know it's important, but this is the wrong time. I'll call you back at the office in an hour."

Dana finally seemed to get the picture. "Okay, Jack, I get it. She's right there with you? Try to get to the office and I'll meet you there."

"Fine, then. I'll meet you there in an hour."

I reached to replace the phone, and Sarah abruptly snatched it from me and slammed it to her ear. For a moment I couldn't tell if she heard anything.

"Hello?" she said. "Hello, Frank?"

Evidently, no one was there, because she violently slammed the phone into the wall, hanging it up.

"What is your problem?" I said, trying to take the offensive again, although now it was with more caution. I had an inkling of the minefield I was in. "I come home from work and for no reason you attack me. Then you grab the phone like I'm some little child. You're the one with some explaining to do."

"Don't lecture me, Jack. In all the time I've known you, you've never lectured me, so don't start now."

"Maybe you need a lecture. And I have lectured you before. Now you're starting to forget things. Maybe you need more than a lecture. Maybe you need a tour of the past. Maybe you need...something else..."

"What are you going to do—hit your pregnant wife, or slam her against the wall?"

"I don't throw forks as hard as you do."

"No, you just, just..."

Again, she couldn't summon the simple words that might explain everything.

I shook my head in disgust and went back into the living room. When she followed and saw that I was getting my coat out, she flew into another rage.

"You're not going anywhere!"

"Sarah, you're pregnant, and I work. I have to do my job. I'm certainly not needed around here."

"Is your job more important than our marriage?"

I shook my head. "This is sad, Sarah. You always said I had the flare for melodrama. Now it's you. If our marriage doesn't survive this, it will be because some Collins' gene in you prevents you from coming out and telling me what's wrong. The truth is what we need. It's not melodrama, anymore, its tragedy, and you are the author."

"Screw yourself, you, you...cheap Hemingway-imitation!"

I probably should have been hurt by that, though it almost made me laugh out loud. To my credit, I kept a straight face and held on to enough anger to head for the door. Hemingway-imitation?

When I put my hand on the knob, however, she lunged across the room and her features turned more desperate. Her demeanor instantly softened, as if she knew she had pushed the limits.

"If I tell you why, will you stay?" she said, almost pleading. "I'll talk, I'll talk."

I wasn't used to seeing her desperate. Going back to the beginning of time for us, it was totally out of character for her. Sarah, begging? I had no concept of such a thing.

"Yes," I said, nodding slightly; dazed.

I walked back over to the couch. She sat down across from me and stared at me with a sadness like the day she had confessed her affair. For a fleeting moment, I thought that was what had happened again. The tips of my ears began to redden, remembering those thoughts I had felt in Somerset about how eastern Kentucky folks handle unfaithful wives. Some instinct must take over; some primitive anger—and I felt it welling in me. I was ready to embrace it.

Something in her eyes, though, was more desperate this time, if possible. We were not in Somerset.

"Go on," I said, still angry, and my voice clearly conveying it.

She wrung her hands, then turned very emotional again, as if giving in to something beyond her control. She looked like she was ready to have a breakdown.

"Jack, I can't believe you're letting her stay in your father's house! That is treacherous! How could you do that to me?" She squealed like a little girl.

For a moment, or two, I tried to be completely flabbergasted. It was not the last thing I would have guessed, though, and I had forgotten (or conveniently ignored) that conversation with her father earlier in the day. The Collins network worked very fast. I should have known that the man who didn't care about the exposure of his own dirty laundry would have no rational reason to keep it clean for anyone else.

I laughed out loud, incredulous. If any man should know how to keep his mouth shut, it would be him! Then again, I told myself, I had nothing to hide. Unlike Mr. Collins, the truth could not hurt me.

I shook my head, still mute.

"Jack, that's your father's house! You asked me to live there with you. We own that place—it belongs to us. Just because I refused to live there doesn't mean you can shack a girlfriend up in there! What were you thinking? And why did you lie, or neglect to tell me?"

Finally, I mustered a response, still somewhat astounded by the enormity of the anthill.

"It's my place, now, Sarah. I can do what I want with it. I want to live there someday, but for now I have to find other ways to manage it. She'll pay me rent; it's part of our agenting agreement. There's absolutely nothing unprofessional or personal about it."

"You just don't get it, do you? I don't care about the arrangements. I care about the fact that you would let her live there at all! Your father was very important to me. My God! How do you think he would feel about this? How do you think it looks to other people? It looks like you're putting up a mistress. Other people would react the same way I am!"

"What other people, Sarah? Who have I offended, or will offend?"

"Your father, I'm sure."

She shouldn't have brought him into it. "My father would approve of it completely. He would welcome the chance for someone to stay there who appreciates the place for what it is. And he's not exactly able to voice his opinion anymore, so I don't think he needs you, of all people, voicing it for him!"

I didn't mean it in a hurtful way, but I immediately sensed that I had dropped an A-bomb on her, unintentionally or not. She wilted, folding in on herself, closing up completely. She didn't cry, or gesticulate—she simply ceased to interact in any fashion, happy or sad.

"I—I didn't mean it that way, Sarah. I'm sorry. My father loved you more than he loved anyone, including probably me. He used to lecture me for hours about how I needed to take care of you right. He took me on many tours of his own shortcomings, just so you wouldn't have to live through them again, with me. Don't use my father as a variable in this equation. I shouldn't have said what I did, and you shouldn't have brought him into this."

There was still no response.

"I have to go to the paper," I said lamely.

No response.

Then I realized I was lying. I didn't really have to go back to work at all. What was I doing? There was no work awaiting me at the newspaper. Dana Beech would be at the newspaper. Another woman who needed emotional buttressing.

What was I—the rock of Gibraltar for everyone?

The words came out again, I think it was because they were easy, and convenient, and because I really did need to step back from Sarah and put things in perspective, so the words just slipped right out, all slimy like some of the things Sarah had said to me right after the affair.

She didn't stop me from going out the door. On the way out, the phone started ringing again. Surely Dana was smart enough not to call back.

Chapter 13
Mountains

MY OLD CAR was in the parking lot when I pulled in. Dana Beech was standing beside it, leaning against the door. She ran over to me as I got out.

"Is she okay?" she said hurriedly.

I blinked. "Sarah?"

"Yes! When she slammed the phone down on me, she was screaming about killing you—and me, too, I might add. She didn't do anything stupid, did she?"

"She talked to you on the phone?"

"Yes. Is she okay, Jack?"

I shook my head limply, sitting down on the pavement. Dana reached over and pulled me up, or tried to. I ended up tumbling back to the ground. Dana was not as smart as I had hoped.

"Jack, you don't look very good to me. Tell me that Sarah's okay, then we'll talk about everything."

"Yes, she's fine."

"What about you?"

"I'm fine. I don't understand why she's reacting this way." I shook my head and blinked. "I don't understand why all of this is happening. What on earth took place on the phone?"

Dana Beech looked around at the nearly empty parking lot. "Do we have to talk here? This probably isn't the best place, is it?"

"No. I've got a key. Let's go up to my office. I'm supposed to be there working anyway."

She didn't comment, or even seem to register the lie that I had told Sarah. On further thought, it seemed ridiculous for me to pretend I was going back to work anymore. Sarah was too smart to believe that. Maybe. Maybe not.

The thoughts that filled my head were like ghouls in a nightmare swirling around without substance.

As I passed my security card through the slot on the door, I thought about the fact that it was the first time that I really hadn't told the truth to Sarah. I think it was the first time in years I had lied about anything. It was a complex feeling. I felt like it was justified by the situation, but not totally justifiable, either. How many times had she lied to me? And hadn't they been bigger lies than this? Wasn't I due one tiny little lie of my own to save everyone's feelings?

I had forgiven her. She could forgive me this time. It was a lie designed to protect both women. She would see that after a while.

I remembered something my mother had told me long ago. "When you start keeping score, you know the game is over." She had said that sometime during the divorce proceedings, when it was getting ugly, and the words had stayed with me. Now they were jumping out to haunt me. What was the score?

Dana was dressed in sweat pants and a UL T-shirt, as if she had left in a hurry. Her hair was a little frazzled. She watched me fumble with the door in deep contemplation, as if weighing the wisdom of something that had already too far gone. Finally, she spoke again.

"You can't start lying to Sarah about us," she said as we entered. "That's not acceptable. You can't ever lie to her about us."

"Us?" I replied. "What is 'us?' Why is a lie about that worse than any other kind of lie? And besides, I think it's too late. Your call shot me down. I'll never be able to convince her of the truth."

"I am your editor and agent. It's a strictly professional relationship. Am I not correct, Mr. Baird? And we haven't discussed or done anything in secret."

I punched the elevator button sharply. "That's fine, Dana. My trip to Cincinnati was strictly professional, wasn't it? I didn't do it out of friendship or concern for your situation."

"Jack," she said, growing more intense, "it's not like you to cash in your chips. If you didn't want to do it, you shouldn't have. Don't come back now and try to use it for something. I never needed your macho male sympathy."

I didn't say anything. The elevator reached my floor and we entered the darkened hallway near my cubical. A cleaning woman at the end of the hall paused in mid-mop and studied us cautiously. I held up my security card and mumbled, "work," and she nodded and resumed her duty.

I turned the small desk lamp on and sat down behind the computer, while Dana sat in the seat across from me where Mr. Collins had rested earlier in the day. Dana was staring off into the wall, as if dreaming. Then she abruptly resumed the conversation.

"It's just not like you, Jack!"

"What's not like me?"

"It's not like you to, to—" her voice trailed off again and she resumed staring.

She looked to me like one of those postcard flappers from the roaring twenties. She had her black hair bobbed, the front strands curling forward with a trace of insolence, and she liked big earrings. Her complexion was very white, and more so in the incandescent light of my tiny desk lamp.

It's funny how your impressions of people change over time. My initial images of her were so very different from her current look. Had she changed or I had I changed? I wondered. Maybe both. My perception was perhaps what was different. Perception is reality most of the time, too, so that makes change a shadow in the light, an earthquake in a fantasy.

"Why did you go to Cincinnati?" she said, interrupting my ludicrous thoughts.

"I went partially to protect my book, and partially to protect you."

Without warning, she reached for the closest object—a dull pencil—and flung it full force at me. It connected with my forehead with a painful whack.

"I don't need your protection, Mr. Baird! You're just not getting it, are you? How can someone so smart be some damn dense!"

I thought she was going to leave, but she elevated herself back in the chair, staring at the wall again like a female Buddha.

"I know you don't, Dana. But I really do appreciate all that you've done, and I owe you more than that. I wasn't trying to be gallant. I was just doing what's right. I wasn't trying to be Sir Gallihad. I was attempting to be your friend. I wasn't out to get something."

She finally looked at me—a sharp, piercing glance. "You weren't? You could have fooled me, and I've got Hemingway's shit detector to back me up."

I stopped for a second. Both of them mentioning Hemingway— what did that mean? Could there be some darker reason for that? It was unsettling how one would mention something, or make an allusion, and then the other one would do almost the same thing.

"Explain yourself," she suddenly demanded, intruding on my mental wanderings again.

"Well," I said, stumbling, "I mean, I was only trying to do what anyone should do. I consider myself a good person, or I want to be..."

"Protect the weak, and all that crap. So you didn't really want to do it?"

I threw the pencil back, purposely missing, and without any real force. "Ms. Beech, I must counter your argument by noting that you are acting most out of character yourself. It's not like you to neglect to offer me a way out. If you insist on trapping me, then offer me a way up and out."

"Give me a break, Jack. You dig your own way out."

"I can't believe I'm in trouble with you, too! You're the last person I thought that would happen with. I've been around you a lot in the past months, and I thought I was starting to get a handle on you. Do you know what my first impression of you was back in Somerset?"

"What?" she said slowly, giving in a little, unavoidably curious.

"I saw an attractive professional woman, who was no-nonsense, had no-pretensions, was independent, opinionated, educated, and unintimidated. I was a little intimidated by you. You were slick and efficient."

"So what am I now, besides unemployed and unhappy?"

"You're a real person now. You're not an image anymore. The fact that I know more about you hasn't lessened your worth in my eyes, it's only increased it. You've told me some things that take away professionalism between us. But I want to know them, Dana. I like who you are. I think Sarah senses that and is jealous of it. In fact. I know that's true.

"On the book side of it, you've earned your way in the business, and that's worth more than money. Hell, I'm a little jealous of you, too. You know a lot more about the mechanics of writing than I do. Sarah is good at that, also, and that's probably another reason why she's so jealous. She's not my editor like she used to be."

"Yes, judging from our phone conversation, I'd say she's jealous. What did you mean about 'saying things?' Have we been unprofessional, or too personal, Jack?

"No, dammit."

We lapsed into silence for a while. Then I brought up the phone call again, dangerously curious about details. I needed to examine what made Sarah jealous in more detail, so I could appreciate it and understand it. The devil, I had heard, was in the details.

"For the record, can you remember what Sarah said in that phone conversation?"

"She said that she didn't want me staying at your father's house; that it was a desecration of his home; that I was leeching off of you; that I was your little agent on the side; that you didn't take her editorial advice anymore since I was around; etc., etc. Do you really want to hear it all?"

"She has no right to talk to you that way."

Dana laughed, tritely. "How are you going to stop her, Jack? If you'll pardon me being so bold, I don't think you have much control over her. Does she listen to you at all? Has she ever? There comes a point when you stop talking if someone doesn't listen to you."

"Do you listen to me?" I countered.

"Do you want to have control over women, Jack?"

"Am I supposed to?" I replied. "What kind of control is a man supposed to have over his wife?"

She frowned. "Wait a second. I heard a change in your voice. I don't think I like where you're going with this..."

"Can you answer me? I want to know. Draw on your own experience and tell me how much control I should have over my own wife."

She hesitated, then spoke very slowly and clearly.

"A husband and wife should exercise mutual influence over each other. It should be a two-way street. Even if the husband is the so-called head of the household, they should be equal partners. Let's not stray from the subject here. You asked me about the phone conversation."

"I'm not through with the marriage thing. I'll buy the influence definition. You're just saying that Sarah exercises more of it than I do. Is that the way it has to be?"

"I don't think so. It's none of my business, Jack. Let's leave it at that. Get back to the original topic."

"Dana, it's time for me to exercise some control." I stood up and put my jacket on. "I'm an equal partner, and the head of the household. I have the authority to make certain decisions."

"What are you doing, Jack?"

"I'm taking you back to Mount Sterling."

"What do you mean?"

"I'm driving you back to the farmhouse. I'm not going to let my wife kick you out. I'll drive the Escort and fly a commuter back to Louisville in the morning. I'm exercising control. This is my right."

"Jack, it's almost ten o'clock. And do you really think Sarah is going to accept that reasoning?"

I pulled her up by the hand. "I'm exercising my authority here, okay? I'm taking you back to Mount Sterling."

She looked unsure, but it suddenly seemed like the necessary thing to me. Actually, it seemed like the right thing, too. I needed to make it clear to Sarah that my father's house belonged to me, and that I chose to help Dana Beech. Sarah had no right to be unfaithful, then tell me I couldn't help someone I cared about.

"You have to sell my book." I reminded her.

Dana Beech looked at me and snorted. "That's what all of this about? Do you think your book has wreaked that much havoc on all three of us? Or is it something else going on here?"

"Are you my agent?" I asked.

"Yes—barely."

"Okay. Let's go back to Mount Sterling, then."

IN THE CAR ON Interstate sixty-four, our conversation continued, a little more like old times at the nightclub, or in Somerset.

"So," she said, "why are you really doing all of these things for me, Jack? Am I that good?"

I laughed—slowly at first, and then with more spirit—then I had to look at her to see if she was being serious. I turned the dome light on and saw that she was smiling broadly. There was a naughtiness in her eyes that you couldn't really pin down on her and make stick. It was there, though.

"Yes, Ms. Beech, you're that good. As soon as my book is published, we'll renegotiate."

She laughed again, then unexpectedly sobered. "What are you going to tell Sarah?"

"I am going to call her from the rest area at Frankfort and tell her what I'm doing. I'm not going to lie."

"You really believe she won't think something is going on with us?"

"No. I'll tell her that I'm restoring you as matron of the plantation, and that it's my authority and decision. Isn't that within my domain?"

"Why is she so jealous of me? We've never done anything like, well..."

"Like what she did?" I finished.

"I didn't mean it that way, Jack. I just don't want her to be jealous. It's a bad emotion—it's not healthy for anyone. And the hell of it is, I really like Sarah a lot."

"Don't you think you're someone to be jealous of?"

Dana Beech seemed to think about that one for a moment, then meandered onto a different subject, yet again.

"Hey, Jack, since you're coming over here, let's look at those chapters you fixed. I worked with them, and I'll show you what I came up with. I think we're almost ready to start showing some people.

Seriously."

"Seriously?"

"Seriously."

"That sounds good. And," I said with special emphasis, "since our relationship is purely of a non-sexual, non-romantic variety, I'm counting on you to be totally honest with me."

"That's interesting," she said, almost wistfully. "So you think a relationship can't be honest when sex or romance is involved?"

I nodded my head vigorously. "I'm convinced of that."

"You're right," she said, deadpan. "Sex is dangerous, Jack. Sex messes relationships up."

"That's certainly true," I said, and lapsed into a long silence.

When I next looked over at her, she was fast asleep. When in that state, she really did look like a vulnerable little girl, and it made me feel very sad for a moment. That man who had abused her belonged locked up. Maybe he was. I hoped that I never met him.

I thought of Sarah, and it occurred to me that most of us end up marrying people who know how to hurt us, and we end up watching them do it repeatedly, like some cheap television soap opera. Did I do that to Sarah? Dana hadn't hurt her husband, or done anything at all to deserve his wrath. She was better than all of us, wasn't she? She had survived far worse than Sarah or I had, and she didn't really complain that much.

I allowed myself the thought that if I hadn't been so fortunate as to find Sarah Collins, I could have done far worse than Dana Beech. She was hard on the exterior, but all soft inside, and that was something I couldn't help but admire. That was the best way to deal with the world. It was a lot like my father.

Of course, like she said (and I agreed), this was dangerous thinking. Just when you think you can trust someone, sex and romance get in the way.

I rolled down the window for cold air.

THE CONVERSATION with Sarah was very short.

"Sarah? It's me. I'm taking Dana Beech back to the farm. You had no right to talk to her the way you did. She's my agent, and I expect you to treat her with a modicum of courtesy. I'm doing this as a favor to her because she is getting my book published, and that's all there is to it."

A tremendous weight fell off my chest. I waited for the explosion. Silence, then: "When will you be home?"

"I'm staying at the Hotel Eight in Mount Sterling after I drop her off. I'm taking the first commuter into Louisville in the morning."

More silence, then: "Well, fine. Whatever you think is best. I trust you, Jack."

Her voice was so syrupy sweet that I knew she was not being frank with me. I shrugged and gave up. I didn't know what else to do.

"Good-bye, Sarah. We'll talk tomorrow."

There was a click on the other end.

I STOPPED AT the Hotel Eight first, reserving a room, then headed out to the farm several miles away. Dana was still fast asleep. It was about two in the morning.

I hadn't called the Hawkins, so when I pulled into the maple-lined entrance to the farm, I was somewhat hesitant to disturb them. But Dana had been living there, so they shouldn't have been totally surprised.

She was still fast asleep. When the car was parked, I reached over and gently shook her awake. She opened her eyes and looked confused for a moment until she recognized the farm. Then she smiled and closed her eyes.

"This is a great place, Jack. I think even I could be a writer here."

She was almost asleep again, so I shook her once more.

"Come on, Dana, you've got to get inside. We'll work on the book some other time. Tomorrow you can get back to work on it."

That seemed to rouse her from slumber, "No, I'll wake up. You said you're leaving in the morning, so we've got to get some things done now. I'll be okay. I can sleep all day tomorrow. We really need to talk about a couple of things. The first phone call I make to an editor at a big publisher may be the most important call I make in the next couple of months."

I was skeptical, but didn't say anything else. We slowly walked up the sidewalk to the back porch door and a spirited Border Collie, Alford (named after a basketball player, I think) loped up to us. Al was my father's dog, and of course he was happy to see me.

"There's a note here," Dana said as she reached the kitchen door. "We've gone to Danville to be with my sick cousin. Signed, Bill Hawkins." She shrugged. "At least we won't wake them up."

In the kitchen, she went straight for the coffee machine.

"You've done this before," I joked, noting how familiar she was with everything.

"Bill says my coffee is better, and he gets me to make it every day."

"It's an automatic drip machine, so there's not really that much that can go wrong."

"Even so, it takes a special touch to make it just right. The pot must be clean, the water cold, and the amount of coffee measured out just right."

I shook my head. "I'll let my taste buds be the judge."

While I was watching her make the coffee, she absently lifted her sweatshirt an inch or two, and then dropped it. I was certain it wasn't an intentional action on her part, though the effect on me was somewhat unexpected. I found myself really looking at her profile, trying to remember whatever she had worn in the past, and what it revealed. A physical stirring that I had not felt in a while demanded my attention as I sat down in the rocking chair near the back door.

She continued to make the coffee. When she turned to say something to me, I considered the sweatshirt again, remembering what I had just seen, and wondering beyond that. She looked at me funny and whatever she was going to say seemed to stick in her mouth.

"I don't think you should be wearing University of Louisville colors around here," I said quickly, trying to cover up for something I had probably already been caught in the act of. "The Hawkins won't stand it, I'm certain."

"True blue Wildcat fans, I know, and they've already discussed it with me. What they didn't realize, and you didn't either, is that Indiana is my Alma Mater, and first loyalty. This sweatshirt was in a closet they said had your old stuff in it."

"Mine?"

"I assume so."

The sweatshirt suddenly was familiar.

"You went to Indiana?" I asked.

"Yes! I've told you that before."

I made a face. I never could stand Bobby Knight. I don't suppose, however, you should judge a university based on the personality of their basketball coach. In the case of Indiana, however, I would make an exception to that rule.

She turned back around and dug through the cupboards for two coffee mugs. When she leaned over to retrieve them, I found myself looking again at her the way any sane man knows he shouldn't.

"I love this house," I heard myself saying. The emotion in the statement, though, was from another feeling altogether. My eyes were still glued to her.

She turned around and poured the coffee, then handed me a mug. She noticed something wrong, and pulled a chair over beside me. She sat on it backwards, arms draped over the top of the ladder-back slats, one hand precariously balancing the coffee.

"What's wrong, Jack? You look agitated."

I sipped. "It's good," I said.

"Maybe you should call it a night. We can work on the book some other time. Maybe you and Sarah can—"

I stood up abruptly and starting pacing, carefully, since the mug was still almost full. The last thing I wanted to talk about was Sarah.

"What did I say?" she asked.

"Nothing."

"Come on, I obviously said something."

I knew I was setting myself up, but I went back and sat down in the rocking chair inches from her face and decided to release the truth and see what disaster could unfold.

"Dana, tonight I'm starting to find that attraction to you is interfering with my judgement. It's a discovery I've just made, right now, this moment."

She looked stumped, then practically spit her coffee on me, laughing. "Did I just hear you correctly? Jack, you are married to the most beautiful woman I've ever seen. Don't tell me I'm more attractive than that. Does Sarah interfere with your judgement, too?"

"I don't want to talk about Sarah."

She weighed that cautiously for a moment, then seemed to let it go by. Then, the words abruptly tumbled out of her like water. Her voice was trembling, and now her arms were behind the chair, wringing in agitation.

"So you did go to Cincinnati for some other reason. You relocated me in your father's house for some other reason. You've listened to my intimate conversations and secrets for some other reason. You've made me feel obligated to you because of your acts of kindness. You've watched my life turn upside down. You've watched me go bankrupt for that same reason."

"No, Dana. You've got it all backwards. All of those things are what brought about these feelings. The feeling wasn't first. The acts of kindness and the professional respect came beforehand. The friendship came first."

"Oh!" she said, throwing her hands back, "so you weren't even attracted to me at first. I'm just the old shoe that's grown on you little by little. Familiarity and all that. That makes me feel real good..."

"Dana, part of the reason I'm so attracted to you is because you avoid most of the little games Sarah plays with me, and now that I tell you the truth about what I'm feeling, you're starting to play those very same little games yourself. That's not what I expected to see. I expected you to be honest with me. I expected you to respect my feelings—not tear them to shreds, or pretend they aren't what they are."

That seemed to jolt her. A tiny tear appeared at the corner of each eye, smearing her mascara. For many minutes, she didn't say anything. She just stared at me with wooden eyes, that neither accused or affirmed, but instead reflected pain and past suffering. She sniffled quietly, never quite giving in to the physical act of crying. That quiet defiance was one of the things that I loved about her.

When she finally spoke again, her voice was barely above a whisper, and crackled uncertainly. Her words were heavy.

"I don't have that much energy left in me, Jack. I know thirty doesn't sound that old, but I've been through a lot in those extra years that you haven't lived yet. I can't let myself out on a limb again. I can't love someone and have them suddenly not love me. I promised I would never put myself in that position again. You can understand that, can't you?"

I didn't answer, so she continued.

"I've loved you from the moment I set eyes on you..." Suddenly, she did burst into full-fledged tears, and her body rocked with spasms.

I was still feeling foolish, and yet something in me finally aroused itself from lethargy and caution, and my hands reached out and grabbed hers. I felt her tremors vibrate through my arms.

"If this about sex," she said between sobs, "then tell me now. Is that what you meant by the word attraction?"

I shook my head. I didn't want to lie, and I didn't want to tell the truth, either.

"Dana, physical attraction doesn't mean just sex. It's an outward manifestation of something inwardly occurring. I was falling in love with you before tonight. But tonight, I can't take my eyes off you. Not just your body, but your hair, and your eyes, even your hands. I can't help it."

"You'll never leave her," she whispered. "This is going to be worse than what happened before. You're setting me up. You're setting her up."

"No!" I said, feeling anger at the mention of Sarah. "Leave her out of this. She doesn't have anything to do with this. If she does, then it's not love."

"She does have something to do with this! You belong to her, Jack. Even if we never have a physical relationship, don't you see that you're already cheating on her?"

I tore my hands away from hers' and tumbled out of the rocking chair, sending it sideways to the floor with a loud clatter. I took a deep breath and counted to ten, then opened the back door a crack. I was gulping for air, like a person just bursting to the surface from a great depth.

"You're killing me," I said. "I wouldn't have thought you would be the one to do it, but you're killing me."

"I'm telling you the truth, Jack. We can't live in a fantasy world. You can't fall out of love with one person, then decide you're in love with someone else like it's all just a Sunday stroll through Central Park that happens every week."

I looked her in the eye. "You're right, Dana. I can't decide for myself, can I?"

"None of us can, Jack! What kind of world do you think this is? It's a low-down, rotten, stinking filthy place where people get used and abused, and then die, often unhappy. I can't look at you without dreaming, but Goddammit, I know what the world does. If you have any courage left in you, you'll turn around and walk out that door and forget this ever happened. I'll get back on my feet quickly, and then you won't have to think about it anymore."

I felt rooted in place.

"I'll still work on your book. That's my project, too, now."

I still couldn't move.

"Go on!" she said, starting to cry again, "You said you respected me because I wasn't like those other slobbering, whimpering women— get out of here so you can keep that picture of me in your mind."

I shook my head.

Of course, she was right. I still loved Sarah, and had a hard time imagining life without her. Sarah was my dream from the beginning. And yet....

"She's pregnant!" Dana screeched. "What would people say about you, or me, if we were screwing while your wife is expecting your first child? Do you see what a slimy thing it is? It's contemptible. I can't believe we're even talking about it."

"Okay," I said, my voice probably too loud. "I know how awful it is. Condemn me to hell for those thoughts of you. Never mind that the love I feel for Sarah is probably the infatuation of first love, and the dream of the impossible conquest, while what I feel for you grew out of friendship, and compatibility. Never mind. The world will not tolerate a man who loves two women, so off into the night I go, banished to hell for my sins."

Dana looked at me, nonplussed. "That's pitiful, Jack. That's absolutely wretched for someone who claims to be a writer. I didn't say it was impossible to love two people, and I'm certain Sarah is more than a simple infatuation. Anyone can look at the two of you and see that you are like beer and pizza. You complement one another. Just leave before something happens that we'll both regret."

"Beer and pizza?"

"I never claimed to be a writer. That's why I edit. Now go before we both lose our resolve."

"So, you do love me," I said slowly; deliberately.

"Yes. And I knew months ago that you were feeling kind of funny about me. Why are you acting so shocked? You write about love—don't you recognize it?"

I almost smiled.

"Now get out of here," she said, turning away from me.

I walked out the door, though part of me knew that I wasn't really leaving. What I was really doing was plotting the next scene. Somehow, we had to arrange things so that it was a simultaneous gesture. I couldn't go flying back in the door; she couldn't swoon, and come running down the driveway after me. We couldn't have it so one of us appeared to be the one who first committed the crime. It couldn't be like an old movie, or a cheap magazine story.

God, I wanted to walk back in that door. I had only taken two steps beyond it onto the darkened back porch, where cans and jars of fruits and vegetables glistened in the moonlight, but it seemed light years away from her. I couldn't understand my feelings.

"How are we going to do it?" I said out loud.

"Do what?" came a voice from the kitchen.

"How are we going to arrange it so that neither one of us is the one that runs after the other one?"

There was silence for a moment, then, "Why don't we accidentally meet somewhere?"

"Like where?" I said. "Supposedly, I just walked out the door and returned to the Hotel Eight."

"We'll I'm supposedly in for the night, so I can't go outside, or I'll be the one chasing."

"I can't go back inside," I said. Then slowly, an idea began to form. "You can't go outside: I can't come back inside—what if we meet, accidentally, on the veranda beneath the balcony? Technically, you'll still be under roof and in the house. I'll still be outside, technically."

"Jack, you are twisted. I guess you are a writer."

I didn't reply, choosing instead to run around the corner of the house to the darkened patio area in the open end of the "U" shaped part of the house. The veranda was like a brick porch beneath the balcony, with a staircase to the second floor, and several benches to sit on. There was also a giant ceramic toad, an erstwhile gift from my mother to my father long after the divorce.

I thought I had moved swiftly, but a shadow caught my eye just as an invisible arm spun me around.

"You realize that this can't have a happy ending," a voice said in a whisper.

I drew her to me and we kissed for the first time. It was a warm, gentle feeling that flowed over me like a blanket on a cool summer night. I felt my hands gliding over contours that were no longer mysterious and elusive.

"It can have a happy ending," I said.

Chapter 14
Prefatherhood

AT THE OFFICE, I stared off into space, daydreaming about that night in Mount Sterling from four days past. I still hadn't recovered—physically or mentally. I was oblivious to the chatter and ringing of phones around me, and to my boss who was staring down at me.

"Jack, snap out of it!"

I fell forward in my chair with a jerk and faced Frank, my superior and mentor at the paper. He was a handsome man in his mid-fifties, a little bit heavy, though in a way that gave him more mature credibility. I could never be as respected as him until I added a little to my non-existent gut.

"Sorry, Frank. What's going on?"

Frank pulled out his reading glasses with a snap, then mounted them carefully on the bridge of his dignified nose.

"Look at this." He flourished a newspaper. "Other papers are writing about you."

"About me?" I leaned forward and noticed that the newspaper in his hand was not our own—it was an Indianapolis paper. Of course, in my dubious state of mind, the first thing that popped into my head was the fact that Dana Beech called Indiana home (or had until her parents adopted Cincinnati).

"This is good stuff, Jack. This guy, George Preston, he's been following your Sunday features and he wants to talk to you in person. He wants to reprint some of your work."

"That's great!" I said. Then I frowned. "Is that okay, Frank? I mean, I work for you, not him."

Frank removed his glasses and grinned. "Of course it's okay. It's great for us. We can work on our circulation in southern Indiana, and I pay you much more than the Indianapolis Star can. Hell, Jack, I'm even paying for you to go up there and let him talk to you. He doesn't want to steal you from me—he's interested in helping you syndicate." Frank looked away, as if he hadn't really uttered the last sentence.

"Syndicate? Are you serious?"

"That's what he said, my boy. I've got you on a Friday commuter flight up there."

I grinned stupidly. I couldn't believe it. Someone wanted to syndicate my writing? That was bigger than a book deal. It was a huge deal.

Coupled with my already sky-high emotions, this was almost more than I could bear. How many great novelists got their first break the same way?

SARAH, HOWEVER, did not take it well.

"Jack, I'm scheduled to get my ultrasound Saturday morning. I was counting on you being there."

"Can't your sister go with you?"

"Jack, it's your child we're talking about here! It's the nineties now, and father's are supposed to be involved in this process. They'll probably be able to tell us for sure that it's a boy. How can you miss a moment like that?"

I didn't have an answer. I realized that I was getting wrapped up in me, and I wasn't really trying to get out of it. The old Jack crawled out for a second and questioned it, and I chose to ignore him.

Sarah continued. "That's all you can do is shrug? I know we have our ups and downs, Jack, but this is something for both of us. Just because I'm the one carrying the baby around in my stomach doesn't mean that you're not fifty percent of the team. I need you; the baby needs you. How about telling me why this is so important that you have to do it right now?"

I hunched my shoulders over defensively and tried to think of how to word it. I spoke very slowly; very cautiously. "A man in Indianapolis is interested in syndicating my Sunday features for other papers."

She looked at me nonplussed, and I noticed for perhaps the first time that her perfectly smooth cheeks were looking a little bit swollen. To this point, she had been one of those amazing women who only grew in one place—where the baby was. No spreading feet, or extra layers of "protection," or sympathetic swelling of hips and buttocks. Her cheeks did, indeed, show signs of puffiness.

"Why?" she said.

I laughed. "Because it's good? I don't know. That's why I need to go and talk to him. To find out what it's all about. It's a big deal in the newspaper world to become a syndicated writer. You know that."

"Well, reschedule it. Your baby is first priority. I'm your first priority."

"That's it? No compromise, or middle ground? I thought we'd

been discussing how to satisfy the needs of both parties."

She shook her head. "No. You're coming with me. I won't compromise on this issue."

"Fine," I said, standing up and not having any idea where I was going to go. Maybe to the greenhouse.

"Well, Jack?"

"I said okay."

I supposed she was right. Still, a part of me remained in rebellion, wondering if I was blowing my first big opportunity in the world of journalism.

THE ULTRASOUND was an interesting experience. This specialist was a moderately middle-aged woman with the reassuring tones of a mother. She handled Sarah as if she were the only patient she would see that day.

I was fascinated with the clear gooey mess they used to lubricate the sensor wand, though Sarah initially complained of the cold. Beyond that one minor physical discomfort, she seemed rejuvenated by the whole process. She was visibly excited as the doctor explained the functioning of the tiny heart, referring to the screen next to it full of blinking numbers, and pointed out various body parts that were visible.

I was excited, too, and also a little frightened. There was a living person inside of Sarah that suddenly bound us together with chains of a different metal. I couldn't pretend that I wasn't just as responsible for it as she was, and I couldn't pretend that it didn't signal a fundamental change in our relationship. Somehow, pregnancy had been more like a game up to this point; a chess match between Sarah and I, and now it was real; flesh and blood.

"Do you want me to make a tentative sex determination?" the doctor asked.

I studied the screens carefully—there was definitely one prominent part missing.

Though the baby's heart was strong and everything else very nicely arranged, there was no evidence of male parts anywhere in sight. I craned my head at every conceivable angle, seeing all kinds of shapes and shadows on the screen, but none of them correct for the anatomy we were looking for.

We were both disappointed, and both felt foolish when we glanced at each other, knowing that we were not reacting the right way. Besides, maybe we were wrong. Maybe the doctor would show us what we couldn't see.

"Go ahead," Sarah said quickly.

"Looks like a girl."

Sarah and I locked eyes, trying not to be upset.

The doctor didn't seem to notice. "But I can't say for certain. Sometimes boys just aren't pointing the right direction, if you know what I mean. I won't say that it can't be a boy. Everything else is perfect!" she said cheerily, smiling down at Sarah. "I don't see anything out of the ordinary."

Sarah fidgeted nervously on the bed. "You're sure it's not a boy?"

"I didn't say that..." the doctor said slowly, returning the wand to Sarah's stomach. "Nobody can say that with absolute certainty..." Her voice trailed off and the wand continued to work in circles. "But I don't see anything at all. There's got to be something there for it to be a boy, unless it's small, or hidden by the angle of the wand. I don't see it."

Sarah looked at me again, and I shrugged with an, "Oh, well," expression, then moved over to hold her hand. Her hand was limp, and mine was, too.

The doctor suddenly seemed to pick up on the issue.

"I take it you wanted a boy, Sarah."

"It doesn't matter," she said quickly.

"Well bear in mind that ultrasounds can be wrong. It doesn't happen often, and I don't see any evidence of a boy. We can shoot for another ultrasound in a month—and then we could definitely tell for certain—though your insurance probably won't pay for it."

It shouldn't have been a big deal. The more I thought about how we had played the whole "boy" thing up, the more foolish I felt.

In the car on the way home, Sarah vented about the gender news. I listened to her politely, though I caught myself several times thinking about the interview I had missed. I wasn't bitter. I just felt dead in the water.

"Are you mad?" Sarah said.

"No. I'm just sorry we made such a big deal over it. We won't be able to name a girl after my father."

Suddenly Sarah burst into tears, and I had to pull the car over to attend to her. In her expanding state, there was not a whole lot of room for her to gulp down air. She began hyperventilating and I had to roll the windows down and take her seatbelt off.

"You, you didn't make a big deal out of it," she said, "I did. I was the one who did this. I wanted a boy, Jack! What did I do wrong?"

"Sarah, you didn't do anything wrong. For God's sake, neither of us have any control over it."

"Then who does, Jack? Did I make God angry or something?"

"God? It's the male cell that determines the sex of the baby, anyway. The doctor told you that. It's not your fault."

"But I shouldn't have led you on like that." She began crying more loudly. "I wanted you to have a son, so you could name him after your father. I was so sure it was a boy. I was absolutely positive!"

It just wasn't like Sarah to accept being wrong about something. This time, the odds were stacked against her. That did pull at my heart a little bit, and I leaned over and cradled her face next to mine and rocked her back and forth. God, how she made me feel the desire to comfort her. How I could contemplate hurting her was beyond me at moments like that. Sarah seemed to have some kind of invisible rope tied to me, and whenever she pulled on it, I just loved her in spite of it.

Sometimes, Sarah could even almost make me forget about the terrible affair I was in the midst of.

DANA AND I ended up in Indianapolis the following weekend for a second attempt at my interview with George Preston. The night before the big meeting, we shopped downtown, ate in a bistro beside the Market Square Arena, then took in a Pacers basketball game.

Naturally, we rooted for the Pacers, who obliged us by winning easily.

We returned to the hotel room a little drunk, laughing, playfully pushing and prodding at each other. Dana pushed me onto the bed and I happened to notice a little red light blinking on the nearby phone.

Sarah had called. The blood rushed out of my head and into my arms, leaving them dead weights on the comforter.

Dana instinctively knew what was wrong with me, and it didn't faze her. She had presented my new book to a big New York editor, and had received promising feedback. Nothing could touch her at the moment.

"I have to call her," I said.

"Why?" She jumped onto the bed, nearly bowling me over. Her short black cocktail dress was certain to rip if it hadn't already. She kicked her shoes off and laughed when one of them landed in the trash can. She straddled me and began to massage my ears.

"She's pregnant, and she's alone."

"God, you're making me feel bad now. Just call her and get it over with."

"I think you should leave the room while I do."

"Oh, Jack," she said, pouting, "I promise I won't make any noise."

"I mean it, Dana. It's not funny."

"Okay, okay, I promise. Just hurry up before I get depressed and fall asleep. I don't want it to ruin the evening."

She smiled and started to get up, then plopped back down on top of me.

"I'll be quiet!" she whispered.

I smiled, too, in spite of myself.

I dialed the number and listened to it ring. I hadn't intended for her to stay so close, and before anyone had even picked up at the other end, Dana curled up on my stomach and closed her eyes, looking dangerously sleepy.

"Hello?" a groggy voice said on the other end.

"It's me, Sarah. Everything okay?"

"Yes. Why are you still up, Jack? You've got to meet Mr. Preston at nine, don't you?"

"Yes, I'm going to sleep soon. I just had to check on you."

"Thanks. I'm fine. I'm exhausted. But thank you for calling. My sisters were here to keep my company, but they've gone home. Mother wanted to come over, but I told her I'm fine. Be careful up there."

"Goodbye, Sarah."

I placed the phone back in the receiver, then noticed a strange tingling in the palm of my hand, almost like a burning feeling. I shook my hand and it went away.

I poked at Dana. Her only response was to roll over, so I pulled the comforter over her and turned on CNN. There was a report about a terrorist attack somewhere in the Middle East dominating the broadcast. Then something about a Presidential scandal.

While I sat there, not really paying attention to the story, I began to think about where exactly I had come to in all of this crazy adventure called life. I was convinced that I was in love with two women. I was in denial that the situation couldn't continue beyond a certain point. The reality was that the baby was a living clock—when Sarah gave birth, I would have to do something.

Wouldn't I?

Until then, I was actually content to play a double-life. There was a perverted, sick satisfaction in part of my mind taken from the fact that I had done exactly what Sarah had done to me, only I had done it better. I was managing it, and painting it like an artist. I was getting away with it. I was making something out of it. I was getting a book published. I was getting syndicated.

I couldn't imagine any future, though, when I tried to. I could only picture the next morning, or the next day. I attempted to imagine leaving Sarah, and moving in with Dana in my father's house, but the baby (soon to arrive in person) was an ever-present barrier to that. Sarah, too, wouldn't leave the picture no matter how hard I tried to think it. I also tried to invent a scenario where Dana faded away from the scene and Sarah and I became a normal, happy family. I couldn't see that, either.

I looked down where she was sleeping on my midsection. It was a beautiful, tragic woman I saw. My success would really be her success, and she was the one I really was in danger of cheating on.

There was no future. There was only the now. That was all I could comprehend.

So the present was where I lived. The present was the place where everything was holding together, even if it was temporary; even if the glue was really dissolving. The present was where I could take a breath, smile, and relax a little bit—it was a place where things made a little bit of sense.

Maybe.

WHEN I WENT to the Reds game with Al, Sarah was getting closer to her due date. The weather had turned very warm, and things had been quiet for a long stretch.

On the ride to the stadium, Al wanted to talk about my new book. I should have been flattered, though for some reason I wasn't really wanting to talk about it. I wanted to talk about baseball, instead.

"This book is much better than your first," Al said, popping open a beer can beside me. "You want one?"

I declined with a shake of my head.

"Much better," he continued, "I think you've really improved. It's almost classic in style. Sort of like—well, hell, I don't remember any of those guys I had to read in college—but it's good, really good. It's just like a classic. Maybe you'll be read in college lit classes someday."

"Thanks," I said. "Dana is really the one responsible for it. She edited it mercilessly, and she pounded doors in New York. I don't know what I would have done without her."

Al shifted gears in the car. I could see gears working behind his eyebrows, as well.

"Yeah, she is something special. I could tell by watching her that you really trust her. Even Sarah seems to respect her, and that takes something."

"Why wouldn't Sarah respect her?"

Al smiled and took another drought. "Come on, buddy. Sarah's told Carla how jealous she used to be of her. You should know that. How many writers get to work with a pretty female agent? Besides, I was making a more general reference. I've always thought of Sarah as a no-nonsense type who doesn't have the time for any fluff. She would hate living with me, for example. But if she says Dana Beech is okay, then hell, she must be."

I shrugged. Al was unusually full of praise for the woman he had so often warned me about. And there were more female literary agents and editors than men (I wondered why that was?) so in theory it didn't have anything to do with how we got along professionally (at least at first), or how we went about our tasks (at first). I was starting to get annoyed with the topic. Baseball would have been much better.

"I mean, tell me," Al continued, "have you ever had the urge to..."

"To what, Al? Pay Sarah back?"

He laughed and spilled his beer. "I didn't mean it that way... Jeez. Why would it have to be revenge? She's good looking, buddy. Don't you agree?"

"Certainly."

"Well, I'm just trying to make sure you still know how to look. You can't get married and suddenly act like women don't exist anymore. I still look all the time."

I wasn't sure how to respond to that. Dana and I had gone to great lengths to maintain our discretion, and I could sense Al fishing for something in his playful, outwardly friendly way. Dana and I had shared our relationship with no one. Al couldn't be an exception— especially with Carla's loose tongue.

"I still know how to look," I said, feeling an obvious lameness as it came out.

"We'll see today. This will be a test of your manliness. There will be some real babes at the ballpark."

I looked at Al carefully. He was truly in a good mood, practically swaggering at the prospects of a day out, away from the normal duties. I wondered how much he meant all of the things he was saying, though, and how much of it was a smoke screen.

"Would you ever step out on Carla?" I asked.

Al's face turned abruptly black. "What? Are you serious?"

I nodded my head. "I'm totally serious. Would you sleep with someone else, if you were given a rock-solid guarantee that it would stay confidential?"

He snorted. "The confidentiality has nothing to do with it. The issue is the act itself. Does that make it okay if you don't get caught? Are you asking me a serious question?"

"Yes, completely."

In response, he crushed one can and opened another. We were nearing downtown, and the oily smell of the Ohio River was wafting into the car through the open windows.

Al was staring out at the church spires and sagging slum-rows of Covington.

"I don't think I would do it," he said quietly. "I love Carla too much. Hell, I know she's not perfect, but what would be the point? Even if I was rocking and rolling with some Hollywood superstar, it couldn't end up in anything but disaster. Have you ever seen a purely sexual relationship last forever? Look at the people in high places, too—do you think the President is happier now?"

He didn't look at me as he spoke the words, and for a minute or so I didn't know whether to take him seriously or not. Big Al, the party animal in college, the man who was never serious about anything, was suddenly acting like my father. He was the perfectly loyal husband. He had scruples.

I was slightly offended. It was not the Al I remembered as my wild college roommate.

"Oh, come on, Al," I said. "You're the one taking me out to the ballpark to watch the girls instead of the game. Are you going to tell me that you wouldn't even think about it?"

He still didn't look at me.

"Think about it? Maybe. Do it? No, Jack. I would not do it. I did it lots of times with other girls before Carla and I got married—hell, half of them I can't even remember their names. But now that I'm married, and have a kid, now something's different. I couldn't do it."

We crossed the old suspension bridge and entered Ohio. The exit ramp to Riverfront Stadium was crowded with afternoon traffic, even three hours before game time.

"How about you?" Al said a minute later. "You've got a motive, after what Sarah did to you. Would you do it? Would you step out on her?"

I shrugged. "I don't know. My experience wasn't the same as yours."

Al guffawed. "You mean you didn't get as much as I did!'

"Shut up. You know what I mean. I just don't know."

"You don't know?" He snorted derisively. "Come on, Jack. You were the collective conscience for all of us in college. We'd all have died if it weren't for your common sense, and some brand of decency we all secretly respected, even when we were making fun of you. You wouldn't do that—not even to Sarah after what she did."

"What makes you so sure?" I said.

"It's not in you, Jack. I told you from the beginning that you and Sarah were opposites. Her, I understand. You, never. You're too good, and that's why I like you." He slapped me on the back, and then had to slam on his brakes to avoid hitting the car in front of us. "Jack, I've always admired you for your common decency."

I scowled, and tapped my fingers on the dash. Common decency? Was I still the decent sort now?

I wondered if I was lying to Al. I didn't want to avoid the truth, and neither did I want to tell it to him. I was dead if he knew the truth. Of course I was lying to him.

His blind trust in my innocence, however, was both insult and compliment. I should have taken umbrage over his comments about Sarah, as well.

Instead, I found myself yearning for another beer. Strangely, too, I started thinking of Dana Beech, and she was all I could see in my head. God, I wished how I could tell Al about Dana Beech. It brought a stupid smile to my face.

No one could possibly understand my world except Dana. She was the only one who could see that I loved Sarah despite what I was doing. No one knew all of me like Dana did. Because Sarah was who she was, there was that little piece of me that Al called "decent" that she would never pander to. It was the part of me that Dana needed so badly, and was risking everything to have.

Al started howling at some girls in the parking lot. They laughed and pushed their sunglasses up. One twitched her backend at him suggestively.

"Alone, ladies?" he said.

"Yes," they shouted back.

Al slapped me on the shoulder. "Let's park this thing, buddy!"

I shook my head in wonder. If Al wasn't a walking contradiction, I didn't know what was. Maybe it was the beer in him.

Or maybe there was a part of Al that I still didn't appreciate for what it was—simple, but basically good.

BY THE EARLY summer, the first royalty check arrived. The first real review came out. The first appearance for me on television came about (just in Louisville, but still exciting).

Sarah was really large by this time, and she stopped going into the insurance office altogether. She stayed at home and watched television, or called me on the phone to converse about mundane matters.

It was harder for me to see Dana, though Sarah surprised me often by bringing her up in conversation.

"Are you coming home for lunch, Jack? My cousin, George, brought some catfish by if you want me to fix them."

"Actually, I can't, honey. I'm swamped here."

"Well," she said, "why don't you get Dana to come over tonight and I'll fix them then? She can celebrate your television stardom with us."

"That's great," I said. I was really thinking that Dana and I had already celebrated...I suppressed the thought. It was a terrible thought. "I'll call her and invite her."

"That's okay. I'll do it. She's at your Dad's, so you go ahead and work. I'll tell her and see what's up. Who knows—if your royalty checks increase, she'll even be able to give you your car back."

"...What?" I stammered.

"It's a joke!" she said, shaking the phone with laughter. "Let her keep that old thing. You'll get a new BMW like you want. I'm just kidding."

"Okay..."

"You get back to work. I'll call her."

After the phone was back in its cradle, I immediately dialed Dana's number. It was busy. Sarah had beaten me to the punch. I wondered if she was suspicious, or if it was the "new" Sarah just like I had witnessed after our reconciliation.

Sarah was so nice to me that I just couldn't trust her. It was as if she knew, and was pretending not to, just to torture me.

The remainder of the day passed nervously as I waited for dinner. Dinner was an event were many dubious events in our marriage had transpired before. Dana had been over many times by then, though this time felt different.

Chapter 15
Dirty Secrets

THE CATFISH were delicious. I was eating my third one when Dana said something very strange. Until this point, the conversation between Sarah and Dana had been like two old college roommates, or a pair of sisters that had not seen one another for six months. Not just cordial, but warm and sincere.

"I don't think I was designed to handle being pregnant," Dana said.

Something about her tone of voice caused me to look up. Sarah was twirling her fork in some seafood sauce. They were complete opposites in appearance. Dana had worn my favorite black dress, and was more heavily ensconced in makeup than normal. Sarah was distorted, her hair tied up behind her head to expose her oval face, her shape hidden beneath wide swatches of flannel overalls. She had a glow about her cheeks, but no makeup on her face.

"Oh, it's not so bad," Sarah said slowly.

"I guess I'm too wimpy," Dana continued. "I like the idea of finding a mate, but the concept of children is so, so—scary, and permanent. Plus, I don't know if my body is built for it."

Sarah finally looked up. "You did a great job on the book," she said, her voice flat. "I want to thank you for that. We, want to thank you."

By this time, I had stopped eating catfish and was trying to figure out what was going on. There was definitely a hint of discontent lingering in the air. I couldn't tell which army was on the offensive. Things had gone so well that I had been lulled into a sense of peace and tranquility.

"Am I missing something here?" I said quietly. Both of them looked at me like I was crazy, or maybe living dangerously. I couldn't tell which. Their expressions clearly conveyed the command to be quiet.

"Being pregnant grows on you," Sarah explained, "no pun intended. The more time that passes, the more you seem to be in harmony with it. Your initial excitement eventually wears off, and then you're left with a warm, pleasant, contentedness. I'm not designed for it, either, and I've survived. Some days I actually enjoy it."

"But the physical discomfort—"

"Yes," Sarah agreed, "that's not fun. Your body, though, adapts."

Dana smiled. "You're good at it, Sarah, I don't care what you say. You'll be a good mother. A great mother."

Sarah suddenly smiled, too. "Thank you. I'm sure you'd find a way to do it, too."

"We'll see... I've made it the first few weeks."

In the movies, the man always drops his fork at the delivery of that line. I held my fork, true, but my grip on it suddenly tightened until my knuckles turned flash white. The catfish, fully masticated but unswallowed, almost exploded out of my mouth.

I dared a glance in the direction of Sarah and found her beaming at Dana. I couldn't see anything but surprise, pleasant at that, written on her features. She let escape a girlish giggle.

Then I looked at Dana. She was smiling, too, a shy, girlish grin that implied a reserved excitement carefully restrained.

"Who's the lucky guy?" Sarah said.

"Oh, you don't know him. It's someone I've been off and on with for a long time. I'm not even sure we'll get married...It's a funny situation."

Heat flushed through my cheeks. I wasn't certain for a moment or two whether there maybe was such another mystery person responsible. Gradually, I realized that I was the man she was talking about. I was the only one it could be.

I blustered a little bit foolishly, without understanding the possible consequences.

"Dana! What a surprise. I'm in shock."

She raised an eyebrow, then nodded. "This is probably the last time I'll be able to wear this dress for a while."

"I'll say..." I muttered.

Sarah looked at me. I shrugged helplessly, my heart pounding.

"You could at least congratulate her, Jack."

"Yes!...Congratulations, Dana."

I forced the catfish down as Dana grinned at me. Her eyes only caught mine for a slender moment, yet in that breadth of time, she convinced me beyond any doubt that I was the one responsible.

I knew in my heart, anyway, that she couldn't have been with anyone else. Dana was not like that. Sarah and I obviously were flawed, but Dana was not that way. She couldn't have loved anyone else enough to do that.

"So when are you due?" Sarah asked.

"Excuse me," I said, standing up carefully. "Would anyone else care for another beer? I'm going to get one..."

Sarah glared at me. "Jack, neither one of us should be drinking. You know that. No alcohol when you're pregnant."

Dana smiled sheepishly and pushed her mostly full glass of beer aside. "Do you have any tea, or Coke?" she said.

"No caffeine," Sarah said sternly.

"I'm not that far along, Sarah..."

"There is decaffeinated tea in the fridge, Jack."

"Sure. I'll bring you some, Dana."

Once in the kitchen, I buried my face in my hands. Sarah had committed adultery. She had not, however, had someone else's baby. Somehow, the enormity of the situation could not fit into my world, or into my head. The possibility had never been conceived in my mind, no pun intended.

In the other room, I heard them giggling like girls again. First gaiety; then later Sarah had been somber and moody—now she was giddy once more. Dana, for her part, was playing along like it wasn't really Sarah's husband that had done something to her.

I needed someone impartial; someone far away from my life; someone who could look and things and tell me where I stood. I thought of my father, of course, and my anguish grew more alarming. He wouldn't have had answers—but he could have offered sympathy and opinions, and that was more than I had at the moment. I thought of prayer, but my faith deserted me in times of crisis. I couldn't connect.

I can't seem to face God when I've screwed up.

Maybe Al, I thought. At the baseball game he had displayed more personal morality than I had given him credit for, despite his outward boisterous behaviors. He would probably know what to do, and he probably wouldn't be too harsh on me.

I had to tell someone.

"YOU DID WHAT?"

I had never heard Al's voice express true incredulity. I explained it again. There was a long sigh on the other end. It was the morning after the dinner.

"What in the hell are you going to do, buddy?"

"I don't know," I said. "That's kind of why I called you. I can't wait until Dana has the baby, though, and I really should do something before Sarah gives birth. Two days ago, they were eating dinner together. Maybe I should move to Utah, or something."

Al did not recognized the humor; or maybe it wasn't funny. "When is she due?"

"Who?"

"Sarah, Jack!"

"About another month."

Al whistled on the other end. "You have got more guts than I thought."

"What do you mean?"

"I mean Sarah is going to kill you. You're a brave man to slap her with this."

I shifted uneasily. I was in a payphone on Bardstown Road, the closest place I could find any privacy.

"Don't you think I have some ground to stand on?"

Al guffawed. "She made a mistake, Jack, a stupid little one night stand with some guy she probably can't even remember now. You, on the other hand, are deep, deep into a relationship with a woman who is not only your editor, but is also going to be the mother of your child; another child. You don't think there's a little bit of a difference there?"

The hairs on my head stood up a little in rankle. "I don't think we can start judging which affair is less moral or harmful than the other, Al. If it's wrong, then it's wrong, dammit, and we're both wrong."

"Of course. I'm just saying that Sarah is going to kill you, especially when she finds out it's Dana. I just can't believe it, Jack. I never would have thought you had it in you."

"Give me some help," I said, feeling foolish as I said it. "Tell me something to do. Come on, Al! You're the brains between the two of us. Quit talking about how shocked you are and tell me what to do. What would you do?"

Al sighed again. "Go tell Sarah the truth right now."

"That's the best you can do? She's likely to miscarry, after she kills me."

"The truth is the best policy. Didn't I say that when Sarah was the one on the other side of the fence? The rules have to be the same for everyone. Tell her the truth."

"Thanks a lot," I said, probably with too much sarcasm. "You're a big help, Al. I need something to hang on to, not to hang myself with."

Al didn't seem to hear. "She is going to kill you! Jeez, good luck. Call me if you need a place to stay. Man, oh, man."

WHEN I ARRIVED home that night after the conversation with Al, I had chickened out on the notion of the truth. I immediately sensed something was wrong, though, when Sarah met me at the door. I was convinced beyond a doubt that something was wrong when I saw Dana sitting on the couch behind her.

"What's this all about?" I said, trying to take the offensive, but knowing deep down that it was too late. I was cooked. It was all over. My house of cards was about to come tumbling down.

"Yes," Sarah said quietly, sitting down beside Dana on the couch. "What is this all about." It was a statement, not a question.

"Come on, Jack," Dana said, "have a seat. I told her everything."

"Why?" I said loudly. "That doesn't make sense!"

I could feel my heart pounding in my chest like a baseball bat. It felt like it might burst. My head started to spin in circles.

Sarah raised an eyebrow, and I had to look away, confronted with more guilt than I could process. She was so pregnant that it made me feel ten times worse. There really wasn't anything else I could say, so I decided to just shut my mouth completely.

Dana wouldn't meet my eyes.

"When were you planning on telling me, Jack? Before or after you were a father with two different mothers?"

"He won't be a father with me," Dana said quietly.

My no-talking strategy quickly died a painful death. "What? What are you talking about, Dana?"

"I had a miscarriage. I was going to tell you tonight, anyway. But something in my head told me that Sarah and I needed to talk first. I came over, and everything spilled out. I couldn't let it go on any longer. It wasn't fair to Sarah."

Again, my jaw fell downward.

"I am mad at her, Jack," Sarah said, "but not nearly as mad as I am at you. Dana and I have talked it all out. Now I'm ready to hear your explanation."

"You did this first!" I blurted out.

Sarah was ready for that one. Her voice was calm and steady. "I made an uncalculated mistake. You burrowed deeper and deeper into this, and you took Dana ransom in the process."

"What do you mean I took Dana for ransom!"

Sarah's countenance suddenly wavered, and she covered her face with one hand and waved Dana Beech forward with the other. Dana looked at me as if I had just died. It was the look people throw on the embalmed body as they pass it at a viewing. I pleaded with my eyes for some kind of mercy, or some form of vague understanding. She responded only for a moment with a deep, terrifying frown of unhappiness, then looked away as she brushed past me and walked closer to the door.

"Sarah and I worked a big part of it out, Jack. Now you need to work out the rest. It's up to you now."

It didn't sound like her voice. It was strangely husky. I looked into Dana's eyes and this time she met my gaze. I saw something there that I had seen that night on the veranda at my father's house. I lunged after her and accidentally tripped, falling facedown on the carpet. Tears were in my eyes.

She left.

I couldn't imagine any scenario where Dana would be the one to come and tell everything to Sarah. It was the opposite of the promise she made me commit to with her. It was contrary to everything I knew about Dana.

Sarah's bluster and confidence seemed to drain away further with the sound of the door closing. It was as if she had been drawing strength from Dana's presence. Maybe we both had. She drew her other hand to her face, then groaned and reached around her swelling stomach.

"I'm not feeling too hot..."

The baby.

"You'd better sit down,"

She didn't answer me, though she did flop onto the couch.

When she looked up at me, I almost blacked out. There was something in her face that I had never seen before; something terrible; something awful that she had never shared with me; something worse than what I already knew. Perhaps it was even one of those things I had wanted her to tell me about, or give me from the very beginning of our relationship; answers about her father, her mother, or her strange childhood, or even why she showed so little direct affection to me sometimes.

Her breath was coming in quick, shallow bursts. The health of the baby was of primary concern, and Sarah definitely didn't look well, either.

"Sarah, I really don't think you should be pushing it right now. Please sit down. I'm going to take you to the doctor in just a second. I need to say something to Dana before she leaves."

She immediately came to life with a hiss. "And you were the only person in the world I really thought I could trust! That was a joke, wasn't it? I'm so dumb...I'm so goddamned stupid! I actually thought there was one person in the world I could count on. I thought that maybe there was one man that could be different. I looked at all of them, and you were the only one I thought could understand me, or at least accept me—"

"Sarah, this isn't the time—"

"No! You just be quiet!" She sat on the couch, ramrod straight, stiff, barely moving, except to take rapid, short breaths. "I should have been able to read the signs, Jack. I should have known that I couldn't really trust you. I should have been able to tell it was her, too. I should have learned from my father. The way he looked at Dana gave it all away. What is it about her, anyway?"

"Sarah!"

I shook my head and ran out the door. Dana was just pulling away in the old Escort.

"Dana!" I yelled, running down the street. The car slowed and I charged up to it, watching her slowly roll the window down.

"I thought you loved me, Dana! How could you do this?"

Her face was streaming with tears.

"I do love you, Jack. That's why I'm doing this. The miscarriage was a sign; a clear message about what is happening. Can't you see it? It's wrong, Jack, all wrong. You can't love me..." she said the last words bitterly, her voice wavering up and down uncertainly.

"That's not true. How the hell can you say that?"

"Now that your book is done, where does that leave me? I'm just your little agent/editor on the side, right?"

"Dana, that's not true! You, of all people, know me well enough to know better!"

She suddenly whispered and looked me dead in the eyes. Her stare reached inside of me to my pounding heart, where I expected it to tear. It didn't rip, though. It hugged.

"I do know, Jack. I love you. And you love me. Now let me go so I can finish putting things back the way they are meant to be. I see the way you and Sarah are, and I'm not big enough to stop it. I don't want to."

"What's that mean?"

"Sarah told me her secret, Jack."

"What do you mean?"

"She told me something I think you need to know. But she needs to be the one to explain it."

"What in the hell are you talking about?"

"Ask her, Jack."

The Escort slowly began rolling away. She stared straight ahead, and said again, "I love you." I could just barely hear her saying it as the car pulled further ahead, with me still jogging, then running behind it.

I kept on running, crying at the same time, but the Escort reached ahead further onto the horizon, and eventually turned left onto the main thoroughfare and disappeared. I sat on the street in a daze. Then I remembered how I had left Sarah.

She was prone on the floor when I returned to her, hyperventilating and holding her midsection as if in pain. I struggled to get her into the Sunbird, and it seemed to revive her spirit a little.

The verbal jousting resumed.

"Did you catch her, Jack?"

"Be quiet, Sarah. I'm getting you to the hospital."

"Did you listen to what I said earlier, Jack?"

"About what?"

"I was trying to talk to you about my father."

I thought about that carefully. It wasn't obvious to me what he had to do with any of this, beyond some twisted Freudian sway he held over all his girls. Sarah and I were the main players—criminals and victims, both and each responsible for our own behavior. It did make me slightly curious, though.

"What about him?"

"I was trying to protect him."

"Protect him?" I laughed, a single, loud exhale. "From what? He doesn't need any protection. He needs to keep his—"

Tears of a different sort appeared on Sarah's cheeks. She had that old emotional pull on me again, and I relented. That look made me stop before I could actually say it.

"Yes..." she said slowly, almost whispering. "You're right about him. You saw it practically the first time you met him. But he's my father, and while I can't use it as an excuse, it's at the heart of my shortcomings."

"Your father isn't in this story right now. Dana said you had another secret. And if it's anything like the first one, I don't want to know about it."

"Jack, my father is the equation. I'm admitting it."

I pursed my lips together and gave it a moment of contemplation. Were there more dirty secrets that I wasn't privy to? Maybe he had been physically abusive, or worse yet, sexually abusive. Maybe it was worse than that.

"What has he done now?" I asked.

"Jack, I never had an affair. I made that story up. I've never slept with anyone but you."

I pulled over to the side of the street and jammed the Sunbird into park. Her hyperventilating had lessened, and she was staring at the people walking up and down the sidewalk.

"You expect me to believe that?"

"Yes."

I laughed again, rapping my hands on the steering wheel. Then I closed my eyes. "Sarah, I don't believe you."

"I'm not absolutely sure why I told that lie to you, Jack, but it never really happened. It wasn't an act of malice, and I didn't set out with the intention of ruining our marriage. But it was a lie. It didn't happen."

"So," I said slowly, "do you think telling me this right now is suddenly going to undo everything that's happened? Do you think you can stop the avalanche from crashing down the mountain?" I still didn't really believe her.

"No, of course not."

"So what am I supposed to do, Sarah? And why shouldn't I blame your father? One lie is the thing that—"

"Okay!" she said, gasping. "We don't have to go through all of that!"

"And why shouldn't we? If you lied to me, I have a right to know why, don't I?"

"And I have a right to know why you were a sneaking, skulking, filthy cheat, too, don't I! Would it make you feel better if I just came out and said that you and my father are exactly alike? Does it feel good to hear me say that?"

I didn't respond. I pulled back out onto the street.

"Answer me, Jack! Wouldn't my father be proud of you? Go ahead and say it, since I know you've been dying to say something really bad about him ever since you met him. Here's your big chance to tell me how truly despicable he is!"

Her eyes were so wide that I could see the whites around the pupils, and her hair was starting to fall through them. Her hyperventilating grew more intense.

"Just rest, Sarah. Take deep breathes and close your eyes. There's no reason to cause a miscarriage..."

"Did you catch up with her, Jack?"

"Sarah, stop."

"You never forgave me did you, Jack? Even though I didn't really do it."

"Sarah!"

"Well I'm going to say it again because it's true. I never had an affair. I just made it up because I knew you were waiting for it to happen."

"What?" For the first time, it seemed like it might be possible. It was as if she had suddenly quoted every macho male friend of mine from college who had warned me about pretty Sarah. A sharp, stabbing pain traveled from my head to my heart, and I felt tears welling.

A ringing grew in my ears. It was the first outward sign of my inward shock. I looked at her and she was completely serious. Everything seemed to slow down. The vehicles on the road were crawling. My hands on the wheel were barely moving. Sarah's lips were slowly parting and I realized she was speaking again, though I couldn't hear anything.

She made it up? It was a preposterous suggestion. Yet it crawled into my brain and lodged there, and aspects of it made sense. I had never once heard the man's name; never seen a picture of him, or a letter from him; never had any concrete detail offered up. I had just assumed that he was real; flesh and blood like the rest of us.

As we pulled into the emergency ramp at the hospital, I didn't know what else to say. Half of me believed her, and half of me would never believe another word she said the rest of her life.

PEOPLE STARTED TO gather outside of the room as the slightly premature labor began. The doctor checked Sarah over several times, reassuring both of us that it was not unusual to go into labor this early, and also questioned us carefully about the stressful events leading up to the current situation. Neither Sarah nor I admitted to what had really happened. He finally pronounced everything okay, and promised that the birth would proceed as it normally would have had she held out several more weeks.

I played the part of Mercury, with clipped wings, delivering the news to those waiting beyond the door.

Sarah's mother, sometimes so mindless and colorless, jumped at me as if angry, though she couldn't possibly have known anything about what had transpired in the last twenty-four hours.

"Why aren't you with her?" she asked. "Who's in there right now?"

"She's fine. The contractions are still about fifteen minutes apart. The doctor has checked her carefully and everything is normal."

"Is she alone?"

"The nurse is in there!" I said, exasperated.

"Why did she go into labor early?"

"Everyone has to go into labor sooner or later. Sarah ended up being sooner. The doctor said that nothing is wrong."

She squinted at me, and behind her Sarah's sisters followed cue and frowned.

"Are you trying to be smart with me, Jack?"

"Of course not. I just—"

My mother chose that moment to lunge into the fray, leaving behind the lawyer (soon to be step-father?) who was gaping at the headline news on the wall television, either totally oblivious or totally unconcerned about the family drama unfolding before him.

"Jack, honey, is everything all right?"

"Yes."

Sarah's father arrived, and his eyes roamed up and down my mother as he greeted everyone. That brought a swift response from the lawyer, who abruptly appeared at her side.

"Have a cigar," Mr. Collins said, shoving one into my hand.

"The baby hasn't been born, yet," I said.

He shrugged. "I'm sure my little Sarah will take care of that in no time."

A question mark passed over both my mother's and Mrs. Collins' faces, though neither one seemed willing to challenge him.

The lawyer tried to make polite conversation.

"Jack said that he and Sarah think it's going to be a boy."

Mr. Collins chuckled and held another cigar up, which the suit curtly declined.

Things were spinning too fast for me again. I needed to jump back into the more sane company of a woman in labor. I pushed the door open and found the nurse watching the monitors. Sarah was breathing quickly, eyes closed, obviously in the middle of a heavy contraction.

"They're speeding up," the nurse said quietly. "Your regular doctor is on the way. It shouldn't be too long now."

"How are you?" I asked Sarah.

Her eyes opened partially and she seemed confused by the question. She moved her face one direction, and then the other, as if she couldn't scratch an itch there.

"Jack...I'm getting irritated. Will you please ask the nurse to leave?"

The nurse, who overheard, said, "I'm on my way out, sweetheart, and don't worry—I won't take it personally. I hear it everyday."

This seemed to irritate Sarah further, although she couldn't channel the energy away from the contractions to say anything to the woman as she disappeared.

"Put the television on, or something. Read from your book. Just do anything to distract me, or I'm feeling like I'm going to do something really mean to the next person who happens to be right beside me."

I was the person right next to her.

I opted for the television. I found the remote next to her bed and clicked on the power button. "There," I said, watching the screen glow to life. "That ought to do—"

My car was on the television screen. My Ford Escort was right there on the Ohio River Bridge downtown, parked in the middle of a group of police cars with sirens flashing. The driver side door was hanging open. Cars were backed up on both sides. One cop was staring over the side. A talking head suddenly filled the screen.

I leapt up and ran out the door, pushing aside every person I least wanted to see at that moment. My mother trailed after me more doggedly than the rest, yapping like a small dog.

"Jack! What the hell are you doing? What's wrong? Did something just happen in there? Where are you going!"

I began running and soon outpaced her, flying out the emergency doors practically before they could open all the way. I found the Sunbird and ripped it out of the parking lot.

Chapter 16
The River

I CAN'T EXPLAIN the way I felt. There was an emptiness, a terrible pain, yet there were other emotions as well. There was a wicked happiness, because I still had Sarah. There was an angry bitterness, because Dana had taken herself away from me without my consent. There was a terrible guilt, because I was the main cause of her final unhappiness. There was a pang of euphoria every time I remembered that night at my father's house when we had first made love. There was a slice of triumph when I remembered the accomplishment she had made out of my second book. There was an awesome weight that descended over my throbbing head every time I remembered that I loved her.

I was on the Watterson Expressway before I realized that I had no idea what I was really doing. Acting on impulse, I called Al.

"Jack?"

"I'm on the freeway."

"Are you crying? What's going on?"

"I'm driving very fast, and I don't know where I'm going."

"Just calm down and talk slowly. What's going on?"

I explained things as best as I could.

"You left Sarah in at the hospital?" he asked.

"I couldn't take her with me," I said angrily.

Al paused, then listened carefully. He started to talk me through it.

"There's nothing you can do, Jack. You'll just get in the way of the police. Either the worst has already happened, or they've pulled her out. Don't do anything rash."

"I'm not feeling that stupid," I said.

He didn't believe me. "You can't let your feelings influence what you do now, Jack. Be rational. Is there a good reason for you to be there?"

"Yes, I owe that to her."

"Stay on the road, Jack. Drive slowly. Talk to the police when you get there. Call me back after you talk to them. Okay?"

"Okay."

Al hung up. Then I recklessly swung the car onto Dixie Highway. A few minutes later, the traffic turned heavy, and I nearly ran into the car in front of me several times. Part of me stared ahead and tried to see what was holding traffic up. Part of me was dead.

Soon I sliced back onto the Interstate and headed for the bridge. Traffic slowed. I wanted to shout, "Move, you bastards! My girlfriend's up there!" Yet, I still didn't believe it. Dana wouldn't really do it...Would she?

As I drew closer to what I wished was a wreck, or a disabled vehicle, I slowed down. What I saw didn't fully register for several moments, despite the fact that I had just witnessed it on TV. When it did hit home, I slammed the brakes on, nearly starting another pile-up behind me. A symphony of car horns immediately started up.

I parked on the narrow emergency berm and scrambled out. An ocean-like breeze was blowing through the steel girders of the bridge, almost stinging my eyes. It was so incredibly easy to climb up onto the lip of the wide concrete guardrail and stare into the water. I glanced around and saw that people were slowing down, but not stopping. Only a few of the police cars were left, which meant I was too late.

The scene was more proof of utter insignificance. Al was right. There was nothing for me to do. I almost laughed. Complete insanity.

The Escort was parked next to the chipped and weathered concrete railing, its four-ways blinking weakly. The driver-side door was slightly ajar, and there was no trace of Dana anywhere in sight. A perplexed police officer was walking around the car slowly, as if leery of a fugitive about to jump out at him.

I scrambled down, stumbling right into the middle of the crawling traffic flow, and shouted at the officer. "Where is she?" More car horns than ever were honking, and I wasn't sure if he heard me.

The officer moved closer. "Do you know the driver of this car?"

"Yes! Where is she?"

The officer must have sensed my desperation. He was drifting over to the edge of the bridge. "Did she have any reason to jump?" he said slowly.

Bits and pieces of Dana's last words came back to me; how she was going to set everything right again. I could hear her voice speaking as if from a distance. "I see the way you and Sarah are, and I'm not big enough to stop it. I don't want to."

The corners of my eyes were melting. Or maybe it was my brain melting—I couldn't be sure.

I moved over to the side where the officer was still gazing

downward. The river was dark and ominous. It had a rotten smell about it. The road was a good eighty feet or so above the concrete-like surface. At stretches, including this one, the water was over fifty feet deep. It was an extremely long fall for anyone, and if you hit just right—I couldn't finish the rest of the thought....

"Are you okay?" the officer said.

I moved closer to the crumbling concrete edge and he suddenly grabbed my arm. "You still didn't answer my question. You're obviously a boyfriend or husband—do you think she would have jumped?"

"Maybe," I said, my voice weak and disconnected, and distracted.

The phone in my car began ringing. Neither of us moved to get it. It was overload for me.

"I called a river rescue squad," he said slowly. "I want you to sit down in your car and wait. They're going to go down there and look around."

The river below looked deceptively smooth and slow. In actuality, that water was moving at about the pace a healthy man could jog. In certain currents and eddies, it would take you under and down fast.

I closed my eyes.

I sat above the river for a long time in abject depression. It was a funny contrast with the first lunch Dana and I shared at the Cumberland River, many, many months prior. The Ohio River was dark, muddy, and foreboding. The Cumberland was green, sunlit, and jewel-like. One was a beginning; the other an end.

Al had once made a joke about jumpers in the James River in Richmond that ended with the fact that they often got stuck in the bottom mud when they jumped, and might otherwise have floated up and been rescued. It made me stand up and scream, and a bolt of agony surged through me.

One of the remaining police officers came over to make certain that I wasn't planning on joining her. He stayed near until I looked like I was going to leave.

As soon as the officer had disappeared around one of the blue and white cruisers, I slid back behind the wheel and jammed the car back into the crawling traffic. I was surrounded by cars, each with a driver staring at me like I was crazy, leering at me—everyone loves to see a freak. Everyone revels in somebody else's misery. Rubbernecking.

Here I was, some guy in an red car, bawling, pounding my steering wheel in frustration...But, screw them—I didn't care what they thought.

All I could think about was Dana...And Sarah back in the hospital with my baby. I drove to the other end of the bridge, near the Indiana shore, and pulled over again. When I jumped, it would be a one hundred-foot plunge into the concrete surface of the swirling river. I probably wouldn't even surface to see the light of day again. I would be where the catfish could keep me permanent company.

At least I might be where I could cause fewer harms to everyone.

It's funny the thoughts that go through your head. I took me back to where I started—the day I meet Sarah. It was one of those soul-defining moments. Yet, since then, lives had been torn into shambles, pains left as road markers along the route of our marriage. There was one victim floating around the river already. There were also children: an unborn child who would remain nameless, and another about to enter a world of confusion and pain.

I thought about God, and all of the crazy things I had heard about suicide; about how Catholics believe you would go to hell if you did it. Did that mean Dana would be there? I wasn't sure what I believed.

God was too heavy to think about. If I thought about God too much, it would pull me over before I was ready.

The wind seemed to be humming a toneless song.

I also thought about perfection. Sarah had been perfection to my foolish eyes, and I couldn't remember the exact moment when that changed. Would it have been on that cold highway when she told me about the affair? Or had it happened long before that, when I saw how she pitifully protected her unfaithful father? Perfection was certainly a great irony, for if the Sarah in my mind was perfect when I met her, then the Sarah in reality had so many hidden flaws that I almost didn't recognize her anymore.

It was true that I loved Sarah from the beginning, and I still loved her. My heart ached as I thought about it, and like the thought of God, the idea of how much I loved Sarah almost dragged me right off the ledge into the abyss. It made me seem so flawed in comparison. Love is such a pure thing that anything else turns yellow in the snow beside it.

Another ache, though, close on the heels of the former one, was the problem of how Sarah felt about me. Before I jumped, I had to admit to myself that I didn't think Sarah really loved me as much as I loved her—past, present, or future. I even tried to say it out loud.

It came out as a moan: "You never loved me." There wasn't much heart in it.

I thought about family history. Sarah and I both came from families where marriage was a failed experiment. Our parents had both screwed it up so badly that it would be easy for us to blame everything on that. But it did matter, and my mother cowering away from me when I needed her was proof of it.

I screamed in anger and anguish.

If my parents had maintained a normal relationship, my father would still be alive. I believed that at that moment.

There was so much blunt trauma. Sarah had never gotten over the living room incident with her father, and I hadn't been able to shake it either. No little girl (or girls in this case) should ever have their father killed that way in front of them, as they stand there helpless to fight it.

There were so many thoughts swirling around my head. I kept seeing Sarah in that sweater she used to wear back at Virginia Tech; back when we had first started studying together and she had predicted that I would be a great writer someday.

Then there was Dana in her lime green shoes. I laughed out loud and turned toward heaven (forgetting the Catholic nonsense for a minute), and called out to her: "Dana! Is this what you thought I'd become? Is this the great writer you saw?"

The thought of my book made me angry. It made me think of all the stupid, idiotic, insane things I had allowed myself to do, because I was some kind of damned artist, or avant-garde commentator on the human condition, separated from the real effects of life decisions. What a load of crap.

"Do you like this suicide scene?" I yelled to Dana Beech. "I'll write your goddamned suicide scene now!"

Behind me, I noticed that traffic had ground to a halt in all three lanes, and another of Louisville's finest was parked beside me, sirens flashing. Two officers jumped out and ran toward me.

This was it. This was the decision I knew would have to be made. This is what I talked about from the beginning. Was it the chicken way out, or peace?

As I leaned forward into the breeze and threw my hands up in the air, I thought of Romeo and Juliet, and it made me want to puke, or scream, or something, because this wasn't Shakespeare. This was reality; messy; in Kentucky, of all places, on a grimy Interstate highway. I really, truly wanted something that just wasn't going to be possible. No poet had ever penned lines that would describe how I felt.

So I screamed again, then relaxed as weightlessness came on.

WEIGHTLESSNESS LASTED only a nano-second. One of the officers grabbed me around the legs and violently swung me around, clipping my head on the side of the concrete in the process. In my dazed state, I thought he was arresting me.

Beyond him, a funny ringing sound gradually registered in my brain. The phone was ringing in my car again.

I tried to say something, but I was still only semi-conscious. The officer beside me, a young man close to my own age, looked fiercely angry about what I had just tried to do, then glared at the other officer.

"Answer his phone!" he said sharply. "It might be important."

He continued to keep me pinned to the ground, although the honest truth is that I could barely breath. He had completely knocked the air out of my lungs, and they were only reluctantly refilling. The side of my head felt like it was bleeding.

"Yes, yes..." the other officer said into the phone. "Of course. He's okay. We're going to take him to the hospital just as a precaution. Certainly. Give me your number and I'll call back and tell you."

Suddenly, two ambulance attendants were beside me.

"Can he speak?" one of them said.

"I don't know. I've just kept him here so he wouldn't try to jump again."

"Can you hear me?" the attendant said very loudly.

"Yes!" I said, growing irritated. "You don't have to yell." The air was returning in slow gasps, and the policeman shifted some of his weight off of me, to my great relief.

"We're going to take you to the hospital just as a precaution. Are you feeling dizzy, or anything unusual at all?"

"No."

"Okay. Let's get him in the ambulance. He seems okay."

I closed my eyes. It would be the fate of someone like me to botch the attempt. Dana did it right. She was a little like Sarah in that instance; she was efficient and cool when it came to carrying it out. She had made no mistake about it.

Me, on the other hand, I messed up the suicide scene in my book, and the one in real life.

My great soliloquy had run a few seconds too long.

GOING BACK TO the hospital was more torturous yet. I knew that inside were half a dozen people or more who would have nothing kind at all for me. Even my baby, had he been able to say something, probably would be cursing me at first contact. I also had a hell of time convincing the doctors and police to release me. Ironically, it was a whispered word from Sarah's father that smoothed things out.

Damn.

My mother, rest her soul, was the first to greet me. She actually embraced me.

"Jack, honey, we were worried to death about you. We saw the old Escort and didn't know what to think. The camera in the helicopter didn't—"

"Stop talking about it, please."

"—And we though you might have jumped."

"I might as well have! My life is over."

"Jack!" she hissed. "Stop talking that nonsense. They'll put you in a bed somewhere and you won't be able to see the baby. You're a father now. Go in there and start acting like one."

Behind her, I could see Sarah's mother approaching, that maniacal glint of power and anger in her eyes. She wouldn't dare reproach Mr. Collins, but woe to me for the slightest affront to her daughter.

"Does anyone care about me?" I said.

My mother looked confused.

"Jack!" Mrs. Collins said. "Sarah's waiting for you. The baby is waiting for you. You need to get in there and offer some kind of apology to her, even if it's not sincere."

For some reason, coming from Sarah's mother, that comment stung like ice water in the face. The frost on her features would never thaw. She had held me responsible for Sarah's swoon on our wedding day—despite the fact that she had tied the corset-like clasps on Sarah's dress—and it would be no different now. I would be the one to blame for everything.

No one really understood what had just happened to me.

Except Sarah.

She smiled when I entered, and it looked genuine. There was an incredible glow in her face, albeit a redness, too, that signaled the successful culmination of months of hard work. She was crying, too, but with that smile that I had seen before. When Sarah smiled like that, the tears were happy tears.

In her arms was the most beautiful baby I had ever seen. I saw immediately that it had Sarah's priceless brown eyes, and my mother's dimple nose. (I was sure my mother would notice that right away, since the nose was a very important feature in her mind.) It was smiling, if such a thing with a newborn is possible, and Sarah cradled it as if she had held babies for years instead of minutes.

"He's beautiful," I said, sliding over and extending my arms out.

"She!" Sarah said. "She's beautiful."

One last hurdle to jump over. I only stumbled for a moment. Sarah had so convinced both of us that it was a boy that the wish had become a religious belief. I picked my baby girl up and held her toward me.

I burst into tears. Tears of happiness, anguish, and maybe hope.

WE NAMED OUR little girl after my father: Morgan Freeman Baird. Sarah and I hardly had time to talk for several days, as her anxious family (and my mother) hovered over her and saw to her every need and whim, while I was left to feel unimportant and stew in my own juices. They doted on her, stroking her hair, kissing her, spoon-feeding her (which Sarah quickly got annoyed with), and reading to her.

I did note that not once when she was in the hospital did anyone turn the television on again. All of them were probably frightened of what else they might discover there; they might see something else about me.

Perhaps Mr. Collins' dark secret had finally been put to rest by the drama I had unleashed. I had distracted people away from his story. He couldn't have asked for a better script. "Here," he might say, "Let Daddy make it better." Now people would listen to him, reserving their dark stares for me.

Actually, I didn't even rate evil stares. I was mostly ignored. I was only spoken to as a slave in the Antebellum South would have been spoken to. "You, there. Fetch some hot water right away. And don't be slow, or you'll be whipped."

I guess I deserved it. I don't know.

WEEKS LATER, Al was drinking beer with me, and I got a little drunk. The baby and Sarah were fine, and things had calmed down a little bit. Sarah had tactfully avoided any conversation at all about Dana. She hadn't even said anything when I donned a black suit and left for the funeral in Indiana.

I probably shouldn't have been talking, but the alcohol got the better of me. No one had the guts to suggest therapy for me, so I guess I was creating my own sessions.

"So listen to this," I said. "All that time I was so worried about what kind of secret Sarah might have. I never thought that maybe she was exactly what she was on the surface."

"What was she on the surface?" Al asked.

"Attractive, sexy, intelligent, a little bit superior or aloof, unattainable, less emotional than I thought she should be...You know the routine."

"So?" Al said. "I could have told you all of that."

"No, you said she would be stepping out on me. You said I'd never be able to sleep peacefully. You were the one that kept warning me about her."

"Well, I was wrong."

"No, you weren't! I can't believe you're saying that now! Isn't lying about having an affair just as bad as actually having one?"

Al crushed his can and laughed. "You're drunk, Jack. Listen to what you're saying. I don't care if Sarah made up some story about being in love with another woman, or selling herself to hard-up business guys on Broadway, or anything. It's not as bad as actually doing it."

"So where does that leave me?" I asked.

"You're screwed." He said. He left, then returned with another beer. "You are the screw-up. Not her. I still don't understand why she told you such a stupid lie, but it's not the same as what you did."

"I loved, Dana. I don't want to bring her into this, or talk about her. It's not right."

Al laughed again, and I jumped up and pushed him out of the lawn chair into the grass. He was much larger than me, and I was very drunk. He splashed beer in my face and dared me to protest.

"You're pitiful, Jack. This is so sad. You're sticking up for your dead girlfriend when you've got Sarah and a baby in there to take care of. It's sick. Call me when you've grown up some."

He left me there, covered in beer.

AL WAS RIGHT. Sarah and I had completely switched places. The old Jack was a person of immeasurable patience. The new Jack was morose, and quick to lose his temper. The old Jack was cautious. The new Jack was reckless, and angry, ready to fight. The old Jack was tender. The new Jack was hardened, skeptical of happy endings, and jaded about the meaning of life.

Sarah, on the other hand, had transformed herself. The old Sarah had been remote and unattainable. The new Sarah was mine to lose; simple and down to earth. The old Sarah had been scared of feminine stereotypes. The new Sarah wasn't worried about what anyone thought. The old Sarah had used her beauty as a tool. The new Sarah was beautiful because she made people around her feel good.

Everything centered around the complicated, unfathomable

relationship between Sarah and I. That was the flashpoint of the entire crisis; that was the central question that remained to be answered. Was there something worth saving in it, or some merit beyond simply a license that legally declared us partners? What defined Sarah Collins and Jack Baird?

It was a question I decided to spend some time on.

THE NEXT DAY, I ended up at a strange place—my mother's house in Lexington. She was home, and immediately sensed that something was wrong. She was dressed in her nightgown, with a mug of coffee and a murder mystery in hand. The lawyer was out of town.

"Is the baby okay?" she asked. "Is my grandchild all right?"

"The baby is fine. It's Sarah and I that you'd better worry about."

She scowled and pushed me into the kitchen. Once there, she pulled out a chair for me and started some hot tea on the stove.

There was concern etched on the middle-aged lines of her forehead, the kinds of wrinkles that had become more prominent in her own divorce proceedings. I wondered for a moment if she really could help me.

"What did Sarah do now?" she asked quietly.

I took a deep breath. "Actually, Mom, it's not Sarah this time."

She dropped two tea bags into the pan and a sharp, tangy aroma filled the steamy air near the stove. "Okay, what did you do?"

"I had an affair with my agent."

A slight smile creased her lips. "Jack, I don't mean to be rude. But we've all figured that out by now."

"Sarah told you?"

"No, Jack. Give me a little bit of credit. Your scene at the hospital was a little more than an ordinary event. In fact, the footage of you at the bridge made the late news that night, you know."

I fumed in my chair, wincing at the memory. Some sick part of me wondered if I could find a copy of it to watch. "It's not a joke, Mom. I loved Dana."

"She was a nice girl, Jack. Pretty, too. I'm sorry about what happened."

I didn't know how to react to that. It almost sounded as if she approved. I had just announced that I was cheating on my wife, and my mother was not enraged, or even slightly upset. I don't know precisely what I expected, but that was definitely not it.

"I don't think it's a light matter, Mom. I think I've screwed up. I'm trying to figure out where to go from here, and what I can salvage."

She peered at me cautiously, studying the way I was sitting, the tilt of my head, the way I was holding my arms crossed, and seemed to assess the seriousness of the situation anew.

"And of course Sarah knows everything, right? Or you wouldn't be here right now."

"Yes, she knows. Dana went and told her everything. Dana was trying to set things right."

"That's ironic." She pulled the pan from the stove and poured the steaming liquid into a mug that she set on the table in front of me.

"Is Sarah physically okay?" she asked. "Do we need to call someone to check on her? Will she do anything stupid?"

"No, she'll be fine. It's me that I'm worried about!"

"Of course," she said quickly, leaning over and stroking the hair on my head. "You can stay here as long as you need to. Alan won't be back for two weeks. He's in California working on—"

"You don't understand, Mom! I need someone to tell me what to do, and tell me how to feel! Sarah hasn't kicked me out—I need to know if I should leave. I need to know what to say to her. I need motherly advice."

"Oh..."

That seemed to throw her for a bit of a loop. She sat there, her coffee getting cold in front of her, staring into the tabletop. "That little tramp..." she said under her breath.

"Mom, I'm the one who screwed up here. Tell me what to do. I'm afraid something bad is going to happen."

She stood and went into the other room, apparently unable to grasp my needs. I must have recalled some crisis in her life that never had any resolution, and ended up buried in time. I left her alone and tried to sip some of the tea.

Now that I thought about it, I was genuinely beginning to worry about Sarah. Once the affair had started, I had envisioned a thousand different ways the aftermath could be played out, and none of them came close to the reality. There was no practice scenario that could prepare anyone for it. There was more trauma and pain than I had planned for.

The realization struck me that this was not about Dana Beech. It was not about Sarah's father, or her mother, or sisters. It was not about my writing career, or the growing success of my new book (which was lost in the events of the past days). It was not about my father, or my family.

It was about what was inside of me.

I stood up and began pacing around the kitchen. My mother had still not reappeared from her retreat into the living room. Perhaps in the midst of my crisis, she was experiencing regret over the way her own marriage had irretrievably been wrecked on the rocks of selfishness and inflexibility. It made me sad for her, but it was also a clear warning that I was approaching the same rocky shores.

It hurt, too, that my father was gone. Neither of us (my mother or I) could deal with life using fundamental objectivity after that happened.

"I'm sorry," I said, feeling helpless, as if I had come to seek help and instead created a therapy need for my mother. "I'll come back a little later to talk some more. I didn't mean to upset you."

She let me go without a protest, and I was little saddened by that, although you shouldn't say something if you don't mean it, and I never wanted to be accused of hurting my own mother.

I WENT TO ONE of the new fast food restaurants nearby and tried another angle. I called Al on the portable phone.

Al, as usual, did not pull any punches.

"Do you still smell like beer?" he asked.

"I'm sorry, Al. I was way out of line."

"All's forgiven. Tell me what's up."

"I just needed to hear someone else tell me that there's a way out of this. I need to know what to do."

"Well," he said slowly. "Carla just talked to Sarah this morning, and she said she seems to be doing fine. How has Sarah been treating you?"

"Too perfect. She hasn't said a word about Dana, even when I dressed up and went to the funeral."

"Come on, Jack. Don't try to pretend that Sarah doesn't have feelings. Didn't that beer splash any sense into you? Sarah is hurting inside, whether she shows it or not."

"How do you know? She's been perfectly civil to me."

"Come on, J.K. You're not stupid. Just think about it. Would you rather have her ranting or raving, or is it more dignified for her to wait for you to come and talk about it?"

"She doesn't want to talk to me," I said.

"I don't know that I agree with that, buddy. I'd say all of the things she's been through in the last week put her at extreme risk."

"Risk of what?"

"Use your imagination. What do people hurt about?"

I shook my head. I guessed Al was only offering what I had asked for.

"Al—I can't believe I'm hearing this! When she stepped out on me, nobody worried about me. Now, just like at our wedding, and every other time she pricks her finger, everyone's running to her defense. I know I made a mistake, but Sarah is just as likely to throw something at me as to open the doors and welcome me back."

"Jack, some things are bigger than your own petty anxieties. Has she thrown anything at you yet?"

"No."

"Then quit feeling sorry for yourself and go talk to her, for Christ's sake!"

I was shocked momentarily by the force in Al's voice. Friends don't usually hear friends talk that way.

"Okay," I stammered. "I'll try to find her. But I'm sure she's fine. All I'm going to do is embarrass myself some more."

"What's the big loss?" Al said. "There can't be much pride left for either one of you at this point. It's not about pride."

Damn. He was right. Sarah and I had sucker-punched each other about as much as two people can. I couldn't argue.

"I'll go home," I said. "I'll talk to her."

"Good. I'm right by my phone if you need me. Let me also say that I'll beat the crap out of you if you push me like that again."

"Sorry."

"I'm serious. Don't kid around with this stuff. This is not a book, Jack—it's real life, and it's dangerous. You can't write things out of your plot when you don't like them. Go and talk to her."

"Okay, okay. I'll do it."

I DROVE BACK to the little house in the quiet suburb feeling rather foolish. I couldn't please anyone. Even Dana Beech, the one I had thought I could count on, had left me when it seemed I needed or wanted her the most. I expected Sarah to walk away from me at any time; she had every justifiable reason to.

I pulled into the driveway, expecting to see some vehicle parked there, and was mildly surprised when there wasn't one. Sarah had probably made an exodus to her mother's house, a certain haven during any troubling times with me. I parked the car anyway to check for a note, or a phone message.

The house was strangely empty when I entered, and my footsteps echoed with a hollow tap that I had never noticed before. For some reason, it felt like Sarah had done more than just go out—it felt like she had left permanently.

I checked the answering machine in the kitchen—there was nothing new. I jogged into the nursery—only an empty crib.

Then I saw something on the table.

The note was written on a yellow legal pad in Sarah's sweeping, dramatic, feminine script. I started reading, unsure of what to expect.

"Jack: I hope everything's all right. I called your mom and she said you had left a while ago. I'm at my father's house with the baby. Come on over if you wish.

"I know you hate my father, Jack. You know that I love him, and I can't defend that. You know that my family isn't normal, and again, I can't counter that, either. I know that you've tried very hard with me. When I think back over the things you've done for me, I realize how much you've tried to look out for me. I really do appreciate that. I'm sorry for everything that's happened. I hope you aren't angry with me. (signed) Sarah."

I slumped to the floor, clutching the paper.

What she had written was far simpler and better than any novel I could pen. The Sarah I had created in my mind was a myth. This was a person I had no adequate appreciation or understanding for; no words to describe. She had accepted the nature of what she was, flaws and all, and it was I that couldn't accept her.

She had also accepted me even after the terrible mistakes I had made. In her note, I even detected a glimmer of hope, the possibility that everything might somehow work out.

I slowly stood up, still clinging to the paper.

Her father's house. Why did I have to show myself in that lion's den? Actually, the image of Daniel wouldn't work for me, since the real Daniel had carried humility and truth on his side. If I went into harm's way, it would have to be because I was desperate to find the truth, not because I wanted to be a hero or a savior.

For some reason, the image of the little girl at the cemetery in Cumberland, the relative of mine, popped into my head again. She made me think about my little baby girl, Morgan, and about what Sarah must have been like as a child. Life is so much bigger than ourselves...My little girl was only one small square in a quilt that contained thousands of patches, each one connected to the others by threads so fragile when taken singly that a whisper could tear them away, yet strong enough when sewn together to hold back the weight of the world.

I knew what I had to do. I needed to join them at her father's house. I didn't have to like him, and I never would, but I desperately needed to love Sarah. I put the note inside my pocket and walked back outside to the Sunbird. Down the street I smelled hotdogs grilling, and it made me think that my life still probably had lots of memories waiting to be crafted.

~ * ~

Jack Trammell

Jack Trammell has published seven books, ranging from murder mysteries ("Gray") to math text books for middle school students ("Math in History"). His two collections of poetry sold out within a month of publication, and he has published poetry and fiction in several dozen journals including: *Virginia Adversaria, Snowapple Journal*, and *Exquisite Corpse*. In addition, Jack researchs and writes historical articles for magazines like "America's Civil War," and currently has Civil War articles appearing in the *Washington Times*. Jack can be reached at jacktrammell@yahoo.com or see his website at www.geocities.com/jacktrammell

Jack is 37 and lives in central Virginia with his wife and three children. His latest book with HSWF is "Sarah's Last Secret."